A Second Chance

To Philip and John
because they make me laugh

A Second Chance

Marion Smisson

Hornby Publishing

First published in the United Kingdom in 2008
by Hornby Publishing

ISBN 978-0-9553267-1-4

Produced by
Action Publishing Technology Ltd, Gloucester
www.actiontechnology.co.uk

Printed and bound in Great Britain

Chapter 1

Jenny sat in the traffic jam on the bypass, listening to the radio, and raised an ironic eyebrow.

'The Long Ashton bypass is down to one lane due to a head-on crash, causing long delays. Emergency services are at the scene. This is Radio Bristol and Somerset Sound. We'll get you there!'

'But you're not getting me anywhere,' she shouted at the car radio and turned to Classic FM. To the quiet music she let her thoughts turn back to the last hour she had spent with Uncle Bernard at the nursing home. The staff were as kind and supportive as could be, but death is the inevitable end for everyone – the feared anticipation of death and what lies beyond.

As a well-known and over-played adagio came on the air, putting her teeth on edge – could there be a more dreary piece of music? – she turned the radio off and shook herself out of this despondent mood. By the time she arrived home she had to be in a more positive frame of mind, and she sat back, taking in the beauty of the mellow gold and red colours of the autumn trees on the verge. Beyond was a village with an ancient solid square tower of a church, and a farmer checking his cows. On the other side of the road was a golf course where men, clubs in hand, were enjoying their game. Life, Jenny thought, had so many facets – golfers connecting with a good shot, the farmer enjoying the lowing of his herd – and she was a fragment of the pattern, her own family, and life beyond that. Driving past the mangled wrecks of two cars and no doubt the mangled wrecks of several lives she felt an even smaller part of the pattern.

Cherry Avenue was made up of semis built in the 1960s. These houses were now well established, cars washed on Sunday mornings leaving damp rectangles on the road, the residents competitive about their elaborate window blinds and shingle-enhanced gardens.

Turning the key in the lock of number 44 she heard loud music from her daughter's room and found Trevor and her son Dean slumped in armchairs in front of the television, Trevor's beer belly protruding over his brown trousers (he never looks professional wearing brown she thought) and Dean's long outstretched legs ending in frayed jeans and scuffed trainers. They were watching football.

'Where the bloody hell 'ave you been?' snapped Trevor, glaring at her.

'I went to visit Uncle Bernard then got held up in the traffic.'

'Hasn't that miserable bugger died yet? Well, I want my tea. I have to be back in the office for a meeting. Overseas business clients want to discuss our plans before tomorrow's conference.'

'There are three fully-grown adults in this house – you could have easily got yourselves something. It'll have to be baked beans on toast.'

She retreated to the kitchen, kicked off her size 3 shoes that were making her feet ache, but resisted the temptation to slump down on a chair, and set to work putting bread in the toaster and standing on tiptoe to reach the baked beans in the cupboard. She sometimes found her lack of height difficult, but it did help when she felt lost and pathetic, as men felt sorry for her. She tried to curb her irritation as she placed steaming plates before her two male couch potatoes, but made the comment, 'I hope the beans don't make you fart in front of your business colleagues,' making Dean laugh, before he asked, 'Where's the brown sauce?'

'You have legs, use them,' was her reply.

Outside there was a toot on a car's horn and Mandy rushed down the stairs in a T-shirt that stopped at her midriff showing off her navel, complete with a stud, worn over tight jeans.

'That's Kev. We're going to the cinema. See you later, Mum.'

Mandy slammed the door with Jenny wondering why her daughter, dressed like that, never felt the cold. Probably a rebellious reaction against the ill-fitting blouse and skirt she had to wear to the bank each day; and surely that stud was uncomfortable when she slept?

Jenny sat exhausted on the arm of an easy chair, tea towel in hand, no longer hungry, and asked the men about their day – with little response.

'Have you started packing yet, Dean?'

'No,' he answered, not taking his eyes of the screen. 'Plenty of time. Don't fuss, Mum.'

Trevor heaved himself from the armchair, 'Right, I'm off. Don't wait up.'

He combed his ginger hair and aggressive moustache in front of the hall mirror and was gone.

Jenny made herself and Dean a coffee and joined him

watching television. There was a goal and Dean cheered along with the crowd, and then said, 'Dad was in a bad mood tonight. I think that insurance company work him too hard.'

'You may be right,' answered Jenny non-committally.

'When we were little he used to laugh and joke with us when he came home from work, even if he didn't help with the homework like some dads do. But not any more.'

'I don't think he understood your homework. He left school at sixteen with four O levels. Physics and chemistry would never have been his strong point, and he got fed up with you beating him at football. People do get older and more tired. Think of Uncle Bernard – he used to be such a jolly man and kind. Not the way you remember him when you last saw him in that dingy guesthouse. When was that, eight years ago?'

'Pity he never got married, then you wouldn't feel so responsible.'

'It's not so much responsibility, but just being the only one left on my mother's side of the family. You going out tonight?'

'Yes. I'm meeting Sam and Mark at the King's Head. Probably the last time I see them before uni. I'll miss them.'

'We'll miss you. All the noise and racket, but I'm glad you've got this chance. If you ever get packed I'll drive you down to Plymouth on Saturday.'

When Dean had left noisily on his skateboard Jenny felt in need of a gin and tonic to relax after the stresses of the day. She took her drink into the darkening garden, lights already on in neighbours' upstairs bedrooms, and sat by the tobacco plants taking in their evening fragrance, whilst she thought about her present problems.

She hoped Dean would go on thinking Trevor was overworked but from her experience she expected the over-work came from another direction. Sharon, his assistant, was young, blond and full of life. Jenny had met her once at an office 'do'. It had happened before, 'the other woman', but if she kept quiet, however much it might hurt, he always came back in the end. She could accept that, because she still loved him. Not in the way she did when she first knew him, when a tingling affected every nerve if she saw him, but in a deeper way through the times and experiences they had shared together.

Her cat jumped on her lap, brushed against her, purring. Jenny thought of the black cat as her familiar, someone she could talk to when no one else listened, and had named him Pyewacket. Many years ago, in her youth, against her parents' wishes, she had seen the film *Bell, Book and Candle*. It had James Stewart as the hero, Jack Lemmon as a warlock who could change traffic lights at random, and Kim Novak playing the witch. She had a Siamese cat called Pyewacket as a familiar, through whom she hummed her spells.

'Well, Pye, what shall we do about all this? Keep shtoom do you think? Try not to cry when Dean goes on Saturday. Children are not children forever. They have to leave, and make their own lives. Accept with patience Bernard's dying. He was so entertaining and good fun when I was young. I wish I knew more about him, but my father disapproved of him – as he did of most things. And Trevor? Pretend not to notice when he comes in smelling of another woman's perfume? It's worked before – let's hope it works this time.'

Pyewacket, purring, looked at her with large luminous eyes, showing he had understood every word.

*

5

The following Saturday was bright and sunny. Jenny showered, dressed quickly in jeans, a relief after five days of office wear, and realised her bobbed blond hair needed retinting at the roots. She put cereals and orange juice on the kitchen table wondering if anyone would stir themselves before noon.

Trevor wandered into the kitchen with rumpled hair and old trousers baggy at the knees. She made him a strong coffee.

'Looks as though you aren't coming to Plymouth with Dean.'

'No. Thought I would stay here, catch up on some paperwork and mow the lawn. You don't mind do you?'

'I know you don't like farewells. You couldn't cope with taking Mandy to the airport for a week's holiday in Majorca, but I thought you might like to see where Dean is living. I'll feel happier when I've seen the flat.'

'Plenty of time to see it later,' and Trevor buried his nose in the *Daily Mail*.

Dean shouted down the stairs, 'Can I take a spare duvet, sheets and pillows?' So, armed with a black polythene bag, she helped Dean ransack the linen cupboard, standing on tiptoe to reach two pillows from the top shelf. Back in the kitchen she made more coffee but Dean mumbled he was not hungry, obviously feeling rather nervous, and started packing the car.

Mandy arrived downstairs in her dressing gown. 'You're not taking those CDs!'

'They're mine. You'll have to start buying your own.'

'And you're taking your TV.'

'Why not?'

'You'll get done for not having a licence.'

'Now you two,' Jenny intervened, 'just be nice to each

other for a few minutes, then we'll be off.'

Parting hugs and wishes of good luck were exchanged then Jenny and Dean were off down the M5 towards Plymouth. Dean, not wanting to talk, played loud pop music all the way whilst Jenny tried to concentrate over the noise. After a few wrong turnings they found the district of Mutley and the student house in a Victorian terrace. A rather bossy girl in her second year, with short black hair waxed in spikes and black painted fingernails, showed Dean his room. Most of the doors had posters stuck on them, Homer Simpson being the favourite, saying, 'Doh.' There was toilet paper in the loo and washing-up liquid in the kitchen. That reassured Jenny. They hauled Dean's luggage past bikes left in the hall and Jenny decided Dean should be stocked up with food, so they walked to the main road and bought coffee, milk, Weetabix and some frozen meals.

'I think you'll be living off pizza for the next three years,' commented Jenny as she stacked the fridge. Then she suddenly felt she was being a nuisance. He had to start his new life on his own, so she kissed him goodbye, wished him luck and left hurriedly, feeling he was relieved to see her go.

She needed a break before returning to normality, so drove with tears in her eyes to Plymouth Hoe. Here she bought an ice cream, and licking it watched the blue-green waves below her swashing over the brown and grey rocks. Ahead of her was Drake's Island, ships moored in the bay and sailing boats tacking to and fro, the water brilliant in the sunshine.

She thought – this is the end of an era for me. The tiny baby I held in my arms eighteen years ago is now a grown man and off to a new beginning. That's as it should be. I'm pleased for him, but it does leave a big hole in my life. I'll be listening for his skateboard coming down the road for many weeks and remembering.

Driving back on her own she was more aware of the countryside she passed – the grey torrs of Dartmoor, Exeter and the green hills of Somerset. She saw buzzards wheeling overhead and wished she had made time to explore these places instead of incarcerating herself in suburbia.

There was no one in when she got home, just notes on the table.

'Gone to the Mall with Kev. Will eat out. Luv Mandy.'

'Gone to the office – back late evening.'

No love there, thought Jenny – I expect he's at Sharon's but I'll ring the office to say I'm back home. At least he's cut the grass.

There was no reply from the office.

She felt flat and despondent. It would have been good to be welcomed home. Surely Trevor and Mandy would have realised how much she would miss Dean? No longer feeling hungry, she switched on the kettle to make a cup of tea in her own special Wedgwood cup. Pyewacket rubbed round her legs, wanting a meal.

The telephone rang. It was Trevor's sister, Sheila. 'I've just rung for a chat.'

'Nice to hear from you,' she answered and delved into her handbag for cigarettes. She didn't often smoke, but Sheila's half-hour calls filled with neurosis had this effect on her.

'I've been to see the doctor. Had to wait for days for the appointment. It's me stomach playing up again. Stress, the doctor thinks. Gave me tablets and two weeks off work.' She rambled on – how would the library cope without her, but standing all day was a terrible strain on her back. Jenny listened to the saga of ailments saying 'yes' in the right places and watching the smoke from her cigarette making patterns in the air.

'Wondered if I could come and stay for a few days. The change might do me good. Though I'll have to be careful what I eat.'

'Well, if you don't mind us being out at work all day. I'm sure Trevor would love to see you. You can have Dean's room.'

'If you're happy with that, I'll drive my little car down on Wednesday. I think I can cope with the M5 from Birmingham.'

'OK. We'll see you about tea-time.'

'Just a little fish would do me. No red meat.'

Sheila rang off after a few more comments on her state of health. Jenny lit another cigarette and groaned. Sheila enjoyed ill-health. It was her hobby. No wonder she had never married. Trevor would have to put up with her for a few days, if he could tear himself away from the temptations of the office, and it would take her mind off Dean leaving.

Pyewacket looked reproachfully at her and she stirred herself to feed him.

'You know, Pye,' she said as she forked tinned food into a bowl, 'perhaps I'm too dependable. Taken for granted. Always here and being the same. Maybe I should be more neurotic like Sheila. Then people would take notice of me – though in my book she is just plain selfish.' Putting the food on the tiled floor she stroked the cat's back. 'Could I possibly change now?'

Looking into her empty teacup she noticed a crack. The first crack in her family's fragile structure.

Chapter 2

Trevor returned at midnight. Jenny was just dozing off, having spent a dull evening taking her frustration out on the ironing whilst watching *Who Wants to be a Millionaire?*, shouting out the correct answers, and wondering where they could find such stupid contestants.

As he undressed Trevor asked, 'Dean all right?'

'Yes, but nervous about embarking on a new way of life. Who wouldn't be? And the house is fine. After I left him, I drove up to the Hoe. I had to readjust. Dean no longer being here. I looked at the sea. It was a different world. People fishing, swimming, sailing, enjoying the sun, eating ice creams. We should have done more exploring when we were young, seen more of the country, had a bit more fun.'

'Didn't have the time, or the money,' and he pulled the duvet over himself. Jenny tried cuddling up to him for comfort but he just turned on his side and went to sleep, snoring.

He doesn't want to know – she thought – and hasn't for months. That Durex packet I found in his coat pocket several months back was not for my benefit. Lucky Sharon, or whoever. Why can't we turn back the clock ten years? Those nights in the caravan at Windermere, I'm sure we got it rocking, and the days with the kids, jumping from rock to rock up mountain streams. Her tears dampened the pillow as she wept for past times, and she lay awake until she heard Mandy's key turn in the lock, then she slept.

The church bells woke them on Sunday morning, as they had for many years. Trevor turned over and muttered, as he also had for many years, 'Wouldn't be so bad if they rang a proper peal.'

'I think they must be two ringers short today,' answered Jenny. 'By the way, I forgot to tell you last night, your sister is coming to stay on Wednesday.'

Trevor sat bolt upright, 'Which one? Sheila the hypochondriac, or Jane with four snotty-nosed children?'

'Sheila. She has two weeks off work as she's sick – stomach trouble.'

'Make sure it's steak and chips every night. You smoke as much as you like and I'll get a large bottle of whisky. She might go sooner.'

'You can be nice to her for a few days. On Saturday we can take her out somewhere. She likes gardens and stately homes. I'll get you a strong cup of tea for the shock.'

When she returned, he announced, 'I'll be away Wednesday. Meeting in Coventry and I'll have to stay overnight. I'll try to be the good brother the rest of the time. I didn't invite her.'

'She invited herself.'

Dread at the thought of Sheila's visit meant that Sunday breakfast was filled with long silences, and did little for the rest of the day. Jenny looked forward to Monday's return to her job in the Education Department at the Council Offices in Bristol.

It was a dull job, checking on children who had free school dinners, but she enjoyed the company and at lunchtime Edith, a friend for many years, who now worked for Children with Special Needs, suggested they went out to lunch.

As they settled at a table in a coffee shop, Edith said, 'I thought you looked a bit down. Maybe a coffee and a chat would cheer you.' Edith, greying hair, plump and comfortable with it, came from Manchester and talked in a very matter-of-fact way.

'Yes I do feel down. Dean's gone to university. Trevor's in a permanent bad temper and to make things worse his sister is coming to stay. So life will not be easy over the next week.'

'I know the feeling. In-laws can be very difficult. They don't seem to understand other families behave differently and expect you to behave as they do.'

'But Sheila's a hypochondriac and thinks everyone should be at her beck and call. Trevor's too interested in work, or the female attraction at work – you know what he's like – so I will have to be tea and sympathy for a few days. Probably herb tea.'

'Can't stand the smell of it. And you've had problems with Trev and his roving eye before.'

'As they say, "least said, soonest mended".'

'Is Mandy OK?'

'We see little of her. Out with Kevin every night, and they seem to get on well. Now you come to mention it, she spent yesterday afternoon leafing through an IKEA brochure. Have they more permanent plans, maybe a wedding?'

'I doubt it, in this day and age. Judging by the partners my boys have progressed through in the last ten years. Ian, my eldest, is now involved with a divorcee ten years his senior ...'

And so the conversation carried on through their tuna and mayonnaise sandwiches.

Jenny returned to the office.

'I would like to remind you, Mrs Evans, that lunch hour is from one o'clock until two,' remonstrated her manager, Mr Haspen, commonly known as 'Has Been'. He was due for retirement, still lived in the 1950s, and could not, when he was reprimanding staff, call them by their first names. Though he did at other times. But then Jenny called Mandy 'Amanda' if she was annoyed.

'I'm sorry, Mr Haspen.'

'Your timekeeping is getting a bit lax, Mrs Evans.'

'I'll set the alarm earlier in the morning, Mr Haspen.'

She groaned as she sat down at her desk.

'Don't let "Has Been" get to you,' admonished Brian who worked on the opposite desk. He was a quiet, humorous man in his thirties with a twinkle in his mild brown eyes. Too easy-going, Brian never got the promotions he deserved. 'You do your job well. What's he got to look forward to in a few months? Mrs Haspen – "The Nag" – gardening, and a fortnight at Teignmouth every year. What a future!'

Jenny laughed. That's what she liked about the office. They made her laugh.

On Wednesday she bought salmon steaks and green salad in a bag, 'washed and ready to eat' (although she had read in the newspapers of live frogs being found in them), for her sister-in-law's gastronomic requirements.

Sheila was sitting in the car, looking peeved, when

Jenny drove into the small drive at Cherry Avenue.

'I'm sorry to be late. Trev's away tonight in Coventry, some business meeting, but come in, make yourself comfortable and I'll make a cup of tea.' She heaved Sheila's bag upstairs and put on the kettle.

As Jenny dropped her standard supermarket tea bags into two mugs Sheila announced, 'I have brought my own tea bags. They're herbal. Good for my nerves.' Jenny dutifully replaced the bag and as it infused wondered if the smell would make her sick. She grilled the salmon and put together the green salad, whilst Sheila watched the news on television making loud reactionary comments on crime and the youth of today.

'In the library they try smuggling books out, look up pornographic things on the Internet and drop chewing gum on the carpet.'

'Well, they didn't put pornography on the net, adults did that,' said Jenny placing their meals on the coffee table.

'But there is no self-control with these school children. Sorry, I can't eat salad – my stomach, you know,' and she pushed the fresh green salad to the side of her plate. Jenny ignored her and turned the TV over to *The Simpsons*, hoping it would really get on Sheila's wick. As Jenny chuckled to the humour, Sheila kept on saying, 'I don't understand.'

The long evening stretched away in front of them so Jenny suggested a drive to the coast to see the sunset. The gold and silver sky reflecting in the tide was beautiful, with gulls calling overhead. They walked along the shore where children were throwing stones in the sea and climbing on the rocks. It made Jenny smile. 'I remember Mandy and Dean jumping around on the rocks just like that.'

14

'Well they were never very disciplined children.'

Jenny sighed and suggested a drink in the pub. As they reached the bar Sheila said, 'I'll have a tonic with ice and lemon,' and as Jenny was about to order a gin and tonic Sheila's acid tones were heard, 'and of course you have to drive home,' so the order became two tonics. Jenny thought – I'll have a double when she's gone to bed, I deserve it.

As Jenny turned from the bar she nearly dropped the glasses. She felt as though an iced dagger had been stabbed in her heart.

'You all right, dear?' asked Sheila.

'Yes, just felt giddy for a minute.' She couldn't tell Sheila.

'Too much caffeine I expect, very carcinogenic,' was Sheila's comment. If only you knew, thought Jenny. She let Sheila prattle on about her varicose veins.

Yes, it had been Trevor she had seen leaving the pub with Sharon. No doubt about that. What stabbed her to the heart was that he was laughing, and looked so happy, much younger. And Sharon, also happy, not so slim as she had been, maybe four months pregnant?

'And I said to the doctor, what about this pain in my neck?'

Jenny jolted herself into reality – pain in the neck. I must deal with today and Sheila. Live through Thursday, Friday, Saturday, then confront him.

'Yes, of course. What did the doctor advise?' (Euthanasia? she thought.) 'Will you be all right whilst I'm out tomorrow? I'll be back late. I go to see my Uncle Bernard on Thursdays at the nursing home. He's got cancer.'

Sheila's curiosity about Uncle Bernard's illness lasted

the journey home. Jenny made Sheila a cup of Horlicks and took it up to Dean's bedroom where Sheila was wrapped in a woolly dressing gown. She wished her 'good night', without a sisterly hug, and downstairs poured herself a large gin.

She didn't know how she had got through the evening. Seeing Trevor, knowing for certain he was lying. If Sharon was pregnant the situation was very different. Not a short-lived fling. And he looked so happy. That's what made her feel sick to the centre of her being. Her familiar jumped on her lap and stared with large green eyes, 'Yes, Pyewacket, this time I will have to confront him, because other lives are involved. But after Sunday when the neurotic one has gone home.' The cat looked reproachful. 'I'm not a coward, Pye, I just don't want too much fuss.'

She got through Thursday, as after her depressing visit to Uncle Bernard she came home to find a message on the kitchen table saying Trevor had taken Sheila out for a meal, so she went to bed early and pretended to be asleep when he came upstairs.

On Friday after five days' hard work at the office Jenny prepared an omelette for the evening meal. Surely no one could object to this, but it was spurned.

'Eggs are bad for the heart,' declared Sheila.

'You're becoming a bloody anorexic,' shouted her brother, getting red in the face. Jenny tactfully made her a mug of instant soup and suggested an evening at the cinema before tempers became too frayed. The cops and robbers film was humorous, making Jenny laugh, but the other two seemed lost in their own secret silent worlds. At least she had got through another day.

The three of them were sitting down to a breakfast of

indigestible cereal that Sheila found acceptable when the telephone rang. Trevor answered with, 'I'll be right there.' Looking concerned, he faced the two women at the breakfast table, 'Trouble in the office. I'll be back when I can.' He grabbed his coat and left in a hurry.

'Oh dear,' said Sheila, 'maybe there's a fire.'

'Probably a computer breakdown,' replied Jenny, not believing a word. 'What would you like to do today? Would you like to look at gardens? There's a beautiful one at Hestercombe.' Jenny, relieved to be out of the house and the tension, drove along the motorway to Taunton and along country lanes to the garden.

Hestercombe Gardens, designed by Lutyens and Gertrude Jekyll had a tranquil affect. The quiet small streams of water running through stone and plants, and the colours of autumn, calmed the two women. They had a snack in the café and walked along the lake to the cascade. Jenny, watching the white water fall on the rocks below, was enjoying the spectacle, but Sheila, in an aggressive way, said, 'Waterfalls fragment things. Break them up.'

Jenny's peaceful thoughts were destroyed; she looked across at Sheila in alarm. 'What do you mean?'

'Like life,' Sheila explained. 'Yes. Life starts off as a clear stream then rocks build barriers – like illness, drudgery of work, loneliness.' Sheila's expression was bleak, her mouth compressed in bitterness.

Jenny was shocked by her sister-in-law's outburst – to see misery in something so beautiful. What went on in Sheila's mind? Jenny wondered what life she had ever had outside the library and illness? Had she ever had a boyfriend, a lover? Maybe she was a lesbian? Jenny didn't know, but felt relationships were too physical for the desiccated Sheila.

'The water also comes together again, combines in tranquillity in the lake,' Jenny said calmly. They sounded like profound words, but were they true? In her own situation how could she judge? She thought of the crack in her Wedgwood teacup a few days ago, and the cracks in the family. As they walked back to the car Jenny suggested an ice cream – a comfort food – anything to alleviate the grimness in Sheila's tone and attitude.

'No. It might have a devastating effect on my stomach.'

Determined to not let Sheila get to her, Jenny enjoyed a honeycomb creamy delight before they found the car.

Lights were on in every room at 44 Cherry Avenue and the rock music was loud. Mandy bounded out of the house with two pillows in her arms.

'What's going on?' asked a horrified Jenny. Kevin seemed to have lost his limited powers of speech but Mandy butted in, with her pillows.

'Sorry, Mum, I should have told you, but Kev and me have found a rented house in Bedminster, and we thought we may as well move in. It's great – a place of our own. I'm so excited. You don't mind do you? It's not the same here without Dean, and Dad's always bad tempered. By the way, he left a message. The computer at work's still down. He'll be back tomorrow evening.'

Jenny stood bewildered on her own account, and then wondered what Sheila would make of it all.

Aggrieved, Sheila folded her spindly arms. 'I am disgusted. Those two aren't even married. And you are condoning them living in sin. What sort of family have you become! Trevor has hardly spoken to me; Amanda has not even acknowledged my presence and your son could not even come home to see his aunt. The sooner I leave in the morning the better.' Given her bad back and varicose veins Sheila stomped up to the bedroom very swiftly.

'Oh dear,' said Jenny, 'what a scene,' and started to smile. The smile turned to a giggle and then to a chuckle and Mandy and Kevin, unsure of the situation, joined in.

'Silly cow. Take no notice of her. *Yes, don't take any notice of her!* She's never had a life, apart from books. Get out there and live the life you want. If you've both thought long and hard about it, go and be happy.' They both gave her a hug and went on packing the car.

'Don't take all the crockery and leave me a tea towel,' she called as they rushed about the house. Jenny was trying to make light of the situation, as really she was thinking about Trevor. What had really happened? She had to get her brain round her family's situation. She ran the dishwasher, as there were no clean mugs or plates, and to its swooshing noises lit a cigarette and wondered what to do. Trevor and Mandy were beyond her control but she could take Sheila some toast and Horlicks. She carried the plate and mug upstairs thinking of the right conciliatory words.

'I've brought you some toast and a hot drink.' She sat down on the bed. 'Sorry about Mandy and Kevin. They're adults now and make their own decisions. We may not agree, but it's their lives, not ours. They may be right or wrong, but that's how they learn. Parents have to step back, and be there if needed. I hope you understand.'

'Well, it wasn't the way we were brought up.' (Jenny scoffed inwardly. The Evans family upbringing seemed to have had little affect on Trevor and his philandering.

19

His father too had the same reputation.) 'And Trevor has been so rude. I don't think our sister, Jane, will be impressed when I ring her.'

'Don't ring her then.'

'I'd feel so alone if I didn't. A sister can be such a support. I'll leave after breakfast.'

Jenny felt dismissed; she too felt alone, as she walked down the stairs and no word of thanks for a day out. The music stopped suddenly, making the house silent.

'We're off,' shouted Mandy.

'Good luck,' whispered Jenny in Mandy's ear as she hugged her, 'and remember we are always here if you need us.'

She returned with tears in her eyes, not noticing the clear starry sky she usually loved to see. Sheila's light was out and the house seemed cold and empty. Where was Trevor?

A drink would calm her. She took a glass out of the dishwasher, added ice cubes before the gin. The glass cracked in her hand. The second crack in her family's fragile structure.

Chapter 3

Despite Mandy's sudden departure and not knowing Trevor's whereabouts, but guessing he was with Sharon, Jenny slept well, enjoying the space in the double bed. She awoke to a misty, chilly autumnal morning and more discordant church bells. Looking through the kitchen window she saw spiders' webs on the garden shrubs decorated with dew, and the sun broke through the mist to shine on the damp lawn. Though she had problems she could still enjoy the beauty of the morning.

As she was brewing coffee Sheila came downstairs fully dressed and starched, carrying her case.

'Cup of tea?' enquired Jenny, trying to sound bright. 'Cereal, toast?'

'No thank you,' replied Sheila huffily, 'I had a terrible night's sleep. Dreadful stomach pains.' Jenny thought – I went to the loo once in the night and she was snoring deeply.

'Besides, I don't feel welcome in this dysfunctional family. I would rather be back in my own flat where I can be comfortable. So I will say thanks. I know you have done your best for me. Trevor I don't understand. I expected more support from him. And now I will go, the motorway should be clear.'

Jenny, still in her dressing gown, tying it more tightly about her, accompanied Sheila out to her car, and apologised for her family's behaviour just to keep the peace, and to make Sheila feel more righteous. She hoped Sheila's health improved and waved her away with a sight of relief. Now she could go back to the kitchen and enjoy her coffee and cigarette in silence you could touch, with no constant chatter about health and diet.

After a warm bath she dressed in old clothes, stripped Sheila's bed and pottered around the house putting everything in its place. Wandering out in the garden she did some random weeding but could not settle to the usual autumn task of cutting down herbaceous plants. Her mind kept on thinking about Sheila driving back to Birmingham, Mandy and Kev in their new home, Dean away in Plymouth and most of all, what she would say to Trevor when he came home.

She made a cheese sandwich, it being the only food left in the fridge as there had been no time to shop, and besides, what could she buy for Sheila's foibles? Then, glancing at yesterday's paper, she realised it was Trevor's sister Jane's birthday the next day and she had better send a card to keep the peace. She wrote insincere words on a sentimental card and walked to the post box down the alleyway. The walk did her good, and the warm autumn colours on overhanging bushes cheered her. There was a cluster of blackberries on a branch dipping over a wall and she picked some, the taste taking her back to her childhood: cycling with a school friend along the country lanes, stopping to pick the sweet purple fruit.

Mellow thoughts were banished when she saw Trevor's car in the drive. Her mind became cold and detached as she climbed the stairs, hearing the noise of cupboard doors banging. The late afternoon sunlight glowed on the warm colours of the floral print curtains and duvet cover, but the atmosphere turned the colour to slate grey. Trevor's suits were piled on the bed and he turned to her. 'Where are the bloody suitcases?' he snarled.

'We've never had many. We rarely went away and then all our clothes were in poly bags. Dean and Mandy must have taken the cases. You don't know, but Mandy left yesterday, with Kevin, they've found a rented house. Your sister returned to Birmingham this morning.' The words fell on deaf ears. Trevor was pulling underpants and socks from drawers, not listening. He didn't care about his sister or Mandy – just himself.

The ice from the dagger that had stabbed her on Wednesday now sent a chill through her veins. She felt stone cold and full of anger.

'I saw you last Wednesday with Sharon. You weren't in Coventry. She must be four months pregnant. I presume this means you are leaving to live with her?'

Trevor looked up and glared at her. 'Yes. Yesterday she was rushed to hospital with a near miscarriage. The baby might have died.'

'Well that would have got you out of a difficult situation.'

A glass ornament crashed against the wall just above Jenny's head. A shard grazed her arm.

'How dare you say that about my, yes, my child. You evil, wicked woman!'

Jenny felt even colder, and moved to the doorway.

'I have put up with you and your women for years. If you wanted a child we could have had one, but person-ally I don't think you could cope with a baby, let alone a teenage child in your fifties. You never coped with the two you already have. Sharon is welcome to your philandering ways and a baby you will soon lose interest in.'

She rushed down to the kitchen to find a bandage for her cut arm and lit a cigarette to calm her. For the first time in her life she had stood up to Trevor.

He stormed into the room. 'Where are the black bags?'

'You have lived in this house for twenty-two years. You find them.'

As he rummaged through cupboards, he stormed, 'Whatever thanks have I ever had from you? When were you ever interested in me?'

He ranted and raved in a pompous manner, flinging his arms wide in a self-important gesture, moustache bristling.

'Pomposity and insurance never interested me. You and life assurance are boring. And what else have you done, except go to the pub with your workmates, equally as dull as you are? We could've gone places, explored life. You were good with the kids when they were little, until they outgrew you. You should have grown with them.' She did not want to be in the same room with him and went into the garden.

In the end she heard him slam the boot of the car and walking to the front door she calmed down. As he opened the driver's door, she said, 'I should wish you and Sharon well, but I don't. You had better get in touch with your solicitor.'

Trevor nodded, reversed fast into the road and was gone.

Jenny noticed her neighbour, Mrs Simms, intent on weeding her petunias. The elderly lady rose to her feet and Jenny tried to smile.

'Your hubby off to the launderette with all those black bags?' She must have overhead the row, thought Jenny. The walls of the semis were very thin.

'Yes,' said Jenny, 'he always visits his solicitor at the launderette,' and slammed the door.

She found a new bandage for the gash on her arm and took a dustpan and brush to the bedroom to sweep up the broken pieces of glass. The last shattered fragments of their broken family.

With energy generated by fury at Trevor's dismissive treatment she cleared out his remaining clothes, stuffed them into bags, and changed the sheets on the bed. The frantic activity stopped her thinking, but this did not last long and, exhausted, she slumped down on the sofa with a cigarette and a stiff whisky. She was angry. Angry with Trevor, angry with Dean, and Mandy for leaving, angry with Sheila for her rudeness. What had she done to deserve this? She had looked after them as best she could; now she felt abandoned, alone. After all the patience and tolerance she had shown to Trevor, he had now shown his true colours. The bastard. She remembered in recent years the evenings she had spent with the children, helping with homework, laughing with them, trying to understand them, on her own, making excuses for Trevor's absence.

Pouring another whisky she thought, it wasn't always like this, and got out the photograph albums and placed them on the table. Pyewacket joined her, crouching on the polished wood, purring. Jenny stroked his head. 'Look, this is us getting married.' Two young naive people, setting out on life together. The bride in white, the groom in a Burton's made-to-measure suit. The photos were taken outside the local Nonconformist

Church, one with the bridesmaids, Sheila not yet looking sour. Another with her parents, her father looking disapproving, but when did he not? Her mother gentle and smiling, but cowed by life. Uncle Bernard looking large and jolly, his arm around her mum's shoulders, laughter on his lips. Dad had always disapproved of Bernard – that he had spent his youth in the Merchant Navy, liked drink and cards.

'Pye, could I have inherited Mum's personality – let life dominate me? But it was a happy day. Look, there's Trev's dad looking bumptious. I've never realised how alike they are. I wonder what his mother was like? That's always a dark hole, never to be mentioned. It was always implied Trev's dad was a widower, or did his mum just walk out, or run off with the love of her life?' Jenny had never had the courage to ask.

'Edith always says; you turn into your parents by the time you are forty.' She sighed. 'What happened to all our dreams?'

She turned the page, topping up her glass, 'Oh, our honeymoon. We went to Newquay and I got food poisoning. But we did have a good time. Now the babies, they were gorgeous. Mandy taking her first steps. Dean in the sand pit. Then their first day at school.'

At the memories tears welled up in her eyes. The whisky was making her maudlin. 'What went wrong, Pye?' She flicked through more pages. Happy children at school sports day, digging sandcastles, fishing for tiddlers. Her tears were dampening the pages and she closed the album.

Grief for times gone by made her pour another whisky, to either cheer her or give her oblivion. Rising to her feet she staggered to lock the front door, and put the catch down, checked the back door and made her way to bed. Pulling off her clothes and flinging them anywhere, she thought, it's been a long day, in fact, a long weekend. Mandy leaving, Sheila leaving, Trevor leaving. Now she was alone. She no longer cared. Didn't even care enough to clean her teeth, just pulled the clean duvet over her naked body. In her befuddled state she sang to herself, 'I care for nobody, no not I, for nobody cares for me.'

She awoke next morning to grey clouds and drizzle. She sat up, her head spinning.

'No wonder,' she said to the empty house, 'after all that whisky. But at least it got me through the night. What's the time? Nine o'clock. I never set the alarm. Sorry Mr Has Been, can't face you today, I'll ring in and say I'm sick.'

She staggered downstairs, her head thumping, rang the office, made herself coffee, took two paracetamol, and sat down at the kitchen table. Lighting a cigarette she thought, I have a complete day on my own. The first for twenty-two years and I don't know what to do. I'm lost. First breakfast – then she realised there was no food. She made more coffee and dragged herself upstairs to the shower. It refreshed her somewhat and she thought a walk to the supermarket might help her headache. Her head still thumping, she picked items off the supermarket shelves then put them back. I don't need large tins of tomatoes. It's just me. I had better put those bananas back. I'll only need two. Just one pint of milk will be enough; I've got to watch the money. This must be how old-age pensioners feel.

She trudged home along the shiny greasy pavements, head down against the wind and rain, wondering how she would cope in the days to come, but her mind refused to work. These questions would have to be answered another day. She ate cheese on toast and watched mind-numbing daytime television until she fell asleep on the sofa and later with another tot of whisky dragged herself to bed.

Tuesday brought reality back to life. Rain lashed against the window and wind howled around the house. Despondently she put her mind back into gear. She had to go to work to earn money to live. No Trevor to help pay the bills. At eight o'clock she joined the commuter queue, her windscreen wipers aggressively swinging to and fro. 'All the main roads into Bristol are at gridlock because of the stormy conditions. This is Radio Bristol and Somerset Sound. We'll get you there.'

As she hung up her dripping raincoat she surreptitiously looked round the office, relieved to find she didn't have to apologise to Mr Has Been as he was later than she was, but Brian noticed a change in her, the way she stood, the expression on her face.

'Anything wrong?'

'Yes. Trev's left home. I'm on my own now. Not sure what to do.' She burst into tears and Brian, embarrassed, found her a Kleenex tissue, patted her on the shoulder and bought her a coffee from the machine.

'Thanks, Brian,' she said, sipping the imitation drink, 'sorry to be so miserable.'

'In the circumstances you are entitled to be. From what you've said about Trev he never sounded like Mr Wonderful.'

'No, but he wasn't always such a sod. And another thing – Mandy's shacked up with her boyfriend, so I'm all alone.' Tears started rolling down her cheeks again. She rolled the tissue into a ball and threw it vehemently at the bin. 'I must stop feeling sorry for myself!'

'Would you like me to ring your friend Edith in Special Needs? By lunchtime you might have some special needs.'

'Good idea. It's OK. I'll do it,' and she picked up the phone.

Jenny and Edith seated themselves at a table at the Mauritania pub with a gin and tonic. Edith picked up the menu. 'You need comfort food.'

'Yes I do. Haven't eaten much over the last few days what with Sheila's neurotic diet and Trev. I'm having egg, sausage and chips.'

While they waited for the food Jenny told Edith all that had happened over the weekend. Edith laughed at Sheila's outraged reaction. 'Silly selfish cow,' she said, 'living with old-fashioned attitudes. She should get herself a life!'

On hearing about the row Jenny had with Trevor: 'I'm glad you stood up for yourself. Any chance of him coming back, or do you find a solicitor?'

'In the past he has come back, but this time it is different. There's a baby involved. I think he'll stick by Sharon and support her and the baby until it gets too demanding. He'll enjoy being the proud father, feeling dominant. I must find a solicitor. I'll look at the adverts in the local paper this evening. I'm sure I can cope on my own and I've seen so little of him I won't miss his company. It's the children I miss. I hope Mandy's all right. She hasn't rung yet. I should ring her and Dean tonight and let them know their dad has left. I'm not looking forward to that.'

'They may well be aware of the situation and they're old enough to accept it and understand. It's you I'm worried about. Your life was centred about the family. That's why you've stuck at your boring job – to help pay for it all. Now is the time to re-think your own life. What would you like to do at weekends, in the evenings? No more cooking, washing and ironing. Any clubs you'd like to join, evening classes?'

'I was trying to thinking about that yesterday, but got nowhere. One thing I wondered about. I always was interested in art. I was hopeless at everything at school, except art, and never had any encouragement at home. Church was all Mum and Dad did. I could take up drawing and try painting pictures rather than walls. Find out about famous artists.' Her eyes filled with tears at the vision of her now empty life and she was relieved when the waitress arrived, her clumpy black shoes too high and her black skirt too tight, with two plates of food.

Edith dipped a chip into her egg yolk, 'I might be able to help with the art. I go to the Folk House once a week to an art appreciation class. The class isn't full, so come along. We meet tomorrow, Wednesdays. We've had a session on Picasso, he continues tomorrow, then Salvador Dali, so you can catch up.'

'Oh, Edith,' said Jenny resting her hand on Edith's wrist, 'you're such a good friend. I would really enjoy that. I won't come tomorrow. I have to sort out seeing the solicitor, and would I understand half of Picasso?'

'I don't think Picasso understood half of Picasso. Just look at his faces. His paintings are dissected before they start!' They both laughed at the idea.

'Perhaps next week, when I'm not so down.'

'Good. We can have a cup of tea and a sandwich up

Park Street before we go.' Edith smiled, 'Maybe a stiff drink before we start on Jackson Pollock or Damien Hirst.'

'Great. Now I have something to look forward too. Not look backwards all the time.' They left the pub with Edith quietly singing, 'We said we wouldn't look back', from *Salad Days*, which Jenny was too young to appreciate.

The rain had ceased as she drove home but the sky was filled with dark clouds against a violent yellow sky that forecasted wind. Jenny was not looking forward to telephoning Dean and Mandy but she had to face it. Once inside the front door she poured herself a large gin and tonic and rang Mandy. Kevin answered the mobile, his voice sounding more positive than usual.

'How's the house?' Jenny enquired.

'Basically it's fine. Some damp we'll have to deal with before we decorate.'

'No problem with you being a painter and decorator.'

'Yeah, I can visualise it in me mind. Spect you want to speak to Mandy.' She heard him put down the phone. Fancy – she thought – Kev knowing words like 'visualise'. Maybe he isn't as daft as he looks, just terrified of parents.

'Hello, Mum. This place is great and so near Asda and I can walk to work. How are you and Dad?'

'I'm very glad you're settling in, but the reason I'm ringing is Dad has left home. He's got a girlfriend who is having his baby, so I'm not expecting him back.'

'Mum, that's awful! How could he, after all you've done for him? Mind you he's been so bad-tempered for months it must be a relief not to have him there. I was quite glad to get away from him, I can tell you. But that's not the point. How will you cope?'

'Oh, I'll be all right. My job will keep me going financially, though the car might have to go. I'll keep busy.'

There was a muttered conversation in the background, but she could hear Kev's surprised tone and then, 'That's OK, if it's just your Mum.' Then Mandy was back. 'Come and see our new home. Can't be this weekend. We're off with some of Kev's biking friends. Next weekend. After twenty years it's my turn to give you lunch. Then we'll hand you a paint brush.' Jenny was so pleased. Mandy had accepted the situation and was happy to see her the weekend after next. 'I would love that. Now I must ring Dean and tell him.'

An aggressive female answered the phone, probably the one with black fingernails and spiky hair, 'Hello? No, Dean's out playing football. I'll tell him you rang.' The receiver was banged down.

Pyewacket jumped up on Jenny's lap. 'Hello Pye. I'm not really alone with you around. At least I got through to Mandy. Perhaps now she has her own place and partner she will be more friendly. She has been very distant recently, but that could have been Trev, as well as Kevin being around. I'll feed you. Then I must look for a solicitor.'

Solicitors only have answering machines after five o'clock so she wrote down several telephone numbers of local solicitors she could ring the next day and make an appointment for Saturday morning. That night Pyewacket curled up on her bed and purred.

Jenny went through the next three days like a zombie. She coped with work like an automaton and in the evenings drank too much whisky whilst inattentively, mind wandering, watched soap operas and detectives on television until her eyes drooped and she hoped she might sleep. Dreams accompanied sleep. A monstrous Trevor covered in warts chasing the children. Trevor threatening on a cliff edge. Her rushing down streets, frantically looking for Mandy and Dean as toddlers in ruined buildings, full of smoke and fire. She would wake up in a sweat and feeling weary, more tired than when she went to bed. Dragging herself out of bed, she showered, dressed, still slightly dizzy, and hoped she wouldn't crash the car on the way to work.

On Saturday morning she roused herself slightly later to see the solicitor. His drab little office was on the first floor of a utilitarian office block in the shopping precinct. Synthetic granite steps and portaflec walls. Mr Figgis, the solicitor, wore a shiny suit with wide stripes. He dealt with cases like hers all the time and wanted to make the most out of it.

Had he ever hit her? Were there mental cruelty grounds? Jenny kept on saying 'no', whilst he scratched his head with his biro and the dandruff fell on his grey shoulders.

'My husband has committed adultery and admitted it. He is living with another woman who is expecting his baby. I wish to divorce him and our house should be sold. Any money made should be divided between us. That is all that is necessary. Please don't make it complicated to increase your fee. Just get on with it.'

She left the office with tears flowing down her cheeks. He was just a leech trying to make money out of a miserable situation. She would have to get in touch with Trevor and agree to make it as simple as possible. This could have happened a few minutes later in the shopping precinct when Trevor and Sharon passed by hand in hand, carrying their weekend shopping, smiling at each other. Jenny couldn't bear it and had to look away into a shop window, seeing a reflection of her tear-stained face. They looked so youthful and she felt very old, as though every bone in her body ached.

She spent the rest of Saturday in misery. In the past when things had been bad she had shut them out by turning her attention to the children, ferrying them here and there, cooking for them and their friends, gardening, washing, ironing, darning but now there was nothing. Just emptiness. Anger and despair.

Contact the Samaritans – no, she had run out of words.

Why carry on? Would anyone miss her?

She had a full bottle of aspirins and a good supply of whisky. Just swallow the tablets, drink herself into oblivion and never wake up. It would be several days before anyone found her. She filled the tumbler with amber liquid took a couple of aspirins. The television and alcohol lulled her to sleep on the sofa before any more tablets left the bottle.

Bright sun and church bells woke her on Sunday morning. She looked at the whisky and the aspirins on the coffee table. The television talking to itself. What a fool, she thought. I wanted to die. Another failure! She smiled at herself – can't even commit suicide success-fully. I'd better make the best of the rest of my life. If there's a God in his heaven he wants me to live. Time to stop feeling 'poor little me'. She picked up the glass: the contents smelt of cardboard. Disgusting! I've been given a second chance. A life on my own where I can do exactly what I like. First breakfast – sardines on toast, good for the brain, then a long walk, to think. Food tasted so good when there was no pressure to get to work. She glanced through the *Mail on Sunday*, thinking she must cancel the papers: they were too expensive. She felt so keyed up, so different from her mood of the evening, and putting on a showerproof jacket, as the sky was now grey with cloud, set out to walk along by the river towards the North Somerset Levels – and think.

Tramping along by the slow-running stream, the reeds rustling in the breeze, her thoughts turned back to hot summers when Mandy and Dean, with red wellies and fishing nets, had tried to catch tadpoles here. She realised in the morning that last night's dark thoughts of total disillusion were dissolving with the light of day. Her love for Trevor and the children was based on the past, but it was still there, it would always remain, entwined in her memory. There was so much. The children being born. Their pride and enjoyment watching them grow. Laughter at their funny ways and sayings. Their amorous nights once the children were sleeping. Trev's support when her parents died after they had slowly disintegrated and shrivelled away in homes for old people. She had felt very vulnerable at the time, but he had been there. But later he had changed. Was it middle age? Did he have to prove he was still virile with someone else? When Mandy and Dean were older and able to speak up for themselves, it was she who had to ask where they were going in the evening. She who had to be stern advising them to revise for exams – GCSEs were important. Where had Trevor been? Where was the parental support and the mutual love in the night? The children were now adults and had decided on their own lives; Trevor had also gone to his new life. She was on her own and must look to her own future.

She wandered on along the stream listening to the reeds waving in the wind. Could she go on paying the mortgage on her own? No, she should sell the house and they could divide any profit after the mortgage was paid off. She did not want to keep on seeing Trev and Sharon at the shops, all lovey-dovey. She could find a one-bedroom flat somewhere near the office. No more commuting, sell the car and walk to work. She would have more time – new interests, Edith's art appreciation class for a start, perhaps study for a new career, make up for the time she had wasted at school.

A kingfisher flashed past her up river, the turquoise feathers briefly seen, but the vivid beauty remained, uplifting her thoughts. The wind was rising, the reeds now hissing against the blustery gale, and rain was pattering on her coat. The change in the weather changed her mood. She had to move in a different direction. Sail before the wind. There was a whole new world out there before her; hers for the taking. She opened her coat to take up the wind behind her, as a child pretending to fly, and ran home, the rain splashing across her face. No one to tell her what she should or shouldn't do. She laughed and shouted at the freedom.

Chapter 4

By the end of Wednesday Jenny felt more positive. She had found the art appreciation evening mentally stimulating. She could not remember when she had last concentrated so hard for two hours. The lecturer, with the unlikely name of Bartholomew Prendergast, had uncontrolled white hair and beard, and a sloppy cardigan which had seen better days. He talked on Dali with great enthusiasm, showing many slides of his paintings and sculptures, and her mind was in a whirl. She had always thought his painting of the Crucifixion, with Christ looking down on the world, transcended other depressing pictures of the same scene. The melting watches and other surreal images intrigued her.

'Thanks so much for asking me along,' said Jenny, taking Edith's arm as they walked down Park Street. 'I couldn't take it all in. I might try and get a book out from the library tomorrow. It will give me something to do over the weekend.'

On Thursday evening Jenny went to the nursing home to see Uncle Bernard for her weekly visit. He seemed in good spirits, reminiscing about his past at sea, places he had visited, odd characters he had met, so she was surprised when the matron drew her aside as she left.

'Bernard seems cheerful.'

'It's often that way just before the end,' replied the nurse. 'I've got your phone number if he deteriorates.'

'I can't imagine him not being around,' answered Jenny. 'He's the one person left alive I've known all my life.'

On Saturday she visited him again, but he just looked sightlessly at the ceiling, not conscious of her presence, and the change in him saddened her.

In the evening she had the novelty of sitting down on the sofa with her library book on Dali. She had time to appreciate the workmanship of his paintings and sculptures, his little jokes about life's absurdities and the surreal message of the clocks – life is finite. When you are young you think life lasts forever, but there is only so much time to achieve aims and ambitions.

Only so much time, she thought. Assuming I live to about eighty, I'm halfway through my life and what have I achieved? Mandy and Dean, a dead marriage, dull job, even a failed suicide. Now I have time to take stock. Given that time is limited, in a lifetime's sense, and money is limited, I need to think about what I would like to do with my life. Pyewacket was not impressed by all this deep thinking, and the cat flap banged as he went out into the night.

Mandy and Kevin's house was difficult to find in the back streets of Bedminster. It was in a Victorian terrace, the street similar to many others in the area. Mandy greeted her with a hug in the doorway and Jenny presented her with some flowers and a bottle of wine. They excitedly showed her round their living room, kitchen-cum-diner and two bedrooms. They had already made a start on painting over the drab wallpaper and Jenny could see the potential and the makings of a happy home. What a pity, she thought, it is just for rent; but if the relationship doesn't last, it maybe for the best. Mandy had gone to the trouble of roasting a chicken and they both had a laugh about the potatoes boiling dry. 'My first roast dinner,' she said with pride, pouring lumpy gravy onto the chicken on one of her mother's borrowed dinner plates.

'My mum always does a gravy dinner on Sundays while Dad's down the pub,' commented Kevin with his mouth full. A couple of glasses of wine brought him out of himself and he joked about some of the houses he had decorated and the foibles of his clients. Jenny was getting used to his shaven head, studs in his ears and tattoos on his arms. Mandy seemed very happy anyway.

True to their word, Jenny was set to work with a roller and tray of white paint, covering the stained mauve walls of the second bedroom whilst listening to Meat Loaf. A week ago she couldn't have imagined doing this.

Driving home, she was content about their situation and realised she felt quite laid back about it. How times had changed in a generation. None of the trauma or excitement of a white wedding, though that might come later. One day Mandy was a single girl, the next they were a couple. What would her parents have made of it? She could hear her father's condemning voice, 'Living in sin'.

The phone was ringing as she put the key in the door and her light-hearted mood changed to a sense of fore-boding.

'Mrs Evans? This is the matron at the nursing home. I'm sorry to tell you that your uncle passed away this afternoon. The end was very peaceful. I did try to contact you.'

'I'm sorry, I was out at my daughter's. Oh dear, I wish I had been with him. He should have had someone with him at the end.'

'Please don't worry yourself about it. He was unconscious most of the time and his favourite nurse, Mary, was there. You know, the one he wanted to chase behind the screens.' Jenny laughed weakly. 'He did whisper one name, "Eleanor". Do you know who that might be?'

'No. It means nothing to me.'

'Could you come in tomorrow, tell me which undertaker you wish to use and collect his belongings?'

'Of course. I'll come in after work.'

Jenny slumped at the kitchen table, staring into space. She felt bereft. Her family in fragments, shattered and scattered like the glass vase Trevor had thrown at her. Now her oldest blood relative had passed away, gone forever. She felt unaccountably alone. Apathetically she fed the cat then drifted into the living room where she poured herself a large gin and lit a cigarette. Gazing at the swirl of smoke she thought back through her memories of Uncle Bernard. He was a big burly man, with dark wavy hair and a beard. A total contrast to his thin mousy sister, her own mother. On his occasional leaves from the Merchant Navy he had brought laughter into her parents' dull household. He ignored her father's disapproval, cracked jokes, drank beer and taught her how to play Pontoon when her parents were out of the way at church meetings.

When he had left the sea he had bought a rundown guesthouse in Bath, which her mother had pointed out was not in the best part of town. When the children were younger she had taken them to Bath in the school holidays on the train. They had done the tourist bit, visiting the Baths, then went to see Uncle at the guesthouse. He always provided them with jam doughnuts for tea then showed them the canal behind the house. They enjoyed running up and down the towpath and watching the narrowboats in the locks, sometimes helping push open the lock gates. If they were in a receptive mood he would get out his guitar and sing them sea shanties and funny songs that made them giggle. But something had happened in recent years turning him into a gloomy individual. Jenny had never been able to find out what this was, but the guesthouse, which he had built up into a good business, declined and he became an irritable old man. Now this was how people thought of him. Only Jenny remembered the younger, jolly uncle.

Saddened by feelings of regret that she had not been with him at his death, and a colourful life now ended, she rose stiffly from the sofa. The unaccustomed afternoon's painting had taken its toll on her joints. What she needed was a hot bath and bed to enable her to face the office in the morning.

Dreams of surreal funerals – Bernard's coffin rushing off down the road, mourners running after like the Keystone Cops – turned sleep into a nightmare as her brain turned over plans for the coming week; undertakers, solicitors and the Herculean task of clearing out his home.

'You look terrible,' said Brian, looking with concern at her unkempt hair and dark circles under her eyes. Without another word he fetched her a coffee from the machine. What would she do without considerate Brian she wondered?

'What's happened now?' he asked placing the plastic cup in front of her.

'My uncle, the one with cancer, has died. I'm his only relative so I've got to arrange everything and I'm panicking about where to begin.'

Brian looked thoughtful. 'When my Mum died two years ago I had to register the death – you need the death certificate – see the solicitor, in case there is anything in the will about funeral arrangements. If he was a sailor he might want to be buried at sea.'

He started singing 'For those in peril on the sea', to try and make her laugh, and she giggled, 'Don't. I'd be seasick.'

'Then it's the undertakers and contacting other people – neighbours and friends. It all takes time. Have a few days' leave.'

'None left. I used it all up in July. I was so fed up with Trev I rented a cottage in Cornwall and took Dean and his mates surfing.'

'Unpaid leave then, and the wrath of Has Been; though he's usually considerate about family matters. And while you are gadding about town, Mrs Evans, get your hair done. Can't have you looking so scruffy in the ranks.'

'Yes Sir,' she mocked.

Mr Haspen grudgingly gave her three days' compassionate leave. Her final visit to the nursing home was sad as she said goodbye to the nurses, who had been so helpful, collected Uncle Bernard's death certificate and belongings and was relieved when the matron gave her the solicitor's address in Bath, as she had no idea where to find the will.

After the stresses of the day home seemed a welcome retreat where she could cook sausages and beans, zombie-watch television and cuddle Pyewacket. She noticed the Salvador Dali book on the sofa. What had happened to her thoughts on time and the limits it puts on life? Death and practical living had got in the way. Had Bernard felt his life fulfilled? Maybe not from his gloomy mood in old age. But she was not near the end of her life and must look forward. The question was, where?

The next day she contacted the solicitor and arranged to see him on Wednesday morning. There were no instructions on the funeral in the will. So much for Brian and burials at sea, she thought, and she telephoned the undertaker recommended by the nursing home, arranging an appointment that afternoon. Now she had time to get to the local shops and get her hair done. She had it cropped short, feeling that highlights were an unnecessary extravagance, and decided this made her look ten years younger. The undertakers were situated in a suitably Victorian Gothic office and the funeral director, a pompous florid man with a waxed moustache gushed suitable sympathetic clichés that oozed from him like treacle. He arranged the funeral for Friday. 'You're lucky it's a slack time of year,' he smiled greasily, 'not like January, or a flu epidemic. Then they come in quicker than we can get them out.' He arranged for notices in local newspapers and found her a minister willing to officiate at the service. She went home feeling confident Uncle Bernard's farewell ceremony would now go ahead.

Slocombe and Slocombe's brass plate, on a mellow Bath stone terraced building, conveyed they were very different from Mr Figgis, the solicitor she had seen eleven long days ago. There were flowers on the highly polished table in the entrance hall and the grey-suited Mr Slocombe had a quiet, deferential manner. He ushered Jenny into his office where legal tomes filled bookcases between richly embossed wallpaper. Mr Solcombe requested his secretary to bring them coffee and he opened a buff file on his desk. He made the usual sympathetic remarks about her uncle and asked about the funeral arrangements then, smiling in what he hoped was a friendly manner, referred to the contents of the will.

'You will be pleased to know, Mrs Evans, you are quite a rich woman.' Jenny stopped stirring her coffee and sat up straight. Did she hear him say 'rich'?

'Apart from two bequests, you inherit the guesthouse, all his worldly goods and two hundred thousand pounds.'

'Two hundred thousand pounds?'

'Yes. He obviously didn't plough his profits back into the guesthouse. Of course you will have to take into account Inheritance Tax.'

'But it will still be a large amount of money. I'm used to dealing in hundreds, not thousands. What are the two bequests?'

'One of five hundred pounds to Missions to Seamen and the other to a Ms Eleanor Watson with an address in Bath. It is a considerable sum of ten thousand pounds, but unfortunately Ms Watson no longer lives at that address. We shall have to make further inquiries.'

'You said "Eleanor".'

'Yes.'

'I don't know who she is, but apparently Bernard murmured her name to the nurses during his last few days. I wonder who she is? He must have thought a lot of her to leave that sort of money.'

'We'll have to find out. But it does mean, assuming you sell the guesthouse, worth between a quarter and half a million, that you will be a wealthy woman.' He eyed her up and down, taking in her shabby suit and shoes.

44

Jenny gulped the last of her cold coffee, too amazed to think straight. She knew property prices had increased, but a quarter of a million pounds?

'I can't quite take this all in at the moment. I shall have to take everything into account before I decide what to do.'

'Of course. But when you come to sell the property I shall be happy to act for you.'

'Thank you. Thank you very much for all you've told me. I have recently separated from my husband so this will change my situation considerably. I need to go away and think about everything.'

'Back to the more mundane. Have you got keys to the guesthouse?'

'Yes.'

'Would it be possible for you to visit the premises and find any bills, bank statements, any financial documents that might be needed for probate. The quicker these minor items are cleared up the sooner the will can be settled.'

'I don't have to be back in Bristol until this evening. I'll go there this afternoon and see what I can find.'

Still thunderstruck by this news, Jenny left the solicitors, conscious of her dowdy clothes, and found the nearest café and tried to adjust her thoughts. The coffee prices, suitable for tourists, shocked her, but now she didn't have to worry any more. Sipping her drink she thought, I can pay off the mortgage, give Mandy the down payment on a house, pay for Dean's university fees. She felt elated, and finding the keys for Uncle Bernard's home in her handbag, set out down Milsom Street to the railway station. Now she had to cast her mind back several years and find her way to the guesthouse.

She had to locate the footbridge by the railway station, the walkway taking her over the green-brown slow-flowing river Avon, then past depressing shops to another traffic-congested road system. She waited for the pedestrian lights and before her in a terrace of houses was 'La Casa', Uncle Bernard's guesthouse. Four storeys and a basement of grimy neglect. From outside she could see the grey net curtains, the discoloured plastic flowers on the windowsills, the peeling sign. Her feeling of euphoria left her. She remembered a freshly painted front door, geraniums in pots, and a bright sign. Now in less than ten years this had gone. What had happened to Uncle Bernard?

She crossed the road and climbed the five litter-strewn steps to the peeling door. The door was reluctant to open against the pile of mail dropped inside. She picked up the dusty letters, mostly junk mail, and surveyed the hall. Six months' dust covered many months' lack of cleaning. Uncle Bernard must have been ill for longer than she realised. Pushing open the door into the dining room she felt like the sailor who had discovered the *Marie Celeste*.

The six tables were laid for breakfast and dirty glasses were stacked on the bar. Cobwebs dangled from the moulded cornice and once-elegant light fittings. The sofas, slightly greasy, in the bay window no longer looked welcoming, the red velvet curtains tattered with wear. Ring marks on the coffee tables and a *Daily Mail* dated 25th March gave a hint of what might have happened. She must ask the neighbours. All she remembered was suddenly being summoned to Bath United Hospital and several depressing visits to sit by his beside before he was admitted to the nursing home, the cancer too far gone for any treatment. Did he have staff and had they been paid?

The kitchen was at the back of the building behind the dining room but she refrained from opening the door, imagining mice droppings and dead flies, and went downstairs to Bernard's living room and bedroom. Mr Slocombe had asked for any documents needed for probate and these might be in his living room. This room had a comfortable, shabby but melancholy air, as though the room itself was mourning its late occupant. It was cluttered and there were several empty whisky bottles in the waste paper basket. Another sign things had not been well for the old man. Perhaps the whisky had had an anaesthetising effect. As she looked around for anything useful for the solicitor she examined the mantelpiece. People often stacked letters behind the clock but there, to her surprise – and jolting her mind back over thirty years – was the model sailing ship she remembered Uncle making on one of his shore leaves. As a child she had stood wide-eyed watching him cut intricate pieces of wood and threading rigging through tiny pulleys whilst he had explained to her the names and the uses for each rope. She couldn't remember these now but the quiet companionship and the humour filled her with a warm glow. They had been happy times. Perhaps she could keep the ship when she had the house cleared. That would be a job! But the thought of quarter to half a million pounds would be an incentive. She couldn't imagine having that much money.

Wandering through to the back of the basement she unbolted the door and climbed into the back yard. Weathered picnic tables, green with moss, were set on the patchy grass but Virginia creeper glowed red and orange along the wall and some late roses still bloomed giving the place a tranquil air. Beyond she could see the still water of the canal and some black and white lock gates adding to the peace. With hard work, she thought, someone could make 'La Casa' a going concern once more, though they would be wise to change the name.

Glancing at her watch she realised there was no more time to look through Bernard's correspondence if she wanted to met up with Edith before the art appreciation class. She would return at the weekend and continue her search.

The pair of them found a wine bar half way up Park Street and settled themselves on a comfortable sofa with glasses of red wine. Edith expressed her sympathy over Uncle Bernard and was then curious to hear about Jenny's visit to the solicitors, but Jenny found she didn't want to mention the will. She still couldn't believe she had inherited money and a valuable property and by talking about it, it might disappear. She talked about the funeral arrangements and how the guesthouse, now so neglected, had depressed her.

'When he first lived there he worked so hard to make it bright and cheerful, then both he and the business . . .' her voice trailed away.

'It happens when people get old and ill. My dad was a teacher. He really enjoyed his job when he was young but had to take early retirement. He couldn't cope once he got to sixty.'

'Yes, that's one of Salvador Dali's messages – those melted clocks. Time runs out on us all. I'm going back to Bath on Saturday. Want to come?'

'Oh, I'd love a day out, especially if I can do a bit of shopping. Now let's go and see what Bartholomew has to say on Miro.'

Bartholomew Prendergast practically danced with

enthusiasm as he manipulated the slide projector, showing picture after picture, which Jenny had to admit she didn't understand. Despite this she realised there was much to learn. As they walked down the hill after the meeting the two ladies chuckled at the remark of a rather straight-laced elderly man who had said, 'I wouldn't want that on my drawing room wall.'

'What a stupid thing to say,' laughed Edith, 'I wouldn't want most of the great paintings of the world in my living room – fancy having to live with Munch's "The Scream" – but that doesn't stop it being great.'

The day of the funeral dawned bright and clear, a mockery of the event waiting ahead. Jenny pressed the creases out of her only sober black suit, and as the steam rose from the damp towel placed over the old material wondered when she had last worn it. Probably Trevor's father's funeral several years ago. All she could remember of that event was his two aunts having a bitter row over the choice of music. What was wrong with Ella Fitzgerald singing 'Blue skies smiling at me' if Trev's dad had liked it? She should have bought a new suit; she could now afford a new suit. And should she have asked mourners back to the house and provided lunch? Would there be any mourners apart from herself? Too late to worry about that now: she had better get to the crematorium and be ready to greet anyone who might turn up.

Why, she wondered, were crematoriums always built on desolate wind-swept hillsides? Two nurses from the nursing home were waiting outside the chapel, one of them being Bernard's favourite – Mary. They talked with sadness about Bernard for a few moments then Jenny turned her attention to an elderly couple – the only other two mourners. Jenny introduced herself and the old man removed his battered tweed hat and smiled through rheumy eyes.

'We saw you out in the garden the other day. We live next door. We didn't know Mr Ellis, your uncle, very well. He seemed an unhappy man and preferred his own company. In the last few months he was obviously unwell, heard him coughing a lot, but it was us he called on for help the last evening he was home. We phoned for an ambulance.'

'Thanks for helping him. I shall be at the guesthouse tomorrow. Perhaps I could knock on your door and you can tell me more about him. I knew him well in the past, but had seen little of him recently.'

'We'd like that,' murmured his wife, 'I was always concerned about him.' With that the hearse arrived and the small group slowly followed the coffin with a solitary wreath into the chapel. Jenny felt relieved she hadn't chosen hymns – five people wouldn't make a choir. Tears started to flow, as Jenny was saddened not only by Bernard's death but by how few people mourned his departure.

During the first prayer she was aware that someone else had joined the sparse congregation but with head bowed couldn't look round. As they stood for the committal she glanced round and saw a tall woman in her fifties with dark hair piled elegantly on top of her head. Their eyes met, the stranger's a brilliant tear-filled hazel-green, ringed with dark lines of grief. By the time they emerged from the chapel to strains of Elgar's *Nimrod* the mysterious lady had gone. Jenny wondered who she was; perhaps she had come to the wrong cremation, having left early and so distraught. In the rush of thank yous and goodbyes, Jenny forgot about her.

Chapter 5

Jenny and Edith felt like kids on a day out as they set out for Bath. There was a narrow gravel track at the back of the terrace by the canal where Jenny left her car. With the key in her hand, feeling the pride of possession, however brief, the pair walked down from the canal to the main road and the front of the terrace. Autumn leaves floated on the brown waterway and there was the continuous sound of flowing water from the leaking lock gates.

Unlocking the front door Jenny mentioned, 'I've brought coffee, milk and biscuits so I'll be brave and open the kitchen. Let's hope there aren't any mice. When we've had our elevenses we'll explore the upstairs.'

Edith muttered at the dust and the cobwebs, which grew to sounds of dismay at the sight of the kitchen.

'How many guests died of food poisoning?' she asked, picking up a greasy frying pan.

'Let's hope the gas works,' answered Jenny, picking up a dusty kettle and turning on the water tap and letting it run. 'He probably hadn't paid the bills for months.' They were in luck with the water and gas and the kettle was soon whistling.

'This hasn't seen the mighty power of Jif for many

moons,' Edith commented as she peered at the cooker.

'I'll hire a clearance firm to get rid of all this stuff when the time comes,' mused Jenny, 'Ah, found some mugs. Ugh, there's a dead spider in this one. Don't worry. I'll wash them properly.'

They sat on the grubby sofas in the bay window watching the traffic, munching digestive biscuits and sipping their coffee.

'You haven't actually said so,' remarked Edith, 'but I imagine you've inherited this place.'

'Yes. I didn't say so before, because I couldn't believe it. And some money as well. It'll make so much difference when I'm divorced.'

'That's what I wanted to mention. If I were you I wouldn't tell anyone, even Mandy and Dean, until it is all signed and sealed. Probate I think they call it. I would hate to think of Trevor getting his grubby hands on this. Dilapidated it might be, but still worth a small fortune. Keep very quiet and get that divorce through as fast as you can.'

'I hadn't thought of that! Yes, Trev could get greedy if he realised there was money about. I'm used to keeping quiet.'

'You can say that again, after all his affairs.'

'According to the solicitor, he has already admitted adultery. I think he wants to marry the beautiful Sharon before the baby is born. Make an honest woman of her,' and they both laughed. 'Let's look at the guest rooms. They can't be worse that the kitchen.'

The first and second floors had two double and two single bedrooms on each floor. The top floor had two double rooms and a single room with dormer windows set in the roof. Edith and Jenny tramped up the threadbare carpet, which had once been patterned with pink roses. Examining the brown stained wallpaper and the damp floral bedspreads covering thin moth-eaten blankets and saggy pillows Edith expressed the opinion, 'My mother had this design many years ago. It must be at least twenty-five years old, maybe more. What are the bathrooms like?' These were of a similar standard, done in turquoise tiles decorated with angelfish and shells. There were grey-brown lime scale stains in the washbasins from dripping taps and the blue lino floor curled at the edges. On these two floors there were radiators with copper-coloured stains by the joints that Jenny felt were inoperable. If she turned on the boiler there might be leaks everywhere.

The top floor had an extra door at the top of the stairs. Jenny tried the handle and found it was locked. From the position of the two doors adjacent to each other, Jenny guessed the door led to a box room. 'Perhaps I'll find a key when I go through Bernard's bits and pieces behind the reception desk. That's the next job after I've chatted to the people next door.'

'And I'll go and mooch round the shops. I could do with a new warm coat for the winter.'

'Could you buy some sandwiches or baguettes? I shall be starving in a couple of hours.'

'Sure. Hope you have luck with the neighbours.'

The elderly lady Jenny had met at the funeral answered her knock.

'Do come in, dear, my name's Dorothy Worthington. I expect you'd like a cuppa after all that dust next door. Come through to the kitchen. We only live in the base-ment. The rest is rented out to students, helps with our pension.' She bustled to the rear of the house overlooking an attractive walled garden. Her husband lowered his *Daily Express*. 'Look, Tom, here's Jenny we met at the funeral.' He rose and shook her hand.

'I expect it's a mess next door.'

'Yes, it's awful. So depressing. I can remember when Uncle kept it really smart.' Dorothy handed her a cup of tea and a plate with home-made cake.

'This cake is lovely,' Jenny said through a mouthful of crumbs. 'It is so sad next door. Something happened to Uncle Bernard about ten years ago, I don't know what. I used to visit him with the children when they were small and had some happy times. He used to get out his guitar and sing them songs. Then suddenly he didn't want us there and was quite rude. The kids didn't want to go after that. I visited a few times but he was always morose and bad-tempered. I asked him if anything was wrong, if he was ill, but he just told me to mind my own business. Did you live here then?'

'No, we moved here seven years ago and he always kept himself to himself. Even at Christmas and New Year he would never come in for a drink or a chat – not that he was rude.'

'No,' added Dorothy, 'he was polite, but distant. But we could see the guesthouse going downhill. The guests weren't as smart – seedy commercial travellers and there was often a "vacancies" sign up in the window. Then he didn't even bother with that.'

'Then about a year ago I was in the garden pruning the roses and Mr Ellis was sitting at the tables smoking his endless cigarettes and coughing. I asked him if he was all right and he told me to bugger off. Not like him at all.'

'He never used to smoke much,' Jenny commented, 'but he liked a drink.'

'Yes, we think he drank quite a lot, usually with the guests, and it kept him cheerful,' interrupted Dorothy. 'It was the smoking made him ill. Then back in March, early in the morning he banged on our door, his chest heaving and gasped "please help", and we called an ambulance.'

Jenny sighed. 'If only he had asked for help sooner.'

'It could have been pride,' said Tom, 'or, though we shouldn't say this, had he just had enough of life? Old people do get like that.'

'Yes, I remember my father-in-law saying that. But Uncle had such a zest for life in his younger days. A spark that died.' The remark triggered a thought in her brain.

'Did you ever meet anyone around here called Eleanor?' They shook their heads. 'He left her some money. I think she must be important, but I know nothing about her. I've found it helpful talking to you about how he was. But I must get back now and go through his office stuff. Thanks for your help and that cake, Dorothy. You're a good cook. Hope to see you around before I sell the place.'

Aware she had little time to examine Bernard's small office behind his reception desk she hastily made her way back to the guesthouse. Behind what had been an attractive reception area, the desk had become a giant waste paper basket. Bills and receipts had been shoved anywhere. Office 'know-how' came into play and she put everything in date order before putting them in categories. It was rather like playing Patience. Edith returned and showed off her new winter coat and a sequinned top she might wear to impress a new gentleman friend.

'You're a dark horse, Edith.'

'And why not? Few years yet to my pension. I'm more attractive than you think. Got any paper clips? I'll help you sort these.'

Whilst munching their ham baguettes the two efficient ladies had tidied up Bernard's clerical mess and Jenny had an envelope of bills to send to Slocombe and Slocombe. At the back of the last drawer they found several unlabelled keys.

'I'm too tired to bother about these now,' sighed Jenny, sagging in a dilapidated chair. 'Tell you something I'll take, if you help me carry everything. I'd hate the clearance people to take it. Uncle Bernard's ship. Come down to the basement.'

The two ladies clattered down the stairs. Edith took in the dank damp smell but her eyes lit up at the sight of the ship.

'Yes, you have to take that. That sums up Uncle Bernard,' and her eyes swept round the room, 'and the guitar. We can wrap them in old sheets off the beds.'

Later that evening Jenny arrived home at 44 Cherry Avenue to a house alight and the beat of music. Dean had come home for the weekend.

'Hello Mum. Thought you might need cheering up after Dad and Uncle B. Besides ...'

'You've run out of money and you'd like some food.'

'How did you know?'

'After eighteen years I can read you like a book,' and she gave him a grateful hug. Oh how she had missed him.

After they had eaten a large English breakfast, despite it being the evening, found some cans of beer and opened a bottle of wine, Dean talked about college life. He was enjoying the course, had made new friends and seemed so confident compared with the nervous boy she had left at the student flat a short time ago.

'Last Saturday I went canoeing up the Tamar: it was great going under Brunel's bridge then exploring the little creeks. We nearly got stuck as the tide was going out. I've got a nice girlfriend called Cassy who's studying marine biology. Might bring her home next time I come.'

'Well that's something we need to talk about. Your dad and I won't need this house any more. We'll have to sell it, halve any money there is after paying off the mortgage and I'll rent somewhere in Bristol and sell the car.' She deliberately didn't mention Bernard's will. No doubt the children would be getting in touch with their father and she didn't want him learning about a sudden windfall.

'That means I won't have a home.' Dean sounded crestfallen.

'I'll find somewhere with two bedrooms. You'll need a base, somewhere in the holidays.'

'Vacation, Mum.'

'When you will probably find a temporary job, which could be anywhere. Things will have to change.'

'Yeah, sorry Mum. Dad's walked out on you and I must see it from your point of view.' (How adult Dean's become in so short a time, thought Jenny.) 'Think I realised, I was about thirteen, he wasn't around when he should have been. He said it was work, but perhaps it wasn't.' He looked sad and wistful for a minute and got himself another beer and filled his mother's wine glass.

'Thanks. It's been a difficult time and not easy to come to terms with. I've felt very bitter the last few weeks.'

'I'm not surprised. You were always here, nagging

57

mainly, but we understood why,' and he smiled. 'But what about you? You're going to have to move, but stay working for the Council, a good safe job, pension in twenty years time or what?'

'I've been wondering that. I've been going to these art appreciation classes and studying Dali.'

'Well, that's a positive move.'

'And I've come across these melted clocks in his pictures.'

'Yeah, remember them from some art trip at school.'

'They convey you only have so much time, and I'm wondering what I can do with the next twenty to thirty years of my life. I'm not going to do anything very dramatic, like discover penicillin or run the Bank of England, because I haven't the education or the time, but something more that checking who has free school dinners.'

'Is that what you do all day? As far as I knew you just went to the office. How boring.'

'Someone has to do it, but not me any more.'

'How about caring for people. You do care for people, like Uncle B and Sheila. VSO, or working for a charity, or the elderly.'

'If I'd cared for Bernard earlier things could have been different. Can't see me doing VSO: tramping through darkest Africa to help the starving.'

'No, you're right, the mosquitoes might get you. I remember you in the caravan. Zapping them with the spray can.'

'I need to do something different. Very different. Now please help me bring a couple of things in from the car.'

Dean carried the sheet-draped ship whilst Jenny brought in the guitar.

'I remember this,' exclaimed Dean. 'It was on Uncle Bernard's mantelpiece.'

'Yes, and I remember him making it. Isn't it a lovely reminder of him? I shall put it on the sideboard,' she said as she pushed Trevor's skittles trophies to one side.

'And the guitar. He used to sing songs to us that were funny. One of the students at the house has taught me the three-chord trick. I wonder if I can remember the songs.' He twanged away at the guitar, tightening the strings, then started singing, tentatively as first, then more confidently,

'What shall we do with the drunken sailor,
What shall we do with the drunken sailor?
What shall we do with the drunken sailor?
Early in the morning.'

Memories flooded back into Jenny's mind too. She could see Bernard and the two happy excited children watching him closely.

'Hooray and up she rises,' she joined in, happy that Dean remembered the old man in earlier times.

On Sunday Mandy and Kev were very pleased to see Dean and Jenny with a large Chinese meal in a brown carrier bag that accompanied them. There was more painting, loud music, jokes in bad taste and Jenny was very content to be in the company of young people. It lightened her mood. Yes, somewhere outside her office/domestic prison there was a life and she would find it.

Monday morning had been its usual dull self, except for Brian's dubious pub joke, which was not politically correct. At lunchtime Jenny was rummaging through her bag for change for the coffee machine when she came across a red electricity bill. In the past Trevor had paid the bills for the house as it made him feel in control – the master of his household. Jenny had seen the first red bill, well more pink and polite, lying around on the kitchen table. Obviously it had not been paid. This was the third reminder, after which would come the threat of the bailiffs, and this bill was three weeks overdue. She had intended to pay it ten days ago but with more important events on her mind she had forgotten. Now there was a real threat of bailiffs knocking on the door and the supply being cut off.

Jenny felt that if she went home to a dark house with not even a kettle to make a cup of tea she might again take to the whisky bottle.

'Brian, I've forgotten to pay the electricity bill. I may be cut off! No lights, TV, hot water, cup of tea.'

Brian looked thoughtfully at his ham sandwich. 'You've got twenty minutes before Has Been starts looking at his watch. The nearest bank is just across the Centre. You can nip over there, write a cheque and be back in fifteen.'

Jenny ran along the hard pavements as fast as she could. Being lunchtime, there was a queue in the bank and she fought with her impatience for ten minutes. The clerk then did a very good impression of this being her first day in the job and computers being a mystery to her, so Jenny left half an hour later in a state of anger and frustration.

'You're late back from lunch, Mrs Evans,' reprimanded Mr Haspen.

'Sorry. I had to pay the electricity bill before I was cut off.'

In a cold voice her boss continued, 'You were given

three days last week to deal with domestic problems. Your timekeeping during the last few weeks has been very irregular. I cannot run an efficient office if my staff are always late. I will now give you an official warning, Mrs Evans. It will be put on the records.'

Something exploded inside Jenny. Not the cold ice dagger of Trevor's departure but a bright sparkling crystal of hope. Spangles of light tingled down her arms and legs, and set her aglow. She took a deep breath -

'I don't think you need bother with that, Mr Haspen. You can stuff your boring job and your efficient office. I've had enough of the nine to five existence. Joining the commuter queue each morning. Tired of doing what is expected of me. "Yes Mr Haspen, no Mr Haspen." I'm going to be free. The one who tells other people what to do. I shall be leaving at the end of my month's notice. I'm going to run a guesthouse. The best guesthouse in Bath.'

Chapter 6

'What have I done, Brian?' Jenny asked.

'Am I off to the coffee machine again?'

'No, I'll go.' A few minutes later she handed him a coffee.

'I've just handed in my notice.'

He put his hand on his heart, 'You cannot leave me, my darling.'

She responded, 'Dearest, I have to go. I have just inherited a fortune and can no longer grovel in this servile existence,' and rose from an unbecoming curtsy. They both laughed and Jenny, still stunned, told Brian of her inheritance.

'When I learnt of Uncle Bernard's will and the money involved I thought I would sell the place; but now, I've been there twice recently, the house is calling me, inviting me in. Can a house talk to you or is it the ancestors? The idea of a guesthouse is the challenge I need.'

'Good for you,' said Brian, thinking hard. 'Make a new start. But this has come like a bombshell out of the blue. You need to think and plan. The house is a wreck and you'll have to deal with that.'

'Thanks, yes, I know,' said Jenny with emphasis. 'At

the moment I am on cloud nine but trying to come to terms with no job, no security. I've got the vast future of the rest of my life, which I was questioning, and now it's here, the answer, and I have to say yes. I will take on the challenge and run a superb guesthouse.' She had become excited, bringing animation to her face and a new light to her eyes. 'I can see the guesthouse now, flowers in the garden, bright décor, new carpets, happy guests with eggs and bacon for breakfast.'

'Can you cook?'

'Of course. And I know you have to take tests on food hygiene. You're right – the whole thing needs planning. With the money I should have time to think it out properly. Now I'd better get on with this mundane work for the next thirty days.'

Which she did, despite Brian's occasional interrupting comments about new bathrooms, fire doors, difficult builders.

'Plumbers. Hard to find a good plumber.'

'Damn. Brian, you've just made me delete a child who needed a free dinner. What do you know about plumbers and planning?'

'I've got a B.Tech in Business Studies, and the wife, Liz, is an accountant. She's had a lot of experience setting up new businesses.'

'If you seriously want to help me, come to Cherry Avenue on Friday night for a Chinese takeaway and do some positive planning.' Brian looked at her with concern, as they had known each over the office desk for several years and he cared for her.

'Yes. I want to see you get out of this rut, make a new life. But I'm also afraid you might be making a mistake.'

'Better still, I'll meet you and Liz in Bath on Saturday.

Look at the place and give me your opinion.'

'A day out, and an interesting evening. I wonder if "Has Been" knows what he has done?'

Jenny buckled down to work for the rest of the week. Enjoyed Bartholomew Prendergast's joyful interpretation of the life of Piet Mondrian, who seemed to have started out painting beautiful landscapes and trees then ended up designing what looked like Formica-topped tables and wallpaper. What had happened in his life and thinking? Edith seemed confused as well.

Quiet evenings were filled with thoughts of the future instead of watching TV and being irritated by *EastEnders*. Pyewacket sat on her lap while she stared into space and made planning notes on an A4 pad.

Early on Saturday afternoon she drove up the back lane of the guesthouse and parked by the garage. A narrowboat was sliding into the lock. It was a serene autumn day and tourists were leaning over the white- painted wrought-iron bridge above the lock watching the boat as it was lowered down to the next level. I'll be able to see this all the time, she thought, this will be my home. Her whole body was filled with hope and a bright new future.

Before Brian and Liz arrived she had time to walk around, ignore the dirt and imagine the guesthouse in six months' time. She visualised six double bedrooms and five singles with en suite bathrooms, or showers. It was possible that there was room in the double bedrooms for bunk beds or cots for children. She could see the clean white walls, bright curtains with matching duvet covers and patterned carpets that didn't show the dirt; only the dirty, flyblown kitchen defied her.

Liz turned out to be a glamorous brunette with shrewd

eyes. She was wearing a casual trouser suit and carrying a briefcase, in contrast to Brian's well-worn jacket and grey flannel trousers; but from the way they looked at each other, they were still very much in love.

'What an exciting situation to find yourself in, Jenny.' Liz looked eagerly round the dining-room cum-bar. 'The house is close to the town, bus station and trains. Not the Royal Crescent, but convenient.' She peered out of the window. 'You've got a small play park opposite and a view of the Abbey. If you can afford the outlay you could make this a going concern.'

'Traffic could be noisy,' commented Brian, 'and parking a problem.'

'Not if they come by bus or train. Have to think about that in the advertising. But first let's think about planning.' She emphasised this by making inverted comma signs with her forefingers.

Jenny was impressed by this forthright attitude. It was like being hit by a whirlwind. How did Brian live with it? She went to make some coffee and persuade her mind to think 'planning'. As she returned with three steaming mugs Liz announced, 'First you must get the place surveyed. Make sure it's wind and weather tight and the walls are structurally sound. Are the bedrooms with bathrooms? Need to be in this commercial era. Are the walls load-bearing? Architect essential. Are you taking notes, Brian?'

'I'll find a blunt pencil and the back of an envelope, my dearest,' sighed her husband, producing a notepad and biro from his jacket. Brian had been in this situation before.

As they drank their coffee Liz talked of a client who went bankrupt when he suddenly had to pay for roof repairs. Jenny thought it sounded like 'Street Repairs' in a game of Monopoly when you had a hotel on Mayfair, which made Brian laugh. Jenny wondered how good an accountant Liz was if her clients went bankrupt but kept quiet. After all, it was very good of Brian and Liz to give up their Saturday.

'What about bathrooms?' asked Brian mildly.

'Later, Brian. Let's be methodical. Start at the top of the house and work down.' With this command Liz headed for the stairs. Jenny, relieved she hadn't started in the kitchen, followed her at a run as Liz took the stairs two at a time.

As Jenny reached the top storey puffing, Liz smiled, 'At least you'll be fitter after a few months of tramping up here with the vacuum and clean sheets.'

'I'll feel that's an achievement.'

'What's behind this door? It's locked.'

'I expect it's a box room. I've found various odd keys but haven't matched them to the doors yet.'

'It could be turned into a bathroom for these bedrooms. They're not that big. Brian take notes! Given the building seems sound, though that lies with the surveyor and architect, a good plumber is going to be important.' Again emphasis was given with both forefingers. A good plumber means expensive, thought Jenny, but probably cheaper in the long run.

'Write down tiler as well, Brian.' Then turning to the bedrooms, 'These windows will need attention, dormer windows in the roof always tend to get wet rot, and you'll need new carpets and curtains everywhere and of course beds. Get rid of everything. Rubbish skip, Brian!'

'Strong man also required, Brian,' chipped in Jenny.

'Not me,' he smiled.

The same comments and instructions were issued for the other double bedrooms that were fortunately big enough to

66

incorporate the now necessary en suite bathrooms.

'If you're thinking of catering for families there is room for bunk beds in the double bedrooms. That would increase your revenue,' suggested Liz. 'After all money,' (with more dramatic fingers) 'is what this is all about.'

An hour later they slumped on the tatty sofas in the bay window of the dining room.

'Is the bar open?' asked Brian.

'You'll need to apply for a licence,' interposed Liz.

Jenny paused waiting for Liz to instruct, 'Licence, Brian,' but as she didn't said herself, 'Oh yes. I'll look into that. I expect the solicitor will advise me, as I've no idea how to go about it. But tonight it's drinks on the house bearing in mind everything is over six months old. Let's see what's under the counter. I doubt if this will affect probate.'

'Of course, you can't do anything until that is settled.'

'Mr Slocombe, of Slocombe and Slocombe, says it shouldn't take long,' said Jenny, as she explored the cupboards under the bar. 'Apart from the mysterious Eleanor, no one else is involved. Look, unopened bottles of wine and spirits. I'll wash some glasses, then we can toast the new venture.'

Liz wandered into the kitchen as Jenny was drying the glasses on kitchen paper.

'Don't think your uncle did much cooking over the last year. If you're going to do a full English breakfast, rather than Continental, this will have to be totally revamped. Better get Health and Safety in to see what needs doing.'

'I realised it was bad, but I hadn't thought of Continental breakfasts. It's an idea. I could do that to start with.'

'Fat self-satisfied businessmen wouldn't be content with a croissant.'

'Fat self-satisfied businessmen would be staying in a

four-star hotel. Now talk of food has made me feel hungry. Let's have a glass to celebrate then I'll go to the Chinese takeaway round the corner.' She poured out three glasses. 'Here's to the guesthouse. Think of a name while I buy the meal.' She hurried out into the darkening night.

Brian opened the door on her return. 'Did you know the lights don't work?'

'Damn. I forgot the electricity bill hasn't been paid. I must tell the solicitors. I think there were candles under the bar. Uncle must have had some in case of a power cut.' She got out her cigarette lighter to give herself enough light to find the candles, then lit them.

'I didn't know you smoked,' said Brian.

'Oh yes. I have many bad habits,' she answered bringing out another bottle of wine. In the light of candles she and Liz washed plates and dished out the food from foil trays as Brian opened another bottle of wine. The food, wine and candlelight made them mellow.

'How about "Dunrovin"?' suggested Brian. 'You know, name for the guesthouse.'

'Too corny,' answered Liz. '"Myrtlebank". I remember staying at the Myrtlebank Hotel in Exmouth when I was a child.'

'No myrtles,' said Jenny. '"Canal View"?'

'Many people find canals depressing. Y'know – the grim industrial past. "Happy Dreams"? Guests will think they'll sleep well.'

'"The Wife of Bath"?'

'Too suggestive. She had seven husbands.'

'Only if you're well educated enough to have read Chaucer.'

'"Cosy Cot"?'

'Don't be silly.'

'Will you two stop arguing. Someone's banging on the door. There's a police car outside.'

Jenny answered the door to flashing blue lights.

'Good evening, madam. A neighbour rang the Police Station saying there was intruders in a empty property, and as this 'ouse is down on our list of empty properties we was wundering what you were doing 'ere?' Jenny could feel herself going red with embarrassment.

'I'm sorry officer. The house has been empty as my uncle, Mr Ellis, who owned this house, was ill and died a few weeks ago. I've inherited it and was looking over it with some friends. I shall be moving in shortly.'

'Anything wrong?' asked Brian coming into the hall. The policeman smiled.

'You don't look like the average burglars. It's the candlelight what bothered the neighbours.'

'My uncle hadn't paid the electricity bill. Perhaps you had better have my name and address and I'll let you know when I move in. Thank you for keeping an eye on the place.'

As Jenny shut the door she tried not to giggle. Walking back to Liz she said, 'You'll be pleased to know the police just thought we were burglars. Mind you it is good to know people have been keeping an eye on the place. I could have found it empty.'

'Then it would have saved you the skip,' said Brian. They all laughed. Jenny thanked them with a hug. She drove home carefully after all the wine, but still chuckled about the police thinking they were crooks.

They still hadn't thought of a name.

'Let's think, planning,' Jenny mimicked to the mirror over the fireplace on Monday evening turning her forefingers into inverted commas. That morning Brian had handed her the notes he had made on Saturday. Now she scanned through them but after a hard day's work dealing with free school meals and commuter road rage, her brain went blank. The words on the page meant nothing to her. She sighed, keeping panic at bay, and thought that there were twenty-three days until she finished working for the Council. After that the world was hers and she could give the guesthouse her full attention. Mr Slocombe had told her probate would take at least six weeks so planning could go on 'the back burner' with more inverted commas.

Whilst she was spending the next three weeks coping with work and enjoying the interaction of her office companions, realising she would miss their comedy, Trevor called round one evening.

'Can I come in?'

'Of course. This is your house.'

'That's what I've come about.' Over a sober coffee they talked about the house. Trevor talked seriously in managerial mode, which secretly made her want to smile. Jenny could stay there and provide a home for the children and Trevor would pay off his half of the mortgage. Jenny started laughing.

'Don't bother. I won't need the house. I'm moving away to Bath.' She didn't want to tell Trevor about her inheritance, he could become greedy, so she let her imagination take over. 'I'm leaving the Council. I only took the job to pay for extras for the children. I've never enjoyed it. Now I've found a new job. Guesthouse manager in Bath. I'll be moving out in a couple of months. The children are now adults and can cope on their own. So the house can be sold. You'd better come round some time and take what you want to Sharon's flat.' She pulled herself out of the sagging armchair, feeling in a position of power. She no longer had to do what Trevor said. She could do what she liked. Walking into the hall she said, 'Let me know when you want to collect your things.' Trevor, looking deflated, paused by the sideboard,

'Where did you get that awful sailing ship?'

'Uncle Bernard left it to me in his will.'

'Well, if that's all he left you good riddance to him.' Jenny shut the front door firmly with a feeling of satisfaction.

A few days later he was back, smiling in an insincere manner. 'Sharon and me were wondering, if you don't want to stay here, we could move in when you go to Bath. Of course we'll pay you half the value, taking the mortgage into account.'

'Oh. Really?'

'Besides Sharon is so tired. She couldn't go round looking at houses for sale.'

'And, let's continue the sob story. Her flat is too small for a growing toddler.'

Jenny abruptly went into the kitchen, ostensibly to find a cigarette, but she was angry. She didn't want some other woman sleeping in her bed. 'Hell hath no fury like a woman scorned', she thought. She was jealous. Was it because she still cared for Trevor? But as she lit a cigarette her practical brain took over from emotion. It would make her life much easier with the work involved taking over the house in Bath. She made two mugs of coffee, giving her mind time to calm down.

'Yes, you're right,' she said, putting the mugs down on the coffee table, 'that would be a good idea. And give me some spare cash for my new home.'

'Quite. I'm so glad you are this understanding.' Jenny

71

was smiling, but the smile didn't reach her eyes. Trevor was too dim to realise he was releasing her from the problem of clearing the house and selling it.

'You don't mind if I take a few things?' Jenny asked. 'The television and stereo would be useful.'

'Course not. We should meet again so I know what you are taking.'

'I can leave all your old clothes that I had cleared out to go to a charity shop, and your dreadful Beatles records.' They both laughed but she felt the pain of lost past happy times and her own present loneliness.

The next three weeks went by quickly. The art appreciation class with the influences of Picasso, Dali and Miro were affecting her taste in pictures she might hang on the walls of the guesthouse, but it still remained nameless. On the last Friday of her employment she knew they were going to the Mauritania for a drink, or drinks, at lunchtime so she took the bus into work. Having her licence taken away for drunken driving was something she didn't want to consider at this time. It was now November, dark in the mornings and wet. Since she had a car she had forgotten the dampness and fugg in buses. How the windows misted up and the smell of passengers' wet coats. For the first time in many years she appreciated the Council House's inspiring sea pictures in the echoing halls of the entrance lobby and the solid wood of the doors to the offices.

As a parting gesture she gave Tom Lockett free school dinners as his mother sounded so ill with ME, although she wasn't on benefit, and Shannon Cannon free meals because she couldn't believe anyone could be so stupid as to call a daughter Shannon Cannon. Edith, Brian and many others came to the pub to wish her well and after three gin and tonics she kissed everyone including Mr Haspen. He made a complimentary speech and presented her with a large picture of Bristol's docks with sailing ships embarking to the New World and, joking in forced hearty fashion, a pair of rubber gloves for her future career.

At 4.30 – the Council stopped early on Fridays – Brian escorted her to the bus stop carrying the picture. She was not very steady on her feet and was glad of his assistance. He kissed her as she boarded the bus and she felt, had circumstances been different, her feelings for him could have been more than just a normal office acquaintance. They had been very close but only in a business way and he was happily married. It must be the gin. From the bus stop she staggered home in the rain and was glad of the shelter and warmth of the house. The central heating had come on but she clicked on the electric fire, still feeling cold. She took a close look at the picture thinking with fondness of the fellow workers who had given it to her. On her walk from the bus stop rain had temporarily blurred the colours on the glass. She shivered as she saw her life ahead as another daunting blurred picture. Kitchen paper removed the rain from the painting, making it sharp and clear. She looked at the groups of sailors standing on the merchant ship's deck. They would be looking forward hopefully across an unknown ocean using sextant and compass to make their direction crystal clear. In her new world she must do the same. It was up to her to make the best of it.

Pyewacket banged in through the cat flap, frightened by a firework. She picked up the warm black bundle. 'Yes, Pye, the future will reappear with a spark.' A firework from some display sprayed over the house in gold and green. She brushed her cheek against Pyewacket's damp fur. 'We will succeed and shine, you and I.'

Chapter 7

Mr Slocombe seemed to be annoyed by Jenny's decision to keep the property. She wondered why. Had he other plans for the house, turning it into flats at exorbitant rents? Mr Slocombe's smile reminded her of a chameleon – it changed to suit the client. And his jowls were reptilian.

'Market prices are rising so fast at present, Mrs Evans. You would make a great deal of money.'

'No, Mr Slocombe, I have made up my mind. I need a purpose in life, and the guesthouse fulfils this.' Why the lizard-like smile? She wondered: perhaps he had a friendly estate agent in his pocket and between them they would negotiate a sale. In return Slocombe would get a free week's holiday in his buddy's harbourside home in south Devon.

Mr Slocombe sighed, the jowls sagging, and said that probate would be dealt with shortly and the property should be hers by the beginning of December. In the meantime she was within her rights to allow surveyors and builders to look over the property, to clear out rubbish and she could decorate the basement. He enjoyed her story of the police and the non-payment of the electricity bill, then confirmed that all the bills had been paid out of the estate.

Jenny was now free to start her refurbishment, which she did by mundanely buying black rubbish bags and a sandwich lunch. Then she took Liz's advice and sharpened her approach. The telephone in the basement burred, telling her that it was re-connected, and she arranged for a surveyor to visit the next day. She wandered round Bernard's living space, munching her sandwich, thinking about what she would throw away. The wide windows made the room light and bright, although it was four feet below ground level. She could see the main road at eye level and more importantly the front door. Opening a rubbish bag, she emptied the waste bin of its whisky bottles, and picked up old newspapers dumped on the floor, meaningless letters and ornaments from the shelves, old coffee-stained mugs and dirty ashtrays. Next came the bedroom at the back of the basement. A dark room that never saw the sun but had a view of the garden. Part of the room had been partitioned off for a small kitchen and bathroom. She cleared these and emptied the chest of drawers and the wardrobe of Bernard's shabby clothes. In the top drawer of the chest were photos and papers she could look at later, but now she realised she had to order a skip and returned to the phone. She could now see what needed tipping, and would need a strong man. Where could she find one? Kevin and his biking friends? She would have to let Mandy into her secret, but not yet. Did Trevor have contact with her?

The next two weeks she spent telephoning builders, decorators, plumbers, window specialists and kitchen designers. Showing them round the property and asking for quotes. Some of them were condescending dealing with a woman, making her feel small, which she was, but gradually she became more confident and hardened her attitude, asking her own questions. She wasn't prepared to be belittled or feel pathetic, as she had done in the past. She was a businesswoman now. The surveyor had reported that the building was sound with the exception of the windows that would need attention, and the electricity and gas supplies would need checking.

When she had had enough of domineering tradesmen and too many calls – 'You are now in a queue, please hold', to jingly music, thinking of her mounting phone bill and slamming the phone down – she continued her sorting and cleaning. By the second Friday, black bags mounting in the back yard, she was ready to start painting the basement. The ceilings were low and she could do this on her own.

Next Monday morning when she was enjoying lying in bed, and the thought of not joining the rush-hour queue to the office, Mr Slocombe rang to tell her probate would be through in three weeks' time. She was energised into action. Decorating could wait: now she could definitely assess the quotes she had from the workmen and give them a date to start work. Still in her dressing gown she made a mug of coffee and riffled through the quotes, putting them down on the dining table to get an overall view. Pyewacket was helping by pouncing on turned-up corners of paper. She clasped the black animal to her. 'In a few weeks we will have a new home. It's by a canal with green places. I hope you'll like it there,' and she buried her face in the dark fur.

As she had realised when showing artisans over the house, one-man bands were cheaper to employ and easier to talk to. She began telephoning to arrange prices and dates. To start the refurbishment during the second week in December wasn't the best time as the building industry shut down for a week over Christmas. Who was available, rather than cost, became the essence – and also the ease with which she could communicate with them. It took two days, much coffee, the odd sandwich and several large gins before the plan became clear. The plumbers, Fowler Brothers, would start first, putting in new heating and bathrooms. After Christmas A & R Decorators would follow on the heels of the plumbers, together with window fitters, then the 'Without a Stain, Stainless Steel Kitchen Fitters'. The amounts of money were alarming but easily covered by the two hundred thousand pounds Bernard had left her.

Satisfied that things might actually happen she yelled, fist in the air, 'Yeah, let's go.' She needed to be there and went out to the local DIY store and bought several large cans of cream paint, large brushes and rollers. Then dressed in her oldest jeans and jersey, with her portable radio and sandwiches, like any other workman, she set out to Bath to decorate her new home.

A week later the basement gleamed, the walls cream and the windows and doors in gloss white. She had managed to get the chairs and ancient bed into the back yard, hired a machine to shampoo the carpets and she was delighted with the effect. Now for the first time in many years she could indulge in shopping for herself. A new comfortable double bed just for one, but you never know. Arm chairs and a sofa that did not sag. A small pine table and chairs. The new furniture would be delivered in December and she had over a week with nothing to do.

At the weekly art appreciation class Jenny asked Edith if she had any free time.

'I fancy enjoying my new freedom and going to Paris for a few days. Put our art appreciation into practice. Could you take a few days off and come with me?'

Edith's face lit up. 'What a great idea. I'd love that. Haven't been there since Charlie took me. That was after husband Number Two.'

'Could you afford to go on Eurostar? We'd arrive in the middle of Paris, so less hassle. It would be an experience. A totally new experience for me. I've never been to France.'

'Great. I'll show you around, kid,' Edith said in a phoney American accent.

'I'll get to a travel agent in the morning. Hang on a minute. Passport. Trev and I went to Majorca once – stayed in an apartment. Left the kids with friends. It was the first time we'd been on our own for years. We had a great time.' Jenny's eyes went all misty. 'He wasn't always a sod.'

Edith put her hand on Jenny's arm. 'No. But you have to go forward. Will you be off to Newport in the morning to get a new passport?'

'I'll check when I get home. I would be a good idea to check on all the certificates – birth, marriage, even the kids' GCSE certificates. The lovely Sharon might throw the lot out, just to make the place her own.'

'Get it sorted. Then think about Montmartre, Musée D'Orsay, the Champs Elysées. French cuisine, red wine and real coffee. Paris here we come!'

Jenny did get everything sorted. She left Pyewacket with Mandy with excuses about where she was going. Having parked the car behind the guesthouse in Bath she waited with her case at Bath Spa station. When she returned she could move into her new home. There were, of course, many beds she could sleep in in the eleven bedrooms, try them out, and get a feel for the place, before the furniture arrived. She was excited about this, but realised the hard work ahead, and was more excited about the next few days.

The speed of the Eurostar train excited Jenny but the entry into Paris was like any other city. Graffiti along the walls, factories, apartment blocks. The Gare du Nord was full of bustling people talking incomprehensibly to Jenny. She suddenly stopped still, dropping her bag, 'I can't understand a word anyone is saying. They're speaking French. I'm actually in France. I've come away on my own. It's fantastic! Freedom at last.'

'Well, you're not quite on your own. The metro's this way,' Edith indicated, dragging her through the crowds to the correct station. The hotel was in an old narrow cobbled street in the Latin Quarter near Notre Dame. The houses were so old they appeared to lean against each for support. Once they had found their rooms and freshened up it was time to explore the area and see the cafés, small shops, and cheerful students enjoying a drink sitting outside at tables on the pavement under gas heaters in the cold December night. They found an attractive restaurant with Art Nouveau lighting shaped like flowers and carved wooden panelling. Young couples at other tables were entwining arms and smiling into each other's eyes.

'Don't you wish you were twenty again?' sighed Edith.

'I think I missed out somewhere,' said Jenny in a flat voice. 'Half a pint with Trev at the Rising Sun was never like this.'

'Romance never came into your life much?'

'It was different. I'm just being difficult. It was romantic but ordinary. So were the holidays. It's just being here in such a unique place connected with romance.'

Puzzled over the French menu Jenny realised she had forgotten all her French O level, but did understand 'vin rouge' and 'pommes frites' and hoped she had ordered steak.

'I can't get over this. Two months ago I thought life wasn't worth living,' and she confessed to Edith about seeing Trev and his girlfriend together, the hopelessness and her night with the pills and the whisky. 'And now here I am in Paris sitting in a café drinking wine, looking forward to visiting an art gallery tomorrow. Where'll we go?'

Enjoying a slice of baguette Edith considered. 'I think we should start with the Louvre. We can walk there over the Seine, and Montmartre in the afternoon.'

'I must go up the Eiffel Tower.'

'We could do that in the evening.'

Next morning Jenny eyed her croissant and strawberry jam with dismay.

'How can you eat these without making crumbs? Look at the tablecloth.'

'Makes a change from cornflakes, and the coffee is marvellous.'

Jenny was delighted by the street market they passed on the way to the Louvre. Barrows piled high with colourful varieties of fruit, fish, cheeses and bread. As they crossed the Seine Jenny's obvious pleasure at so many different sights made Edith say, 'Life hasn't been very exciting for you over the years.' Jenny leant over the old stone bridge watching the river flow by.

'No, not exciting, but contentedly dull with the children growing up, until Trev started playing up. We couldn't afford to go away very much, although I wanted to broaden the kids' horizons. A few caravan holidays in the Lake District, that holiday in Majorca and I did take Dean to Cornwall this summer. He and his mates went surfing and I cooked. They got so hungry and eating out was expensive.'

'It'll mean you enjoy this all the more. Open up your own horizons. Come on, I'm getting cold standing here.'

The Louvre, originally built as a palace, impressed them both with grand halls and sweeping staircases. They found the 'Mona Lisa', a must on the first visit, and Jenny wondered what she was smirking about. There were galleries of huge paintings depicting historic battles, monarchies, and religious subjects. Feeling she had had her fill of voluptuous naked ladies, men's buttocks and chubby cherubs, Jenny found herself in a peaceful gallery of still life paintings and sat there for a long time immersed in the colours and light.

Edith was waiting for her in a café in the foyer. 'My feet ached so I came to sit down. Got you a small bottle of wine and a cheese baguette, no point in us both queuing up.'

'Thanks. I'll pay you back.'

'Yes. Not cheap in here. They know they have captive consumers.'

'What did you see?'

'First I went the wrong way and got lost in Etruscan antiquities, then I got mixed up with French paintings, 'The Raft of the Medusa', great but grim, then ended up on the top floor looking at Dutch paintings. And you?'

'I've fallen in love with still life pictures. They have a peaceful effect.' They went on talking on their way to the metro and got on the train to Etoile. Here they walked through underground burrows to find the line to Anvers at the bottom of Montmarte.

81

As the two women rose up over the roofs of Paris on the funicular railway to Montmarte the sun broke through. Jenny gasped in wonder as she looked over the leaded roofs of the tall, thin, wooden-shuttered houses towards the centre of Paris and the Eiffel Tower, then towards the hill and the Sacre Coeur. Edith smiled with pleasure at her friend's delight. They tramped over cobbles to the Place du Tertre and curiously watched the painters at their work in the square, others touting for business to paint their portraits.

'They're not very good,' commented Jenny.

'Just a tourist trap,' answered Edith dryly. 'Apparently there's an exhibition of Dali's work down a side street. Let's find it.'

The exhibits were mainly statues but they both remarked on the quality of the work. 'Look at the curls on this girl. That is quality. The Turner prize should take this into consideration. And these melted watches.'

'Yes,' said Jenny in deep thought. The message was the same. Life is short – there is only so much time.

They looked at an elephant whose legs changed into those of a deer. There was a crystalline pyramid on it back. Jenny peered at the inscription, 'I don't understand, but it is beautifully made. It says, "Dali's love of dichotomy marries the heavy beast with the ethereal prismatic lightness of the obelisk". What's dichotomy?'

'God knows. But it has impact'.

Later they were sitting in a café near the Place du Tertre, dark interior with red checked table cloths, taking in the aroma of Gaulois cigarettes and coffee.

'You're looking pensive,' remarked Edith.

'It's Dali's clocks. Time. There is only so much time. You can't always drift. At some time you have to make a decision and I have done that. Something constructive. But now I realise the watches have done something else. I can see ahead. Be positive. I told you, I took Dean away in the summer and just cooked for him and his mates, read magazines and watched TV.' Jenny waved her cigarette angrily, 'now I am thinking I didn't have to be there for him and his mates. I could have gone walking the coast, so beautiful, but I didn't. Just stayed in and let an opportunity drift away. Realising all this, seeing, thinking, hearing and smelling,' as she drew on the cigarette, 'a new life is opening up. I don't have to be a little mouse anymore. With the guesthouse I can be the boss.'

'Let's go to the Sacre Coeur. It might suit your mood.'

The façade of the building with the great dome was enough to impress any tourist, and Jenny was completely overwhelmed by the interior. First the darkness. Then light. An illuminated mosaic of Christ above the altar rising up to the roof. 'I am the light of the World', as she had been taught in dreary chapels and had not been convincing. Here she could think differently and sat wondering if this was the answer. She lit a candle hoping to bring light and clear thought into her own mind. The church was beautiful; so many people walking past in silence, with nuns getting ready for the evening Mass. She felt there was a presence with her to help her on her way, or it might be imagination.

Edith was waiting for her. She felt dazed as she looked out over Paris in the dusk, the Eiffel Tower now lit up.

'I don't know about you but I am exhausted,' Edith declared, 'I'd like something to eat, then bed.'

'Let's go to the Champs Elysées. There must be lots of cafés there. We can sit and watch the world go by,' which they did, enjoying 'people watching'. They laughed and made quiet comments about the plump middle-aged ladies in fur coats and hats sitting near them sipping coffee. Cups held by fat, ring-smothered fingers. They giggled about the Asian tourists talking on their mobile phones and smiled wistfully at the young lovers arm in arm, wishing they were that age again.

'Bet you'd live life differently if you were young again,' mused Edith.

'Yes, I'd stand up for myself,' answered Jenny. 'Answer back occasionally.'

'You mean be more bossy,' countered Edith.

'Yes, and watch Trev's blood pressure go up,' chuckled Jenny into her second glass of wine, 'but also have more time to do what I wanted to do like an art or craft class. Lack of money somehow drags you down, so your initiative goes. Now I am going to be different. What about you?'

'Not got married so young. Perhaps if we'd been older and wiser. Like you, lack of money was a problem. The boys mightn't have been such delinquents. Wish I'd met Charlie earlier: he was good fun, took me all over the place, and then he met a younger woman. That's life.'

'Anyone on the scene now?'

Edith smiled mysteriously. 'There's Eddie. I met him at the pub playing darts. He's invited me to his Christmas do.'

'Hence the new outfit you bought in Bath.'

'Yes. He's good company. Got a nice home. Works for the Electricity Board. You never know.'

'Hope it works out. How many glasses of wine have you had? Do you think you can find the metro?'

A man was playing jazz on the clarinet in the train back to the Left Bank to complete the picture of their first day in Paris.

*

They were sitting in the café at the Musée D'Orsay, once the frontage of the old railway station, now an art gallery. Jenny was watching the old Railway Clock, that had once summoned passengers to their trains, tick backwards, as they were behind it. It had an odd effect – time going backwards, ticking away. Edith was enjoying her soup and as she dipped her crusty French bread into its depths asked, 'Are you going to serve evening meals in your guesthouse?'

'Evening meals,' mused Jenny. 'Not to begin with. If I'm on my own bacon and eggs was all I was thinking of. But seeing these Continental breakfasts, I'll have to think a bit more.'

'But after you've changed the beds and vacuumed, you've got all day. After all you only got up at six o'clock to get that done. Then in the evening Chateau Briand Steak, Chicken Chasseur, Trout Hollandaise.'

'You're winding me up.'

'Of course.'

'But I could. Now let's go and look at the Art Nouveau exhibition.'

They came to the Eiffel Tower when the sun was low in the sky. Edith opted to stop off at the first level and enjoy the view from the café. Jenny returned from the heights half an hour later. 'There was a wonderful sunset. I could see the Sacré Coeur on the hill, the Arc de Triomphe and the Lourve all illuminated. Tiny boats on the river and clouds floating by below me. It was amazing.'

'Keep it in your mind over the dreary winter. Tomorrow we're back to normality.'

Chapter 8

Jenny frowned at the dark rain-streaked window of the train from Paddington.

'Anything the matter?' asked Edith.

'What if the guesthouse doesn't work? What if I can't do it? Can't cope.'

'Where has the confident, enthusiastic lady of Paris gone?'

'In a few minutes I shall be walking to a cold, dark house on my own. In the morning two unknown plumbers will arrive and take the house apart and I have to be in control.' Edith helped Jenny get her case from the rack and gave her a hug. 'You'll be fine – and thanks for a great few days. Let me know how you're getting on. All the office will want to know.'

The empty pavements glistened in the rain. There were no other people walking across the footbridge over the Avon but she listened out for footsteps behind her. It was dark and she was alone. She pulled up her coat collar and walked doggedly, pulling her suitcase. The canal towpath was the quickest way home but the black water of unfathomable depth pitted with raindrops seemed ominous. She took the long way round, past lighted shop windows though even the fish and chip shop was shut, which made her feel hungry, not having eaten since lunch at the Gare du Nord. A couple of drunks, arm in arm, staggered past her shouting something obscene and with relief she opened the front door to the guesthouse. The damp cold engulfed her, but it was safe. She realised there was no food in the house, not even a biscuit or tea for a drink. Brandy as a medicinal remedy seemed the only option, so finding a bottle from under Uncle Bernard's bar she made her way to a first-floor bedroom. Why had she so efficiently cleared out the furniture from the basement? This damp bed was the only option. What a bleak end to her holiday. She huddled fully clothed under damp blankets, sipping the warming spirit, hoping the alcohol would revive her and renew the sparkle she had felt over the last few weeks. She tried to think back over the days in Paris, the new Jenny willing to explore and discover the world, rather than the old Jenny bogged down in depression and anxiety at the thought of the chaos tomorrow would bring.

Monday morning did not improve her mood. The house had not been heated for nearly a year. A bleak chillness had seeped into every nook and cranny of the old building. She wiped the condensation from the window and looked for the Abbey but it was lost in fog. The bright spark that made her want to change her life seemed lost in the gloom as well. At least she didn't have to dress but just made her way to the small Spar shop down the road to buy provisions for the day and was embarrassed as she tried to pay in euros. The Asian owner laughed and she felt she could introduce herself as a new neighbour. It made her feel better. Perhaps she could become part of this community.

Back in the kitchen she lit all the gas burners to warm the place up and make tea and wait for the plumbers. The Fowler Brothers, true to their word, turned up at nine o'clock. They were like Jack Spratt and his wife. They could not have been more dissimilar. Jake was tall, thin and fair. Zak was short, fat and dark. She filled three mugs with tea whilst Jake explained they would put the boiler in the kitchen first, and work on the heating using existing pipes and radiators where possible, checking for leaks. Add a new system to the top floor then it all might work and be the cheapest option. After this they would attack the original bathrooms, and new en suites in the double bedrooms.

'Last thing we'll do is the tiling,' said Jake, who was the spokesman, 'so if we tell you how many tiles we need you can choose them yourself. And if we get short of time we know someone who'll help us out. Do you want glass doors?' Realising she had much planning and thinking to do Jenny took her tea into the bar but once Radio 1 was turned on and the hammering started her brain stopped. It was a pity she had got rid of Uncle's table and chairs. She had to get out. Of course, she thought, I'll go back to my old home, do my planning in the warm and fill up the car with the TV, the electric fire, duvet and warm clothes. And she had forgotten Pyewacket. How could she! A visit to Mandy's as well. That would cheer her. When her new furniture came next day she would feel more at home. She gave the Fowlers the back door key and left.

Once the heater in the car started working so did her brain. She stopped off half way at the coffee shop by Chew Valley Lake and wrote quick notes whilst drinking her coffee and munching a Danish pastry. The list was getting frighteningly long and expensive. Tiles, mattresses, duvets, curtains, carpets, a hygiene course, probably an accountancy course, the bar licence. Perhaps too much thinking was a bad idea. Only yesterday she was in Paris full of excitement. She bought another coffee and gazed out to the forlorn ducks and the misty lake trying to bring back the positive feelings she had experienced in the buildings, paintings, music, and people cheerfully enjoying themselves. What was the French phrase, 'joie de vivre'? It didn't seem to apply to the English in this gloomy fog. Was it the weather, not philosophy, religion or politics that gave a country its personality? Is that why the Scots were dour, the Swedes analytical, the Germans authoritarian, the Italians operatic? Quiet detached thought, food and warmth were restoring her to a positive frame of mind. Yes, she could cope. Now was the time to collect all she needed from her old home. She said to herself – I won't be nasty like some wives I've heard of, who take everything down to the last light bulb, or cut the sleeves off their husband's suits. I'll only take what I need. As she drove down the familiar road she felt she had been away for weeks, not a few days. It seemed smaller and insignificant. She tripped over Dean's rucksack in the hall. Why was he here?

'Hi, Mum. I wondered where you were.' An attractive blond girl was sitting next to him on the sofa. 'This is Cassy.' Just as well I didn't arrive earlier, thought Jenny. Which bed would I have found them in? They shook hands.

'Why are you here? Have you dropped out of college?'

'No, Mum. It's the end of term. It's different at uni. Cassy's parents are away so she had nowhere to go. I thought she could stay with us.'

'Us?'

'Yes, here. Where's the cat?''

'I'll just make myself a coffee.' Jenny escaped to the kitchen to think. Should she tell the children about the guesthouse? Would they want to stay here on their own? What would Trevor do? Neither of them had told the children of their agreement that Trevor and Sharon would be moving in.

'What's for lunch, Mum?'

'How should I know, I've been in Paris for the last few days.'

'Paris?'

'Why not? I'm living my own life now.'

'Good for you,' said Cassy.

'Lunch at the pub, and I'll tell you what's happening. I'll pay.'

Over their chips with everything Jenny told them about inheriting the guesthouse, and some money to put it right, and how she would hope to open in the spring.

'I don't know what contact you have with your dad, but I don't want him coming round wanting some of the action. He has made his decision and he must stick with Sharon. Now, he and Sharon are going to move into our house when I've moved out. What d'you feel about that, Dean?' Dean was silent for some time, chewing away on tough steak, battered onion rings and chips.

'That explains odd boxes in the bedroom. Full of cuddly toys. I did wonder. Not your scene. No, I wouldn't live in the same house as her.'

Cassy butted in. 'If you have a guesthouse there must be plenty of rooms for us to sleep in.'

'Yes, there are. But they are all bitterly cold and dank. The plumbers will be there for weeks sorting it all out.

What would your parents say if you caught pneumonia?'

'My parents, like you, are separated. When I said they were away, Mum is out in Spain with someone, and Dad's girlfriend has moved into some flat he's got in London. So I don't have a home either.' She sounded aggrieved and angry. Jenny's thoughts took some more rearranging.

'Look, you two. Stay where you are for the moment. Help me get my stuff out of the house. Hopefully the central heating will be up and running soon. Then you can move in. I should talk to your father, though I don't want to. Tell him when I am moving out. But please don't tell him about the guesthouse. I don't want him knowing about this. He thinks I'm just going to be a guesthouse manager in Bath. Let's leave it like that.'

So Dean and Cassy helped her move a small unwanted TV into the car, wrapped in a duvet, a fan heater, the electric fire from the living room, a box of sentimental ornaments, a tea set and some warm clothes.

'I know what you need,' called Cassy, and rushed into the house returning with a hot water bottle. Jenny thanked them. 'I'll be back in a couple of days for the rest of my stuff.'

She drove back to Bath. Was it really home? Yes, of course, her new home. A shining new beginning – but her bright blue sky of newfound freedom had been clouded by grey clouds of responsibility. She would have to make some provision for Dean and Cassy. It would never enter Trevor's mind, although he was equally responsible. In the dim light of dusk two proud horses suddenly appeared in her headlights making her brake fast. Her wheels slid. She could have been killed, and the horses with their arrogant riders. She calmed down, breathing deeply. All she had to do was go to her new home, plug in the fire, the TV, boil a kettle for her bottle and enjoy the warmth. Clouds with silver linings would have to wait on the borderland of grey depressions blowing in from the west.

Tom from next door was out strolling along the towpath as she arrived. He willingly helped her in with the television and the fire. He plugged in the fire in Uncle Bernard's fireplace and the light of the false coals illuminated the room. Although there was no extra heat the room felt warmer. Then he plugged in the TV. There was little of interest in the programmes available.

'Got satellite?' he asked.

'No. Is it important?'

'Very. Guesthouses round here all have satellite for the guests.' He laughed. 'Besides, if you had it, you might ask me round to watch the football, and Dot likes the boxing. Seriously, it's a good selling point.' Jenny added it to her growing list of things to be done. She thanked him and said he and Dorothy would be her first guests when the furniture arrived the next day. Later she made herself an instant soup, a hot bottle and, with the fan heater, escaped to the bed upstairs where she had slept the night before. At ten p.m. she sat straight up in bed. She had forgotten Pyewacket again. She rang Mandy but there was no reply. Her mind was beginning to think in a different way. There was always tomorrow and she was warm.

At nine o'clock the Fowler Brothers, tall and short, awoke Jenny. She greeted them in her dressing gown, put on the kettle and whilst this boiled, they told her the boiler would be finished by today. Then they would start on the heating.

'Whilst we're here in the kitchen have you thought

about a washing machine and dryer?' asked Jake. 'You're hoping to open a guesthouse? Where are you going to wash the bed linen?'

'Oh, my God! There's nowhere. What did Uncle Bernard do?'

'Could have used the laundry or the launderette. Both expensive. Where shall we put the plumbing for you non-existent machines?

'Is there an outhouse?'

'No.'

'Then by the back door. Stainless Steel Kitchen Fitters can move their stainless steel. Thanks for pointing this out.'

'He's clever is Jake,' muttered Zak, as he left with his mug of tea. The first words she had heard him say. She fled to the first-floor bedroom to dress, then more demurely returned to her uncle's basement to telephone and adjust her order to Stainless Steel Kitchens. She looked at the list of jobs she had made in the coffee shop at Chew Reservoir yesterday and tried to keep calm. She was sure she would enjoy today, after all she was now a confident woman, and her new furniture was being delivered. At 10.30, after an hour's anticipatory waiting, the van arrived. She ordered men to put the bed in the back room, the sofa and easy chair by the fire and the table and chairs in the window. She made up the bed, then, laughing wound herself up in her own duvet thinking – this is really mine. Looking out of the window she thought – I must make that garden grow, but in the meantime I'll buy silk flowers to brighten the place up. Put the picture the office gave me over the old sideboard in the front room and Uncle Bernard's ship back on the mantelpiece.

There was a bang on the door. It was Jake.

'Mrs E we need to run pipes along the back walls of the top floor of the house for the heating but the little room at the top is locked. 'Ave you got the key?'

'I know the room you mean, just a box room. I've got all uncle's keys in reception. I'll come up and see what we can find.' Jangling bunches of keys she followed Jake to the top floor.

'It's got to be one of these old-fashioned keys,' said Jake, 'not your modern Yale keys. You're going to have fun finding out which key is which. None of them is labelled.'

'He's smart is our Jake,' commented Zak. They tried many until one fitted.

'I feel like a princess opening a magic room. What treasure will I find inside?'

'Don't be silly Mrs E. It's just a room full of dirty blankets and old rolls of wallpaper.'

The door swung open, 'No, you're wrong, Jake. It's full of pictures.'

She turned one over, 'Look. An oil painting of Pulteney Bridge. What wonderful colours. The artist has the water just right. Not easy to do.' She turned over the next picture of a garden, 'I wonder where this is?'

'That's Sydney Gardens, just up the canal,' contributed Jake.

'I haven't had time to explore Bath yet.'

'It'd be useful to get to know the place,' added Jake. 'Then when your guests ask where they can visit you'll be able to tell 'em. You'll be able to say, "Why not take an evening stroll up the canal to Sydney Gardens." Now we'll help put the pictures in the bedroom, otherwise we'll be here all day discussing the merits of painting. Who do you think painted them, your uncle?'

Jenny peered at the scene of Pulteney Bridge. 'Yes, there's a signature – B Ellis. This is amazing. I knew he was creative. I've a model sailing ship he once made, but I never expected to find anything like this. And look – here are all his paints dried up on the windowsill. He obviously hadn't used them for a long while.'

As they walked back and forth to the bedroom carrying canvases Jenny remarked, 'I could hang these up the staircases. They would be a talking point.'

'Not this one you wouldn't.' Jake held up a large painting of a nude reclining on a rumpled bed.

'Cor,' exclaimed Zak, 'she looks like a goer.'

'Now, Zak, we don't want to upset Mrs E.'

'No, she is beautiful. I wonder who she was?'

'Here's another. Sitting in a chair. You can see her face more clearly.'

Jenny looked at the long black hair flowing over shoulders onto full breasts and the hazel eyes flecked with green staring back at her. Her memory was nagging her. Where had she seen that face before? Realisation changed her thoughts from detached observation to excitement.

'I know her. Jake, Zak, I know who she is! She was at the funeral. She left before I could speak to her. I wonder if she is "Eleanor"? Yes, I bet her name's Eleanor Watson. Uncle left her money in his will.'

'Lucky Eleanor,' said Jake not sharing Jenny's enthusiasm and wanting to get finished. 'Zak, take these and put them on the bed.' There were other canvases of Eleanor, one of just head and shoulders, which Jenny took downstairs to her flat. She gazed again at the face and wondered what part Eleanor had played in Bernard's life – obviously amorous. He had treasured her, loved her. That's why he had painted her. But he had never married her. Why? He would have liked a family. It was a mystery. Was Eleanor already married? Could she find out? She had to. Uncle had left Eleanor £10,000. Over ten years ago when he made the will that was a lot of money. She would have to get in touch with Mr Slocombe. Had he put adverts in local papers? For her own part she could make some local enquiries, ask the neighbours and in the shops. Find someone who had lived here over ten years ago and liked to gossip.

She felt restless, her mind overactive with this new discovery, so walked into town to see Mr Slocombe. She was lucky he was available and after she had explained the situation and the fact Eleanor Watson knew of Bernard's death he agreed with his desiccated smile, which he imagined was charming, to advertise in the personal column of the *Bath Chronicle*. He shook her hand and wished her the compliments of the season, which she found bewildering as Christmas this year, to her, just didn't exist.

Still unsettled, on impulse she decided to drive to her old home and collect Bernard's ship, her picture from the office and more sentimental items to make her basement flat feel like home. Dean and Cassy were out, which meant that taking things was easier, but she missed their carefree humour.

Her next stop was Mandy to pick up Pyewacket. Seated at Mandy's kitchen table with a mug of tea she told Mandy about the guesthouse and her plans. She mentioned Trevor and his expectant girlfriend were moving into their home and she didn't want Mandy's father knowing about the guesthouse. Mandy was horrified,

'That woman has taken away our home.'

'No, Mandy, this is your home. Here with Kev. It's because you have both left home I've agreed to this. Dean and Cassy will probably come and stay in Bath once the heating is in. At the moment it's cold and damp. I hope Jake and Zak get the central heating done by Christmas.'

'Who are Jake and Zak?'

'The plumbers.'

It was too much for Mandy to take in and, bewildered, she started chopping onions in preparation for the evening meal.

'I'm trying to come to terms with you starting a new life. A bed and breakfast lady, running your own business.'

'After all those boring years in the Council offices it is a challenge. Something I can take on, now there are no other commitments.'

'Were we that much of a burden?'

'No. Don't be silly. I loved watching you both grow up. I wanted to make sure you grew up fit and well, then after school find careers and adjust to adult life. Which I think you are both doing. Now that time has passed. With your father gone I must now make my own life. Uncle Bernard's inheritance has made this possible.'

Mandy, bending down to find mince in the fridge, asked, 'Do you want to stay for tea?' Standing up again she said, 'I'm glad you enjoyed bringing us up. We enjoyed it too. But as you say, we all grow up. Are you staying?'

'Thanks for what you said. No, I won't stay for a meal; Pyewacket and I have to accustom ourselves to our new basement home. I'll have to keep him in for some time. There's a main road at the front so I must train him to go out at the back. I'm looking forward to putting on the fire, the telly and snuggling up on my new sofa with

Pye while we share fish and chips.'

Jenny stood up to leave, 'Sorry I haven't found any decorating work for Kev. But I needed someone who wasn't booked up and could get the job done quickly. I'll try to use his services later.'

'No worries. Give me your new phone number.' Jenny wrote it down. Mandy stood back and looked at her mother in a critical manner. 'Y'know, you look different. You're standing straighter. Look taller. You'll make a go of it. I had thought of asking you here for Christmas, but if you have a guesthouse available Kev and I could join Dean and Cassy and try the place out.'

'Oh no. I don't even know if the oven works. The whole house is freezing.'

'Now is the time to find out your weaknesses, catering for would-be guests. We'll be there to help you. It'd be different, exciting. With no Dad around, a new situation is what we'll all need.'

'You're right. A new family Christmas celebration.' Secretly her heart sank. She had wanted a peaceful life, but both her children needed security and this she would have to give over the holiday period. What a selfish swine Trevor was! Never giving his children a thought at Christmas time, too absorbed with his own life, not the lives he and Jenny, in the past, had created.

Mandy hugged her mother in the tiny hall, 'Are you sure this is right?'

'Yes.'

They packed Pye in his basket in the back of the car.

'I just wonder if this is your chosen course in life?'

'Why?'

'You hate changing beds.'

Chapter 9

Pyewacket meowed all the way to Bath but Jenny took no notice. She was coming to terms with the fact that both Mandy and Dean wanted to come and stay. On reflection she was glad she had told them about her expectations and that they wanted to join in, no doubt on the grounds that they would be fed. She would have to turn her spare moments to the kitchen, cleaning materials and rubber gloves. But now all she wanted was fish and chips, Pyewacket on her lap, the telly and then a warm bed.

Jenny lay back on her new sofa, happy and content, watching some dreadful soap but enjoying the flaming rows and neurotic love matches, which had nothing to do with normal life. Tom next door was right. Satellite would be a good idea. The salty chips were good, and the batter, but she left some of the fish for Pye who was still yowling around investigating his new home. Fortunately used to the litter tray at Mandy's he adjusted to this in the small bathroom beside the bedroom. Eventually they both curled up around the hot water bottle, warmth becoming their common denominator.

Her first task the next day was to return Uncle's ship

to the mantelpiece and prop up her picture on the side-board. She realised she hadn't a hammer and nails and must invest in these. Her next job was to review the linen cupboards on the first and second floor landings, and find out what was needed. New duvets, covers and sheets were a must. Babies were something she hadn't considered but she would have to take families into account, and there was a cot in the landing cupboard. As Liz had said, 'These could be family rooms, and after all making money is what this is all about.' Jake was passing with a length of copper pipe in his hand.

'Where is the best place to buy beds round here?'

'Probably up Cribbs,' he said, thinking of the large shopping mall near Bristol. 'Best wait for the sales after Christmas. You can get cheap bedding in a warehouse place just off the A4. I'll show you on the map. While you're out go to Comet and order a washing machine and dryer, then we can plumb them in by the back door.'

'Thanks – you're a mine of information. I'll leave the beds, concentrate on bedding.'

Three hours later she returned delighted with her purchases. The boxed duvets couldn't all fit in her small battered car, so she made two journeys to the warehouse. Jake and Zak were eating their sandwiches in the kitchen and seeing her arrive the second time helpfully came to help her carry them into the dining room.

'These covers have given me an idea for the rooms,' she announced fingering the packets and holding them up. 'The rooms on each floor could have a theme. The first floor will be the poppy rooms, and second honey-suckle and the third wild roses. I could use silk flowers in vases, so I don't have to keep changing them. It would make the whole atmosphere peaceful.'

'Flowers is luvvly,' said Zak gruffly.

'The washing and drying machines will be delivered next Monday,' she added, sounding really efficient.

'How many pillows will you need?' inquired Jake, surveying the fourteen duvets piled by the bar.

'Thirty-four at least. I think we'll need your van to collect them,' Jenny answered with a glint in her eye.

In the afternoon on her way to the Spar shop Jenny knocked on Dorothy and Tom's door and invited them for a cup of tea later in the day. Her search for Eleanor had begun. Next, as she paid for a fruitcake and biscuits, she asked Mr Patel if he had lived here for ten years, or knew anyone who had. He had only come here from Smethick three years ago, but Mrs Trubshaw, at the Post Office on Winchcombe Hill, had been here since the world began. Jenny thanked him and climbed the hill to the Post Office. It was crowded with people sending parcels and late overseas letters and she decided she would call at another time.

Back at the guesthouse she found the Fowler Brothers had turned the water off. In desperation she found bottles of fizzy water under Uncle's bar and filled the kettle in her small basement kitchen to make a pot of tea. She opened a box from her sentimental horde and found the tea set her mother had given her on her marriage. She dusted this off and set cups, saucers and plates on her new pine table along with her cake and biscuits.

When the bell rang she ushered Dorothy and Tom into her new domain and introduced them to Pyewacket.

'I love cats,' said Tom, 'but Dot gets asthma so I've never been able to have one.' Pye rubbed round his legs and as he sat down on the sofa settled on his lap.

Dorothy sat on a chair near the window.

'I can appreciate he's beautiful, but I'll stay over here. You'll have to be friends in the garden. So what are you plans, dear? Are you staying?'

Jenny filled her teacup and passed her some cake, 'Yes, I'm going to try and make a go of running the guesthouse. Bed and breakfast at first, then later, I hope evening meals. The plumbers are here now putting in central heating. They're an interesting couple.' Then she went on to tell them about the discovery of the paintings.

'When I last talked to you I asked if you knew of anyone called Eleanor, but you had never met her.' She produced the picture. 'Do you remember seeing her at the funeral? She left before the service ended.'

'What a beautiful woman. I would have remembered her,' said Tom.

'I'm sure you would,' said his wife with a smile.

'My uncle left her some money so I want to find her. There are other more revealing pictures so she must have been important in his life. You don't pose nude for just anyone. I need to find out who she is. Who can I ask who has lived here for over ten years? I'll show you some of the other paintings, lovely local scenes in oils. But there are no recent pictures and I wonder what happened about ten years ago. Uncle changed and the guesthouse changed. I want to find out why. What happened to turn him from the jovial man I remember to the depressed man you knew.'

'Try Mrs Trubshaw up at the Post Office. She knows everyone. Mrs Barrett at number five, other side of us, has been here some time and is a net curtain twitcher – she might tell you something. If Eleanor came to Mr Ellis's funeral she must have been fond of him, perhaps more.'

'And she must live locally to know Bernard had died,' said Jenny. 'The announcement was only in the local paper. I'll have to play detective. In the meantime I'll show you some of his paintings.'

Since yesterday she had brought down more of the paintings for a closer look. Tom and Dorothy admired them and were able to identify the locations. There was much more to Bath than the Roman baths and Georgian buildings.

Jenny enjoyed their visit and whilst in an enquiring mood went to knock on the door of number five. She introduced herself to Mrs Barrett who looked at her suspiciously.

'Hope your guests won't be rowdy. Some of Mr Ellis's crowd got very noisy as they left about eleven o'clock. Used to keep me awake. Gave the place a bad name. Wasn't like that in the early days.'

'I'm sorry. Uncle wasn't a well or happy man towards the end of his life. I want to run a quiet guesthouse, probably catering for tourists. There was something I wanted to ask you. Do you remember a lady about ten years ago called Eleanor Watson? She had dark hair. Quite a striking looking woman.'

Mrs Barrett gave a wry smile, 'Oh, think I know who you mean. Used to walk past most mornings about half past nine. She was supposed to be the cleaning lady, but I can't see how cleaning takes all day, especially with the curtains drawn all afternoon. She used to leave about four o'clock. Too glamorous for a cleaning lady. Then she stopped coming. Come to think about it that's when the place started going downhill. No more potted geraniums out the front, just litter. Why do you ask about her? It was years ago.'

Jenny didn't want Mrs Barrett getting too nosy so just said Uncle had mentioned Eleanor during his time in the nursing home and thanked her for the information. 'She lived up Winchcombe Hill somewhere.' Added Mrs Barrett, still fishing for information, but Jenny just thanked her again and returned to the basement thoughtfully. Mrs Barrett was the perfect gossip with an accurate memory going back at least ten years. Perhaps she had little else to interest her, but had Bernard had a secret lover? Just as well she had always telephoned before she visited with the children. And he must have been breaking the law. His liquor licence, for which she would have to reapply, was for those staying at the guesthouse, not for his drinking buddies.

After spending two valiant hours next morning cleaning the kitchen oven, which she would have to use with Dean and Cassy coming to stay, she needed a break and walked again up to the Post Office. She queued to buy some stamps and asked the postmistress, an elderly lady with white frizzy hair, if she had ever known someone called Eleanor Watson. Mrs Trubshaw paused, delving in the recesses of her memory, as the queue behind Jenny lengthened.

'Doreen, can you take over for a bit. I need a break.' Doreen stopped stacking rice pudding and took over behind the counter. 'I really do need a break. Come and sit in the kitchen while I go to the lav.' Jenny sat in the neat small kitchen behind the Post Office until Mrs Trubshaw returned.

'You were asking about Eleanor Watson. It took me some time to remember who you meant as I knew her as Eleanor Turner. I've known Eleanor since she was a kid. Her mum and I were friends. I watched her grow up. She was a beautiful child with that long dark hair, but not very bright. Once she had grown up we lost touch. I was too busy here. But I remember her marrying a Ted Watson. Posh affair cos he was a civil servant – only a clerk really – and they didn't have much money.'

'The reason I ask is she used to work for my uncle, Bernard Ellis.'

'Oh yes. He died recently.' Mrs Trubshaw laughed. 'The trouble with this job, what with pensions and child benefit, you know more about people than you should. What'll happen to the guesthouse?'

'I'm going to run it. In time, if I may, I should like to put an advert in your window, but I want to get in touch with Eleanor. You don't know where she is now?'

'No. She and Ted moved away, but Eleanor's mum still lives up the hill. Number 53 Wellington Terrace.' She smiled, reminiscing, 'The number of times we pushed our prams up this hill.'

'You don't think she would mind if I called on her?'

'No. Not if it's to do with Eleanor. She's the light of her life.'

'Well, thanks for your help, especially at your busy time of year.'

'Nice to have a break and think of the old times. Now I'll make meself a cuppa tea. Nice meeting you, and if you've moved into the area no doubt we will meet again.'

Jenny walked further up the hill thinking she had only been here a few days but already she had met several locals and was beginning to feel part of the place. Something she had never felt in suburbia. She found Wellington Terrace, a small cul de sac off the main road, and drew a deep breath before knocking on the door of Number 53. Mrs Turner, old and stooped, had Eleanor's green-hazel bright eyes.

'Good afternoon, Mrs Turner. I hope you don't mind, but I wonder if I can ask you about Eleanor? I'm Bernard Ellis's niece.'

'What did you say? Whose niece?' Jenny repeated her introduction in a clearer voice, and Mrs Turner said, 'Do come in.' She showed Jenny into the tidy but shabby living room. 'Please sit down. Eleanor's away at present. She lives in London, but is well. Why are you asking after her?'

'Am I right in thinking she used to work for my uncle?' asked Jenny in a raised voice.

'There's no need to shout. I'm not deaf. Yes. She did. After she got married she wanted part-time work and did his cleaning. Now she's moved away, I do miss her.'

Clearly enunciating her words Jenny asked, 'Well, assuming I have the right person, Eleanor Watson, my uncle has left her some money in his will. Quite a considerable amount. There will be an advert in the local paper and she can apply to Slocombe and Slocombe, the solicitors. I also have some pictures Uncle painted that she might like.'

'I was so sorry when I read he'd died. Saw it in the *Bath Chronicle*. I told Ellie and she was quite upset.' Mrs Turner was now off. Jenny sat listening patiently whilst Mrs Turner told her about her beloved Ellie. She had their life history – her own husband, who had left for Betsy down at the Old Lion, Ellie's schooling and how the teachers let her down, various jobs as shop assistants and the wonderful marriage to Ted – a government official. Ten years ago Ted was promoted and they went abroad for several years, but now they lived in a smart suburb in London. Jenny listened with interest at first; then got bored as Mrs Turner talked about the problems with coaches getting to London; she couldn't afford the trains. She got no response to questions because of the old lady's deafness. Mrs Turner was probably very lonely and glad to talk to someone, especially about Ellie. Jenny tried to look interested and eventually managed to intervene and ask, 'Will Ellie be coming to see you at Christmas?'

'Oh yes. Got to see her poor old mum!'

'Could you ask her to come and see me about the will?'

'I'll try and remember. You could send her a card, my memory's not very good.'

Taking her hand she said, 'Good idea, and thank you for your time, Mrs Turner. You've been very helpful and relieved me of the problem of finding Eleanor, which my uncle obviously wanted me to do.'

She walked back in the December dusk. There were fairy lights in some windows and the shops at the bottom of the hill were garish with decorations. Usually she would be busy writing cards, making mince pies, thinking shopping lists, but this year she couldn't get her mind into thinking of Christmas. Her thoughts were too busy with 'planning' and at this present moment with Uncle Bernard and Eleanor. Jenny wondered – a love affair that ended in sadness when Eleanor moved away? It would explain many things – Bernard's disinterest in the guest-house and the dried up paints.

The phone was ringing as she ran down the stairs to the basement. It was Edith. 'What happened to you yesterday? You missed the art class. Bartholomew was in good form. We did Lowry. It was great, especially for me having come from that area. Took me back a few years.'

'Oh no! So sorry, I forgot. I've got very involved in a mystery. Remember that door we couldn't open on the top floor? Well, the plumbers, and they're an interesting pair, needed to get in there so we opened it up and it was full of pictures. Some of them were of Eleanor – the mysterious woman I told you about. Uncle left her some money. And now I've found her.'

'Hang on, you're losing me.'

Jenny settled down on her sofa and told the story from the beginning.

'No wonder you didn't come last night. And it's good to hear you sounding full of life. You've still got the Paris confidence and you're on you way. Come next week. We're having an artistic quiz, wine and mince pies.'

'I will. And you must come over at Christmas time. See the flat and the changes I have in mind.'

Later as she lay in bed stroking the black soft fur of her cat, she said, 'Pye, I'm beginning to feel I belong here. This place is becoming cosy and I've met local people. Tomorrow I'll let you explore the house, so you know it's your home as well.'

The next few days were a whirl of organising, planning, clearing and cleaning. The plumbers had nearly finished the work on the heating and would soon start on the bathrooms. She was now looking forward to Dean and Cassy coming to stay. She had even visited Liz in Bristol and discussed the business side of things. Liz bounced about her office dressed in her tailored executive suit, enthusing about all Jenny had done and was curious about Bernard's paintings and the mysterious Eleanor.

'Now, as you've started buying items for the house

and you'll have to pay the plumbers before Christmas, we must get down to money. "Accountancy",' she said, raising her index fingers, 'is now important. I'll show you how to do a basic cash book, but you should do a course so you can do VAT, and annual accounts, then present me, or another accountant if you prefer ...'

'Oh, please, I would like to use you. You understand the situation.'

'Good. I suggest you contact the Technical College in Bath and see what they have to offer. You'll probably have to pay.'

'I've already been in touch with them about their hygiene and catering course. I can't run the guesthouse until I have that. It starts in January.'

'That should be interesting. Make you wonder why you've never poisoned anyone in the past. So after the plumbers, decorators, etcetera in say, February or March, you must think of your future customers. It's a dreary time of year, not many tourists. Where will you advertise?'

'I'm going to contact Tourist Information and the university. Oh, and I told the local postmistress I'd put an ad in her window. I'd like to start slowly until I get the hang of things.'

'A good idea would be to get a computer, then you could have an email address and include it in your ads.'

'I thought I'd got away from staring at a screen all day.'

'Sorry. Computers are the way things are done now. You'll fall behind in the business world if you haven't got one. Once you've got established you can have a website. And you can do your accounts on them.'

After instruction on cash books Jenny left, inviting Liz

and Brian over during the Christmas holiday. 'We'd like that. Brian misses having you around. He has no one to tell his dreadful jokes to. The new girl doesn't understand him.'

Jenny combined her business visit in Bristol with her evening party at the art appreciation class. The students had to identify which artists had painted obscure pictures and there was much laughter at some of the suggestions. There was wine; happy chatter. A middle-aged man made a pass at Jenny, and although she wasn't interested, she was flattered at the same time. It made her feel maybe she wasn't too old to be attractive. She invited Edith over to Bath with Brian and Liz. On the way home she realised she had never done this in her old home. Trevor would never have been interested and would have grumbled. Now that didn't matter.

She panicked on arrival at the basement flat. Pyewacket was not there. She rushed round the house calling for him and after listening for a plaintive mew found him shut in a bedroom. The Fowler Brothers must have closed the door, but it looked as though they had made good progress. Only her flat remained to be heated. Tomorrow she would have to live in the kitchen and keep Pye with her.

'We had trouble with your cat yesterday,' reported Jake next morning. 'He'd gone out in the garden then got into next door's garden. Fortunately the old man brought him back. Perhaps you could pretend he's a dog. Get him a harness and take him for walks to get him used to the area and the canal.'

'What a good idea. You're full of good ideas, Jake. You must find plumbing a rather boring job.'

'Not really. I did go to uni, and got a degree, but I couldn't find any work. We meet interesting people and every job is different.' He looked around to see if his brother was about but he was out with the van. 'Besides I don't think Zak would survive on his own. He had a bike accident when he was a kid. He's a bit brain damaged. He can read, but can't write much, and he gets panicky if he feels stressed. This is a job we can do together and I can look after him. Our mum and dad is both dead.'

Jenny was surprised. 'That's very good of you, taking care of him.'

'Cuts both ways. He does all the cooking.' He looked away, obviously wanting to end the conversation. 'Today we'll put in your radiators and check the system then we'll be finished until after Christmas.'

'When you'll put in the en suites.'

'That's right. Perhaps you could pay us for this part.'

'Of course. And as I haven't much to do today, in fact, I've rather a hangover from a party last night, I'll try the dog-walk bit with Pye.'

'Why Pye?'

'You know you're the first person to ask me that. It's short for Pyewacket.'

'Oh, *Bell, Book and Candle.* Kim Novak. Good film.'

'You know everything!' Smiling, he left to get on with his job.

Pye was shut back in her bedroom and she popped out to find a pet shop. Whilst she was out shopping she bought ingredients to make mince pies before her children's invasion.

The December day was sunny and mild as she dragged Pye, scared but curious, out into the garden and on to the

111

canal path. In the couple of weeks Jenny had been in the house she had not had a chance to stroll along the towpath. She had to pull Pye along the path, but he also tried to jump up on garden walls and had to be pulled back. Jenny hoped in time he would get used to the sights and smells then know his way home. As she walked she enjoyed the sunshine, the locks, the bare trees and wondered about the two brothers, their lives intertwined. Jenny had never experienced brothers or sisters as her parents had married in their late thirties and had not expected children. Jenny had been a surprise her parents never got over, which may have explained their old-fashioned ideas and lack of understanding. But Mandy and Dean, although close, had always argued too much to work together, and Trevor and his sisters had never got on. A gentle caring brother-like relationship she could not imagine, but here with the Fowler Brothers it existed. She looked at the still reflections in the water and remembered Sheila's destructive remark, 'Waterfalls fragment things.' But her comment had been, 'Water also comes together again in tranquillity.' She tried to keep this thought in her mind as she coaxed Pye back home. Why were some people always friends, but others fell out when there could be tranquillity? She had enjoyed her walk and realised she could do this every day.

Later the future landlady felt it was time to get to grips with her out-of-date kitchen. She washed all the utensils, sterilised the work surfaces, then settled down to the satisfying task of making mince pies. Rubbing up the pastry, cutting out the pies, and filling them with mincemeat. Now she needed to put them in this over-large oven, but at what temperature? Gas ovens were a mystery to her, she was used electricity. She swore but then heard Zak saying, 'Try regulo 5.' She stood up and said, 'Thanks.' Zak had come in to make a cup of tea. 'Regulo 5 is the same as 180 electric. Have you just made short crust pastry, or tried using an egg and 50 grams of sugar?'

'Just short crust.'

'Try the other next time. Makes the pastry less bland. Ten minutes in the oven. That's all they need.'

'Got any other tips for Christmas?'

'No Brussels sprouts. A creamy dessert rather than Christmas pud, less indigestion, then relax and enjoy it.'

'You know about food. I might pick your brains on meals when you come back in the New Year.'

Jake arrived in the doorway, 'We're about to run the central heating system. Go and sit down with a cuppa and we'll check everything.'

'OK. Just after the mince pies are cooked.'

Later with the central heating working and the house warming up after many months of damp – and windows open to get rid of condensation – Jake and Zak left after warm mince pies and more cups of tea. Jenny had got used to their company and respected them for their work. Would other workmen be so reliable?

Now the house seemed empty and she realised Dean and Cassy could stay. She gave them a ring and agreed to pick them up the next day, knowing they wouldn't have the train fare. She also rang Trevor to let him know the house was his and that she would like half its value. He stalled when it came to money, as she knew he would, so she put the phone down on him.

It seemed odd visiting her home for her entire married life for the last time. Whilst she was waiting for Dean and his girlfriend to extract themselves from bed, get showered and dressed with the comment, 'The bathrooms are filthy and you're not using my shower every day,' she packed a few last items. Cookery books, dictionary, atlas and other books that would make the place look more homely. The picture she liked of a Cornish fishing village, photograph albums.

At last they were ready and she banged the front door with finality. There were tears on her cheeks.

'This was our home for twenty-two years. Now it's all over.' She blew her nose violently and Dean put his arm round her shoulders.

'We'll make a new home in Bath. Better than living here in misery.'

'You're right. I'll shove my key through the letterbox. You keep yours. After all he'll always be your dad, and you might want to see him.'

Realising the emotion of the moment Dean and Cassy chatted to Jenny as she drove and then she told them about the Fowler Brothers. Over lunch in a pub on the outskirts of Bath by the river Jenny talked about Eleanor and the pictures.

'You must go up to the top floor and look at them, and if Eleanor knocks at the door please ask her in.'

'By the way, Auntie Sheila rang. She was wondering why she hadn't received her present and card. I just said you were both very busy.'

'Well done. As least she didn't ask to come and stay again.'

'No, she's going to Auntie Jane's and the dreadful children.'

'God help them. Sheila and screaming children won't gel.'

'She didn't sound too well,' Dean added. 'Got an appointment with a consultant at the end of January.'

'Let's hope he can sort her out.'

The pub was festooned with streamers and Christmas bunting. It reminded Jenny, 'When you've sorted out where you're sleeping and made up the bed or beds with new sheets and duvets, I've a job for you. Go into the town and buy a Christmas tree, glass balls, tinsel and we'll decorate the house. You can turn it into a Christmas home.'

As the young ones decorated the tree and put it in the bay window of the bar, a brass band played Christmas carols in the park over the road and the holiday had begun.

'Hi, this is great,' called Mandy from the front door. 'Yeah, great,' echoed Kevin, weighed down with cases and polythene bags. With a few beers the two couples introduced themselves and with whoops of exploration discovered the rest of the property. Pyewacket, enjoying familiar company, joined in and bounded up the stairs after them.

'We want the room at the top,' said Mandy.

'Ideas above her station,' grumbled Kevin, stroking Pye who purred loudly.

'Well you are above the station, it's down the canal.' Dean's weak joke caused much beer-made laughter and Jenny sent them off to the chippy for supper. She was so happy to have her children around her – it was home and Pyewacket was purring.

The next day was Christmas Eve. Yes the children were home, but there was no turkey, sausages or sage and onion stuffing. The kids, now thinking they were on

115

holiday, slept late. After Pye's early morning walk along the canal in the misty morning, and enjoying a quiet moment for the pair of them, Jenny nipped down to the bank for some money. When her children arose, grumpy, and had eaten their way through half a packet of Weetabix, all her milk, half of loaf of bread, marmalade, sugar and coffee she sent them out with money and a long shopping list including a turkey.

As she washed the crockery and cutlery, the front door bell rang. Before her stood an tall elegant lady, dark hair twisted round her head, deep green eyes starring down into her own blue ones.

'You must be Eleanor. I'm so pleased to meet you. Come in.'

Chapter 10

As Eleanor followed her down to the basement Jenny said, 'I remember you from Uncle Bernard's funeral and wondered who you were. Then I forgot until I saw Uncle's pictures.'

'Oh yes, the pictures.' Eleanor wistfully surveyed the room, 'This place brings back memories – very happy memories. You've made it look comfortable, and you've kept his ship.'

'Yes, I watched him making some of it when I was a little girl. Would you like a cup of coffee?'

Once they were settled, Jenny told her about the will and the ten thousand pounds. Eleanor looked thoughtful.

'I don't know what to say. It was very kind of him. As you no doubt realise having seen the paintings, we were lovers. Bernard employed me to clear up the guests' breakfasts, change the beds and clean. He often helped me. We would joke and laugh and one thing led to another. In the afternoons we would go to bed. Sometimes he would get out his paints and easel and paint scenes of Bath, then as the years went by he painted me. They were very happy afternoons.'

'And your husband?'

'My husband, Ted, never knew. He was out at work all day, preoccupied with his career and studying for exams in the evening. As long as his meal was on the table when he came home that was all that mattered. We loved each other but it was dull compared with afternoons with Bernard. Perhaps it was the secrecy that made it exciting. We never knew when the doorbell might ring.'

Jenny smiled, 'I remember visiting Uncle when the kids were small. The guesthouse was smart, flowers out the front and a welcoming atmosphere. How long ...?' Jenny didn't know quite how to put it. 'How long were you and Uncle together?'

'About seven or eight years. Things might have been very different had I had children, but I knew I couldn't. Then Ted got this amazing chance with the Civil Service to go to the Caribbean. Half of me wanted to leave him and stay with Bernard, but half of me wanted a more exotic life. The thought of warm blue seas, sun, different interesting people. So I went. It was a mistake. I soon got bored. There was nothing to do and the people rather snobbish, though I did have the odd fling to relieve the boredom. And Bernard? Did he find anyone else?'

'No, sadly he didn't. You were very important to him. He seemed to lose his zest for life. He stopped painting and neglected the guesthouse. I gave up visiting him, as he never seemed pleased to see me. I think he may have had cancer longer than anyone realised.'

'I'm sorry. Although it would have seemed wrong to leave Ted, we all three might have been happier if I had. Ted's work was always more important than his home life. Four years ago we returned to England and he now has a high-powered job in Whitehall and I spend my days in a smart house in Wimbledon.'

'What do you do with your time?'

'I walk the dog on Wimbledon Common and love my garden. Interest in gardens started in the Caribbean where the plants were so different and beautiful. I think it's the idea of nurturing something, watching it grow. Never having been able to have babies it was a feeling I longed for, but could never experience. I lavish care on plants instead. I have so many flowers some end up in the house, which Ted appreciates. I go to a gardening club and flower arranging with a friend. She's called Marie and she's the first woman friend I've made since I was at school. We daydream about opening a flower shop – spending our time in a fragrant brilliantly coloured atmosphere, making floral displays.' Eleanor was suddenly animated.

'I think you feel like I do. Life is short. We've already experienced half of it and it's time to do something different. Tell me – how will Ted react when you inherit ten thousand pounds? Won't he be suspicious?'

'Yes. That's why I wonder if I should take it.'

'If you and your friend are thinking of starting up a business with a separate bank account, and the money was used as capital, would he ever know?'

'What an interesting idea.'

'You get your inheritance and a new future. Think about it. In the meantime come and see the paintings.'

They spent time looking through Bernard's work, Eleanor reminiscing about the times when they were painted in quiet afternoons in the basement.

'Choose one and take it with you to remind you of happy afternoons. That would give you a reason for coming here. Uncle Bernard left you a picture in his will. Then when you have a chance, go and see Mr Slocombe.

He knows all about the will and can advise you on what to do.'

Eleanor browsed through the paintings and eventually chose a scene of a small Georgian street, brightened by geranium-filled window boxes and ornate wrought iron street lamps. 'That will give me pleasure whenever I look at it.'

'You can take the nudes. You look very beautiful.'

'That would take some explaining, but thanks.'

As they descended the stairs the young ones were returning weighed down with supermarket bags.

'That was a nightmare,' announced Mandy dumping the bags in the hall. 'Talk about panic buying, and the shops are only shut for a day.'

'Did you see that bloke buying five loaves of bread and three dozen eggs?'

'Perhaps he's looking after the homeless,' suggested Jenny. 'I would like to introduce you to Eleanor, a friend of Uncle Bernard's.' They all shook hands, and Eleanor smiling all round said, 'Dean, you look so like your Uncle. It's good to meet you all. I'll wish you a happy Christmas and now I must go home to Mum. She'll be wondering where I am,' and she hurried out into the dusk of Christmas Eve.

'The mysterious lady,' said Dean.

'And very beautiful,' said Cassy wistfully.

'Why did she leave so fast?' asked Mandy, 'we're not that awful.'

'I think she was embarrassed and felt awkward,' replied Jenny. 'You've seen the pictures. Besides children, however large, may upset her. She never had any, but obviously would have liked to. Right, let's puzzle out where to put everything, and someone can pour me a gin.

Who mentioned eggs? I fancy scrambled eggs for supper.'

'Let's panic!' Dean threw up his hands in dismay, 'Mum's going to use up all the eggs.'

In common with many families all over the world the rest of the evening was spent in secret present-wrapping with demands of who had the Sellotape, watching television and over-indulgence. Bells began peeling at eleven o'clock and Jenny suggested Midnight Mass but there were no takers. Too nervous to go to church on her own, she went out with Pye to walk by the canal, take in the peace of the night, and the odd feeling of awaiting some momentous event that takes over many people on Christmas Eve. She sat down on a damp bench and let the beauty of the stars sink into her being. After a while Cassy came out to join her. Jenny offered her a cigarette and they sat smoking in silence, taking in the atmosphere.

After a time Cassy said, 'Space is a wonderful thing. All those stars. Studying marine biology I've come to understand how big the oceans are and the variety of life from the smallest creatures you can imagine to the largest. But think how much more there might be in the sky, going on for ever.'

'I'm glad you appreciate the beauty of nature. It's here all around us but many people are blind to it.'

'Yeah. My dad's like that. Belittles such things cos he can't see it. He wouldn't know a dandelion from a daisy.'

'Have you heard from him this Christmas?'

'Had a card and a cheque. Nothing from Mum. And she's got my mobile number.'

'Perhaps you should ring her. Wish her well at this time of year. After all the Christmas message is supposed to be about love.'

'Yeah. Stupid really. We spend all this time buying things and spending money, but it's not about that at all.'

'Well, giving someone a present shows you love them. That's different from commercialism. What we should be doing is celebrating the birth of a man who was happy to be poor and had no time for riches.'

'I hadn't thought of that. Very deep.'

'Must be the drink.'

'Maybe not.'

'Let's get back, I'm tired. I hope the kids weren't expecting stockings at the end of their beds.'

Early next morning Jenny was deep in cookery books finding out how long to cook the turkey, and peeling potatoes whilst listening to carols on the radio. She knew the young ones wouldn't be up early and, satisfied everything was under control, knocked on Tom and Dorothy's door to ask them round for a drink. As their son, Neil, with his wife and four children, were staying, they insisted she have a sherry with them, and she spent an entertaining hour being shown the grandchildren's toys: baby Martin's teddy bear, David's cars and garage, Amy's tea set and Emma's Barbie doll. She in turn told Tom and Dorothy about her meeting with Eleanor.

After two sherries she returned to her kitchen and the turkey. She pushed tables together in the bar and laid them with Uncle's shabby tablecloths and now clean cutlery and glasses, then laid crackers on the side plates. Her young guests drifted down and over more drinks, presents were opened, exclamations of delight were heard, and wrapping paper tossed about the room. They watched *Mary Poppins* on television whilst she battled with roast potatoes, carrots, peas, sausages, stuffing and finally the turkey.

The large oven was a blessing to keep everything warm. She commandeered Mandy and Cassy to be waitresses, Dean and Kevin to deal with the drinks and they all sat down to eat and enjoy themselves. There were jokes and laughter, silly mottoes from the crackers and Jenny was pleased. The effort of the meal had been worthwhile. Content and replete, Mandy told Jenny to put her feet up, made coffee, found chocolates and the others washed up.

The gaiety continued in the kitchen as she dozed contentedly in front of the television. When they returned she suggested a game of Scrabble.

'No, too many of us,' said Kevin, 'besides I'm dys— I can't spell.'

'Monopoly?' enquired Cassy. And to Jenny's surprise everyone agreed.

'Mum's the old boot,' declared Mandy.

'I know my place.'

'But now as you're a hardened businesswoman you should win.'

'I shall.'

She didn't. Kevin won with hotels on Mayfair and Park Lane, and she spent much of the time in jail.

Later they drifted off to bed. Cassy was last, came over and kissed her good night.

'Thanks for a wonderful day. It was a proper family Christmas. I did what you suggested and rang my mum. She was so pleased. She's going to visit me in Plymouth when she comes back in January.'

Jenny lay in her warm bed stroking Pyewacket. 'Pye, it's been a good day. Four pleasant young people and me, all of us enjoying each other's company – shame the old Trev wasn't here as well.'

*

She slept deeply and woke early full of energy. She wanted to walk, walk for miles. The canal path beckoned. She could stride out until she was tired then using her new mobile phone, another move to independence, ring the house so someone could pick her up. She fed Pye on turkey bits, made a sandwich, found an apple and a bottle of water, stuffed them in her pocket then set off. She left a note in the kitchen telling her sleeping guests to help themselves to breakfast and she would telephone.

The morning was glorious, bright and shining. There had been a frost and autumn leaves lying on the grass were edged with sparkling white. The brackish water was so still it seemed like glass. For the first time Jenny noticed the name and number of the lock.

Lansdown View Lock. Yes, as you come up the canal you would suddenly see the Abbey tower and the Georgian terraces on the opposite hillside. What a great idea! Lansdown View Guesthouse. I have a name! She started her walk with vigour. Imagining herself saying on the telephone, 'Lansdown View Guesthouse. Can I help you? Yes I do have a double room vacant for tonight. The price is ...'

She would have to wander round the area looking at the competition.

Deep in thought, she found she had passed the flight of locks and the path levelled out. In front of her was an imposing house that arched over the canal. In the quiet morning the mellow Bath stone building bridging the canal was reflected in the still water. The entrance to Sydney Gardens was on her left but she did not deviate – she wanted to know about the house. It turned out to have been the headquarters of the Canal Company. Like money-makers of the present day they liked their statement of wealth. She had to cross the road, then found the towpath on the opposite bank. There was a boatyard that looked forlorn; holiday narrowboats idle. This would be a hive of activity in the summer. As she walked, more terraces of Bath came into view, set in gracious curves and crescents, the pale golden stone glowing in the sunlight. Beyond gentle hills the fields, green and brown, sloped down to the river. Yes, Lansdown View Guesthouse was a good idea for a name.

Other walkers and cyclists greeted her cheerfully as she walked but mostly she was preoccupied with her thoughts on the work she still had to do with the guesthouse. Before she could open she had to battle through an impenetrable forest of organisation – brambles of licensing laws, thickets of health and safety, fallen trees of finance and the rabbit holes of unknown contractors – and she had no idea what the world would be like on the other side of the forest. As a slight breeze set the reeds rustling her mind went back to the last time she had walked beside a stretch of water after her failed suicide attempt with pills and whisky. Was that only three months ago? Yes, she had come a long way. She was no longer bogged down by work and home. Most of the time she was aglow with confidence. She felt younger and looked younger. Her step became brisker and she soon found herself at Bathampton.

There was an old church and an attractive pub by the canal. It was too early for a drink but not too early for her sandwiches so she walked further and found a bench and ate some of her snack looking at the boats moored along the bank. Most of the boats were old and battered – people lived on these vessels all the time. There were piles of logs on the roofs, and old bikes. From the boat in front of her came the scent of wood smoke and a blue haze issued from a crooked metal chimney. The boat was called *Blithe Spirit*, which seemed at odds with its dilapidated state. At that moment a man in his mid-forties with long curly dark hair, a battered blue woollen Aran jersey and faded jeans bounced out on to the deck of the boat and wished her a happy Boxing Day. He came over to her, talking of the beautiful day. He had a merry twinkle in his eye and Jenny asked him about the boat and its name.

The man laughed, 'I'm the blithe spirit. Moving happily from place to place, as free as a bird. It's a poem about the skylark. It's by Shelley.'

'Where does the canal go?'

'This canal now goes all the way to the Thames, so you can get to London from here. I did that some years ago then came here via Oxford, Birmingham, the Severn and Avon. It took months.'

'It must have been very interesting. Tell me, what is that tower on the hill?'

'It's called Brown's Folly. The hill itself is full of tunnels. They extracted Bath stone from there. During the war they stored munitions in the tunnels.'

'You'd never think that, looking at the peaceful landscape.'

He moved nearer. 'That turkey smells good. I only had baked beans yesterday. Forgot to get to the shops.'

Jenny smiled at him. He had an engaging manner. Despite his scruffy appearance he had an educated accent. So where did he come from?

'Would you enjoy a Christmas sandwich?' and she held out the last one.

'Very good,' he said, munching away, 'reminds me of proper old-fashioned Christmases.' They chatted for a while then Jenny said, 'I must go, get back to the family.'

'Perhaps I'll see you again along the canal,' he smiled.

Retracing her steps to the pub, surprised at enjoying the company of an attractive man, she bought herself a drink and managed to get hold of Mandy. Kevin was the only one dressed and would pick her up in half an hour.

He arrived as promised, bleary eyed, and asked the barman for a black coffee. Kevin was obviously nervous sitting with Jenny with no Mandy to give him support, so Jenny made all the conversation and told him about her walk and the meeting with the canalboat man. Kevin's only comment was, 'Odd he should forget Christmas. P'rhaps he had no dole money.'

'You think he was unemployed?'

'Obviously. If he's bumming round the country on a boat.'

On the way home in the car Jenny broached a subject that had been bothering her. That she hadn't asked Kevin to paint the guesthouse. She explained she needed a bigger firm with several painters to get the job done quickly. Kevin became more embarrassed and just mumbled he had plenty of work. Still, Jenny had done her best to explain herself. Kevin was relieved to see Mandy in the kitchen. She had been busy. Bubble and squeak sizzled in a frying pan. Cold turkey and sausages with pickle were already on the tables in the bar with a bottle of wine. Jenny poured a glass of wine and relaxed, her muscles pleasantly tired. She could hear Dean in the basement strumming away at the guitar and trying out one of Uncle Bernard's sea songs. 'A ship I have got in the North Country, and she goes by the name of the *Golden Vanity*', wafted up the stairs and she hummed along.

Their stomachs satisfyingly filled, the young men and Cassy went off to watch Bath play rugby. For the first time in many months Jenny had time with her daughter and wondered what to talk about and what to do. Mandy suggested shopping. She needed some new clothes so they walked into the town and Mandy tried on various tops and jeans in the big chain stores. Jenny was surprised the shops were open but this was the way of things in this new commercial age. She was glad to get home again and watch TV with a cup of tea. She was worried they had talked so little. Was something bothering Mandy – Kevin or her job? Or was this what happened when daughters had a partner or husband? She had no idea, having never been able to talk to her own mother. Either her mother knew nothing, or religion had been the barrier. She suddenly felt sorry for her careworn mum.

The rugby fans returned home jubilant and over the last of the turkey and beers played Pontoon for pennies. Dean was banker for most of the game, with cheerful derisory calls every time he had to pay out. Jenny suggested a game of Cheat, and there was much laughter. Mandy seemed her usual self and Jenny put her worries about her daughter on one side.

As they were making bedtime drinks Jenny asked if they wanted to do anything in the morning. Her children seemed to pause slightly.

'We thought we should go and see Dad,' said Dean. 'He's asked us out to lunch at a local pub. Sharon won't be there. She's too tired. But we do want to see Dad. He might be like he used to be.'

Jenny took a deep breath. 'Of course you must. He's your father. Part of your life.'

'Then Mandy has asked us to stay with her for a few days over the New Year. If it's OK, Cassy and me will come back here until term starts.'

'Of course it's all right. Bristol will be probably quite exciting over New Year. Fireworks and everything,' Jenny countered. 'Besides I have to go to Cribbs tomorrow and order three double and eleven single beds. Mandy, you know your way about all those shops. Tell me which showroom to go to.'

There was discussion about this, which ended up with Jenny thinking the place was a maze, but the tension had gone and everyone hugged each other 'goodnight' and tramped upstairs to bed. Cassy was the last to go. She took hold of Jenny's hands. 'Thanks for a wonderful Christmas. I don't really want to go to this lunch tomorrow, but Dean wants to see Trev. I met them both once when we were at your old home. He was OK, but she was a silly person. They came to the house to leave of huge box of shoes. I didn't know people had that many shoes – and all impossibly uncomfortable.'

'Must go with the fluffy toys. I've enjoyed having you here. Enjoy the New Year and you're welcome here 'til term starts.'

She took Pyewacket out for a late evening stroll to calm down. They found a seat and Pye purred. 'What do you think Pye? You enjoyed the turkey. I shouldn't have felt so jealous or protective because they want to see Trev. I'd like to see the Trev of ten years ago. Times change. I've changed and I'm strong enough to accept new situations. I didn't think I wanted the kids here over Christmas. I thought they wouldn't be part of my new life but they are. They always will be and I'll always be here for them. Yes, it'll be money for mortgages and uni grants, but I'll be here. Pity they're not as easy as you, Pye. Two cans of food a day and you're happy.' She stroked his arched back, black against the black sky. 'We're very lucky, you and I.'

In the morning Jenny laid out a proper breakfast and had even nipped down to Mr Patel's for some croissants. The children, she still thought of them as children, came down to breakfast carrying their bed linen.

'Perhaps,' Mandy suggested, 'it would be better if we used these machines for the first time whilst people were here. Let's find out how they work.' So to the whirring of the machines they had breakfast, and finally folded the clean bed linen. It seemed odd to end their Christmas celebration with breakfast and the relief that the washing machine worked, but that's the way it was. She waved them all 'goodbye', made sure Pyewacket was safe, then set off to buy beds, double and single, to be delivered on the first of March.

Back in the flat she felt lonely knowing her kids were out enjoying themselves, so she occupied herself cooking for her guests, Edith, Brian and Liz, the following evening. For the first time in her life, apart from children's friends, she was going to entertain people who weren't part of the family.

The evening was a success, in fact such a success they stayed the night. The four of them had eaten well, the wine flowed, they talked about the office, Brian imitating 'Mr Has Been' to a tee so they were all in hysterics, then played card games into the early morning. Then they had hilarity making up the beds.

'We do expect room service,' said Liz. 'Tea at, let's say, eleven o'clock.'

'Certainly, Madam,' said Jenny giggling. When she finally found her bed Pyewacket looked at her with disapproval.

Chapter Eleven

The New Year reared its ugly head. Jenny didn't care for the celebration. Shouting, firework bangs and stupidity over a new day. Now the Fowler Brothers were back with their noise and Radio 1. They had brought along two more plumbers, mates of theirs, Jim and Fred, and a tiler, Mr Giles, to help speed the job along. Now there were five men wanting cups of tea. Jenny went out to buy extra mugs, tea and milk. Although the price would be higher Jenny accepted this, hoping the Fowlers' high standards would continue and that she could open earlier.

She had a week before her hygiene course but there were a hundred and one things to be done. She ordered curtains to match the duvet covers for the bedrooms, and mottled carpets in a peaceful shade of green for the whole house, except the dining room for which she chose grey. Maroon curtains for the deep bay window with easy chairs in the same colour. She found a wholesaler who specialised in hotel equipment and ordered crockery, cutlery, kitchen utensils and bathroom fittings. This was all exciting as she felt she was nearing her goal for opening. Coming in at the end of the day she would tell the Fowlers what she had been doing. Zak was now becoming a little more forthcoming.

'You haven't chosen Willow Pattern for the plates?'

'No. Uncle had that. I can use it for emergencies. This is white with a pastel design as a border.'

'Good. You need white plates to show up the meals. Make 'em look tasty.' Zak really understands cooking, thought Jenny. He had already given her a couple of evening meal recipes.

'I don't want to interrupt you culinary experts but I've realised something important,' interposed Jake. 'I was wondering why this place is so easy to work in. There ain't no fire doors. God knows how your uncle got away with that one. He can't have been inspected for years.'

Never having stayed in a hotel or guesthouse until she went to Paris, Jenny wasn't aware of them. How guests, loaded with luggage, had to battle against wired and sprung glass doors to get to their rooms. But she did remember news reports of a terrible fire when many people died as flames swept through a hotel.

'Thanks, Jake. You know so much. And thanks too, Zak, for your help. I shall go and consult Yellow Pages for a fire door specialist.'

'And while you're doing that Mrs E, think about security locks on the doors,' called Jake as she was off down the stairs. I'm going to miss those two when they've gone, Jenny thought. So far everything has been so easy. It couldn't last. Fire doors were yet another obstacle: barbed wire came to mind, in her impenetrable forest to get to the other side, and the unknown country of guesthouses.

She woke up on Thursday night thinking why is it so quiet? Dean and Cassy had returned but there was no noise. She looked out though the window and snowflakes drifted silently earthward. The world was being transformed into pure whiteness, covering for a short time the griminess of the world; was that the attraction? She had a childlike thrill about snow and stood entranced watching the flakes swirl.

In the morning Jake and Zak arrived on foot.

'You should see the roads. Utter chaos. We're only half a mile away so we walked. People walking are so cheerful. Chatting to people they wouldn't dream of talking to normally. The car drivers look so bad tempered. It's a real laugh. Come on Zak, bathroom number three. I don't think Fred and Jim will get here today. Have you ordered the extra tiles yet Mrs E?'

'Should be here next week.'

It was very cold. Jenny could hear Dean and Cassy moving about and decided a cooked breakfast would set everyone up for the day. Three cooked breakfasts – no five – she had to practice: it was going to be her livelihood. The smell of sizzling rashers seemed to draw people and they all sat down to bacon, eggs, fried bread, tomatoes and baked beans.

'Where can we go tobogganing?' asked Dean of the Fowlers.

'You haven't got a toboggan,' interrupted Jenny.

'All you need is a strong polythene bag,' explained Dean, 'and I'm sure Jake has some of those after all this plastering.'

'You're welcome to them. Put a few stones in the bottom or some sand. Your best bet is Victoria Park up by the Royal Crescent.'

'Can I come?' asked Zak innocently.

'Maybe, when we've finished work.' So the five went in their separate directions, two tobogganing, two to the bathrooms and Jenny for a walk, having given up any idea of planning work today. She wanted to enjoy the snow. Trees covered white, the silent canal with icicles on the handrails. The sun was shafting through gaps in the clouds so branches and lock gates glinted. She could hear tinkling as heat melted the snow – it never stayed long in the South West. At the top lock she turned into the streets, curious to see what they were like. For the most part they were Victorian dwellings, but many of them had bed and break-fast signs outside the door. She stopped outside one where a woman of her own age, auburn hair in a ponytail, and wearing a track suit was sweeping the snow from the path. The B and B was called Rosebank.

'What happens to your guests in weather like this?' was Jenny's opening gambit.

'Two have gone neurotic, one had a meeting in Cheltenham and how could he possibly get there over the Cotswolds. I suggested the train. The other has defied the weather and hopes to make it to the Vale of Pewsey. A third has totally relaxed and said "A day off" and is watching telly. I might charge him for the extra coffee.'

'I was just interested as I'm starting up my own B and B on the main road, by the canal.'

'Not "La Casa"?'

'Yes. It used to be called that.'

'My hubby and I stayed there when we moved to Bath and were looking for a place. Eventually we found this, and it does us well. The old bloke who ran it was so welcoming and entertaining. He looked after our kids while we were house-hunting and was so interested in what we'd found.'

'He was my uncle. He died recently and left me the property.'

'I'm sorry. He was a good man. Would you like to come in and have a cup of tea? You must be so cold.'

'I would love to.'

Over several cuppas and some shortbread biscuits they talked about Uncle Bernard and got on to the nitty gritty of running a guesthouse. Jenny learnt more in an hour about running a B and B than she could have learnt from any course. She now knew what to charge, how to deal with clients who came back drunk from the pub, couples that obviously weren't couples, and unruly children.

'Basically,' said Lyn, Jenny's new-found friend, 'you need to be charming on the outside, but hard as nails underneath. Don't let anyone take you for a ride. Like, "I can't afford to pay. I'll send you the money". Get the money up front. Dodgy salesmen, who haven't got a contract, are the worst.'

As they parted, Jenny shook Lyn's hand in friendship. She had found someone with similar goals. They exchanged phone numbers and agreed to meet again.

'It's nice to meet another landlady,' said Lyn. 'I can't get friendly with the neighbours as the competition for prices takes over. You're further away. We can exchange notes.'

Jenny crunched through the freezing slush to her now cosy home, pleased to have found someone who had enlightened her about her new trade. The Fowler Brothers were just leaving.

'Be a wise move to keep your heating on all night. Don't want any burst pipes, although you have plumbers on the premises. Think I'll take the phone off the hook, otherwise we'll be inundated with calls we can't deal with.'

Fortunately, as Jenny was curled up under a blanket on the sofa as the heating had little effect on the freezing temperatures, Cassy, bright red nose, shiny cheeks, but bubbly, had agreed to show off her cooking ability and did them a risotto whilst Dean and Jenny chatted. They would be around next week before the Ivory Towers of university beckoned.

'You can keep an eye on things whilst I'm out on this hygiene course.'

The following Monday Jenny came back from the college after her first day of the Essential Food Hygiene Certificate and Dean enquired how she had got on.

'It's all so simple really. Don't touch that. Wash it first.'

'It's only a spoon, Mum.'

'But was it clean? When did you last wash your hands?'

Dean sighed, knowing a lecture was about to take place.

'I need loads more chopping boards and sharp knives.'

'Why, who are you going to kill? Or are you going to be the "Mad Knife Woman" at a circus?'

'No. It's all about cross contamination of germs. Cooked meat and uncooked meat. Clean vegetables and dirty vegetables. Making sure the clients don't get food poisoning. Do you know how many germs there are in an uncooked sausage?'

'Calm down, Mum. When in my eighteen years have you ever given us food poisoning? The only time we have ever had that was from takeaways.'

'That's the point!' exclaimed Jenny, waving her hands for emphasis, 'if you leave food hanging around waiting to be cooked. Flies.'

'But you wouldn't!'

'And no animals. Pye incarcerated in the basement.'

'If you were staying in a guesthouse you wouldn't want the cook's animals jumping about on your food. They might have been dancing in the cow shit for all you know. These are just sensible precautions, which you normally take all the time.'

'Yes, you're right. I've never been to a college before. I found it overwhelming. The tutors were frightening.'

'They behave like that so you'll do what you're told.' Dean realised that he knew things of which his mother knew nothing. 'You've got enough understanding about cooking to say. "I know that", and "I don't know that". Make your own judgements and don't be afraid to argue. I'll get you a large whisky, although they'll say it's bad for you. You deserve it. Your first day at college.'

Jenny took a sip of her drink. 'Fowler Brothers OK?'

'Fine. Zak has even put in the cat flap you bought. Pye is outside exploring the garden,' with which the cat poked his nose in, decided this was home and curled up on his mistress's lap.

'Anyone cooked supper?'

'Sorry. Never got round to it. Could you manage a takeaway?'

Three weeks later Jenny was deep into two courses advancing her knowledge on accountancy and computer literacy. The Fowler Brothers and their mates had finished and to celebrate she took the brothers out for a meal at a local Italian restaurant. She couldn't imagine more helpful plumbers. They had always been people, flesh and blood people, and she wanted to thank them. They started talking about Italian food, on which Zak was very knowledgeable, then it progressed to Italian buildings and antiquities and she discovered Jake's degree was in archaeology. Jenny had a very romantic idea of archaeology that extended to the pyramids and Stonehenge and wondered at Jake's willingness to give all this up to look after his brother. What concern and care he must have for Zak. She kissed them both 'farewell', hoping the painters would also be good friends.

A & R Decorators were not available on Friday or over the weekend. She wanted to confirm they would start on Monday. By Tuesday Jenny was getting angry. She had already missed a day of her course waiting for them. They turned up at two in the afternoon. 'Sorry Missis,' said the one in charge. 'Ad to finish off the las' job.' He smelled of sweat, picked his nose and hadn't shaved for several days. His sidekick was missing a few teeth and had trod mud onto her vacuumed floor. They stayed for two hours and got the wallpaper off one of the top bedrooms. On Wednesday they turned up at eleven o'clock and stripped the second bedroom and departed at three o'clock. On Thursday she let them in at 9.30 and went off to her course. When she returned at one o'clock for a snack lunch they were sitting at the bar with their feet up munching sandwiches, the radio blaring and a bottle of Uncle Bernard's wine open on the counter.

'OK.' She stood there, hands on hips, furious. Although she was small, she could be angry. 'In theory you have been here for three and a half days. It has taken you this long to strip two rooms of wallpaper, do some gloss on the windows and cover the floor with paint. You've missed nearly two days' work, and I've probably failed my course. That's not good enough. Perhaps you should get back to work!'

'Look 'ere, Missis. We works our own hours. We don't stand with no messing. Don't you talk like that.'

'I will talk like that if I wish, and if that's your attitude you're out of here. Stop wasting my time. Take your paint and your brushes and get out.' She dramatically pointed to the door, as did the heroines in old black and white films. The men, sniggering, threw their sandwich packets on the floor, called her several four letter words and left with, 'You'll regret this, you silly cow.'

The two men tramped out deliberately treading cheese and pickle into the carpet. As they slammed the door she breathed a sigh of relief. But had she made a dreadful mistake? No! No she was not a silly cow! She was an independent woman who no longer let people walk all over her. If they sent her a bill she would consult Mr Slocombe. She wasn't going to let a couple of crooks take her for a ride. Somehow she would overcome the problem. The businesswoman was in control and would find another painter.

After an afternoon of more mind-sapping lectures on Value Added Tax she returned in the evening to her haven of peace in the basement and she found her Bible – Yellow Pages. After two hours of telephoning – narrating her sob story of being let down by painters, enough to bring tears to the most hardened painter's eyes – no one could help her for another month. Right, she thought, pouring herself a gin, I'll start myself. Getting the wallpaper off the walls will be a problem – and the ceilings – but the rest I can do. I'll start on glossing the doors.

She worked through the remainder of Thursday

evening, studied all day at college on Friday, then painted more doors and scraped wallpaper, so by midday on Saturday she was weary. Her lack of height and standing on steps made scraping wallpaper very wearing and her arms ached. She decided she needed a break and walked towards the Victorian terraces where Lyn lived at Rosebank. Could she knock on the door and ask for advice? Of course she could. A middle-aged bald man answered the door and happily ushered her in. 'A kindred spirit,' he said. 'I'm Ken. Lyn told me about you. I did like your uncle, Mr Ellis.'

'I would like to be Bernard's kindred spirit but I've got bogged down.'

'Come on through and tell us about it. We're having a quiet time until the next invasion about three o'clock.' They sat down with Lyn in the warm kitchen. 'What's the problem?'

'My painters were so bad I sacked them.'

'Brave woman,' exclaimed Ken.

'Now I'm stuck. I can't find new decorators for at least a month so I'm trying to decorate on my own. And I know I can't. D'you know of a decorator?'

'You've made me remember the backache,' said Lyn handing her a mug of coffee, 'but we've always been able to do it between us. Every year we close down for a month. Decorate for two weeks then spend two weeks in the sun. We used to go skiing, but not since I broke my leg. That was an interesting season. Difficult doing breakfasts on crutches.' Both Lyn and Ken chuckled at the memory. Yes, thought Jenny, that's the kind of memory I want.

They talked some more about guesthouses, eccentric guests, and near disasters that made Jenny laugh and lightened her heart. As she was leaving Lyn asked Ken, 'Got time to spare for a few ceilings?'

'Of course. I would be very happy to give Bernard Ellis's niece a helping hand. I'll lend you our machine that steams the wallpaper off. We're very busy next couple of days but I could come round next Tuesday.'

'Thank you so much,' and she gave them both a hug.

Wandering back to the house a solitary boat handler waved to her as his boat disappeared down Lansdown View Lock. 'Hello Christmas Sandwich Lady,' he called. She remembered his cheerful smile but the boat was gone before she arrived at the lock. Invigorated by the thought of support Jenny found the nearest DIY outlet and bought paint, brushes, endless rolls of anaglypta, wallpaper paste and a pasting table, then set to work.

With the aid of Ken's machine she had the wallpaper off three walls in the third bedroom and went to bed shattered. She was up early and had finished wallpaper scraping before breakfast. She was busy gloss painting the window when the doorbell rang. Annoyed at being interrupted, she stumped down the two flights of stairs thinking 'I must get used to this'. Her annoyance changed to delight when she found Mandy and Kevin on the doorstep. 'Thought we'd come to Bath and do a bit of shopping,' explained Mandy. Seated comfortably in the basement Mandy said, 'We've got some news for you.'

'You're pregnant!' was Jenny's excited response.

'Bloody hell, Mum, don't go jumping to conclusions. No, I've left my job at the bank. I was so bored. You can have enough of direct debits, standing orders, banging away on keyboards.'

'You're telling me!' commented Jenny, thinking of the accountancy course.

Mandy continued, 'I was getting quite depressed. That's why I was so quiet at Christmas. Then I thought I'd take a leaf out of your book and branch out. Seems to have done you no harm. So now I'm going to help Kev, join his business and become a painter. He says I've got a good eye for interior decoration. We've just completed our first job – just one room to be wallpapered but I really felt I'd achieved something.'

'Changed the name on me van,' interrupted Kevin. 'It now says "Morris and Evans, Interior Decorators". Doing up a flat in a smart part of Bristol next week. Should get it done in half the time.'

Jenny laughed, pleased for them both. 'I just can't imagine Mandy in overalls. Hope you don't argue over paint colours. I've a bit of a problem here,' and she went on to tell them about A & R Decorators.

'Think I've heard of them,' said Kevin. 'Have a reputation for not paying bills. So what are you doing?'

'I'm stripping wallpaper. I've got all the kit and will do it myself except the ceilings. Some friends I've made who also run a guesthouse are going to help with that.'

'What about the stairs?'

'I'll have to get someone in. Wait for a month. It doesn't matter when I open, but I really want to get the business started. It'll just take longer than I expected, especially as I'm doing courses – accountancy and computing.'

'Good for you, Mum. Six months ago you wouldn't have coped with all this.'

'If you can decorate the bedrooms I think Morris & Evans can help you out with the stairs.'

'But you're very busy, Kev. You said so at Christmas.'

'Now there are two of us, we'll have more time. Let's have a look.'

The three of them trooped up the stairs and Kevin examined the walls and ceiling.

'We could get away with just painting over all this. Use cream, and mushroom under the dado rail. I've got the ladders so shouldn't take too long.'

'Great, ' Jenny sounded relieved. 'You must let me know the price.'

She treated them to fish and chips and after their shopping they returned to help her with more wallpaper stripping. After a depressing week when her plans had all gone awry things were looking up.

On Monday morning as she was about to set out for college, the telephone rang. 'Stainless Steel Kitchen Fitters here. We've had a cancellation this morning. Any chance of us doing your kitchen this week?'

Jenny did a quick rethink. Having missed two days of the course could she afford to miss any more? It was worth the risk to get the kitchen started. 'Of course. I'd be only too happy to see you.'

'Be there this afternoon and strip out the old stuff.'

Thankfully she went to her course and later cheerfully greeted two efficient men in blue overalls. She told them what to dump in the back garden and what was staying. Pots, pans and crockery were removed to the bar and Jenny left them to it and went downstairs to order a new skip. By the end of the week new kitchen equipment gleamed. A shiny gas cooker with six burners and an outsized fridge adorned one wall, along with work surfaces and cupboards. Under the new stainless steel sink and draining board the dishwasher was installed ready for use. A new pine table and chairs in the centre and a dresser against one wall gave it the look of an old-fashioned farmhouse kitchen.

Also with Ken's assistance two bedrooms were painted pristine white.

By the end of the month the bedrooms and stairs were finished, and new windows had replaced the rotting ones in the top storey. A security firm had fitted new Yale locks on all the doors and a carpenter came to erect the fire doors and a new reception desk.

The carpenter was a giant of a man from Jamaica who sang spirituals and gospel songs in a mellow bass voice as he worked. Jenny, who was painting the kitchen, turned off her radio so she could listen to him. He gave her tickets for his choir's next concert in a local church, and she found the performance an uplifting experience. In the audience she greeted several neighbours she knew by sight; something that had never happened when she lived in the suburbs with Trevor.

Electricians came to put in extra plugs and television sockets in the bedrooms and gave her a certificate to say the system was up to standard. Then it was the turn of the carpet fitters who hammered and banged their way through the entire house. The noise and the fluff drove her out of the house to buy an endless list of kitchen and bedroom items she still needed. Finally the beds arrived and she felt she was emerging from the forest to new country only to realise this was a forest glade and a dark fir wood lay beyond. This was the land of fire and safety certificates, and residential drinking licences from the Magistrates' Court with which Mr Slocombe assisted her. The men from the fire brigade, pleasant enough with officious clipboards, pointed out that she had no smoke alarms and no fire precautions in the rooms and they would return. Men from the council came round looking suspicious but only mentioned that she should put a notice of tariffs in each bedroom. The computer had arrived and was installed in the reception area so she could look professional.

At last after four months she was breaking out of the forest of refurbishment and could see fresh pastures ahead of her. She put her advertising in place, then realised she had better put up a sign, and found a sign-writer. To feel she had achieved her first goal she asked all those who had helped her and the neighbours around for a drink and had a party. The Fowler brothers were there with Tom and Dorothy, Mr Patel, Lyn and Ken, Mandy and Kevin. They made a ceremony of putting up the sign saying 'Lansdown View Guesthouse' and opened bottles of champagne. Now her new life could begin.

Chapter 12

Next morning she awoke and panicked – why no door-bell, no workmen? Of course, that part of the work was over. She relaxed; realising for a few days life could be easy before her adverts would come into effect. Get up late, please herself what she did, but explore the city of Bath so she could tell her future guests of the best places to visit.

She cooked herself a full English breakfast to get used to the new cooker, then set out on the Bath Heritage Trail. The Roman Baths she remembered and was then entertained by the street musicians and pavement artists. She had lunch in Sally Lunn's, often having wondered what a Sally Lunn bun was like. The Tourist Information Centre confirmed that they had her guesthouse on their list and she picked up leaflets for her future guests' use. Climbing up Milsom Street and Gay Street she discovered Georgian Bath and Jane Austen. Like many schoolchildren she had been made to read *Pride and Prejudice* and thought it very dull. If fact she was so confused about English literature she thought Mr Rochester had married Elizabeth Bennett, but apparently that was another book entirely, as the assistant in the

Jane Austen Centre tried tactfully to tell her. Deciding her limited education needed broadening, she bought a couple of Jane Austen novels in paperback.

Climbing on up the hill she was impressed by The Circus, a circle of gracious houses, set off beautifully by plane trees, with budding leaves, at its centre. One of the roads from The Circus lead her on to the Royal Crescent and she could see Victoria Park spread below her. Returning by another route past many antique shops she came to the Market and Pulteney Bridge with its attractive small shops set on the bridge. Jenny wondered how many bridges in Britain still had shops on them? She remembered the old nursery rhyme 'London Bridge is falling down', and old prints in history books of London Bridge, but nothing like that existed now.

Leaning over the parapet she watched the Avon, green water turning white, plunge over the horseshoe-shaped weir, and thought about all she had seen and the people she had passed in the street – shoppers weighed down with carrier bags, Japanese tourists in groups, different languages being spoken, down-and-outs wearing odd clothes. She wouldn't have seen them in the shopping precinct of the suburbia she had left behind – well may be the junkies, late at night.

Looking at her map she thought rather than walk to the dreary railway station she could make her way along Great Pulteney Street to Sydney Gardens then down the canal. The clocks having changed to British summertime there would be an hour's extra daylight. The wind was chilly standing by the bridge – British summertime indeed – and a brisk walk would warm her up. Sydney Gardens proved to be another discovery. She was greeted by the sight and scent of daffodils. As she wandered along the twisting paths the huge trees delighted her, horse chestnuts coming into leaf, their sticky buds holding the promise of white candle-like flowers, shrubs she could not name and two buildings constructed with pillars like Greek temples. In the late afternoon sun she sat within one of these houses dreaming of the people who had walked these paths in past times, women in long sweeping dresses, men in top hats – what conversations and liaisons had taken place here? At the top of the garden she came out by Cleveland House and walked down to the towpath.

A stooping figure with a worn blue jersey was tying ropes expertly to bollards as he moored his boat. He straightened up, stretching his back and she recognised her canal boat acquaintance. She bid him good evening and he asked, 'Fancy a beer, Christmas Sandwich Lady?'

She paused, wanting to get home as her feet ached, but a beer was inviting. 'Yes, thanks.'

He helped her on board and put out a couple of folding chairs on the stern deck. Trees and bushes in new leaf formed a temple roof over them and mist was rising from the still water as they sat drinking beer out of cans and smoking cigarettes to keep the midges away, whilst she told him of her day. He laughed at her not knowing about Mr Rochester and Jane Eyre.

'I'll lend you a copy,' and he vanished into his cabin. Handing the dog-eared book to her he said, 'You'll find the bits about Grace Poole and the first Mrs Rochester quite creepy.'

'The first Mrs Rochester?'

'You'll have to read the story and find out.' She took the book, looking forward to some interesting bedtime reading. He smiled at her with eyebrows raised in a questioning manner.

'From our last conversation you're curious about the area. Have you just moved here?'

'Yes. Four months ago. I live in a house by Lansdown View Lock.' He was a stranger and didn't need to know her business.

'If you're not busy tomorrow would you like to come on *Blithe Spirit*? We'd get as far as Dundas Aqueduct. Then you could catch a bus or get a taxi home. It's beautiful at this time of year.'

The thought of a day away from the guesthouse, no telephones, no planning, no thinking, sounded wonderful. 'What time?' she asked.

'Ten-thirty. Come rain, come shine.'

'Ten-thirty, come rain, come shine, it is.'

This was going to be an adventure. She was going out with an unknown man for the first time in over twenty-two years.

It was a clear bright April day, but being sensible she packed a waterproof at the bottom of her knapsack, a bottle of wine and some turkey rolls. From her Boxing Day conversation he might well not have any food. Mr Patel at the shop was amused and curious. 'Perhaps also some Bombay mix and poppadums? I shall worry if you don't come in tomorrow. You may have been whisked away to Bradford-on-Avon.' They both laughed at the joke.

She was a little late walking up to the top lock; her legs ached after yesterday's exercise. He was untying the boat ready to leave, obviously not waiting for her.

'Time and tide wait for no man,' he said helping her on the boat.

'But there is no tide.'

'I have to be at certain places at certain times. I deal in ancient and second-hand books and there are clients I need to meet.'

'Ay Ay, Sir. You must have a name, Captain?'

'Of course. It's Ben. Ben Robinson.'

'I'm Jenny Evans. Not Mrs Christmas Sandwich.' They both chuckled and he kissed her.

They chugged off along the canal sitting side by side in the stern of the boat watching the ever-changing scenery. From field boundary banks primroses and violets showed, rabbits scurried under hedges and an occasional buzzard soared overhead. The air was warm and summer was on its way. They moored for lunch near an old building that Ben said he would show her later.

'I haven't got much for lunch, just sardines on toast and beer.' Jenny produced her bottle of wine and rolls. 'Ah ha,' announced Ben. 'Sardines for hors d'oeuvre and turkey for the main course. Would Madame wish to sample the wine?'

Ben showed her down the narrow steps, past his hastily covered unmade bed into his living area. It was stacked with books. She asked to go to the loo and realised canal boats were different from ordinary homes, more like floating caravans.

'I make a little money buying and selling books. Even some paperbacks are in great demand over the Internet. That's why I need to be in Bradford-on-Avon by tomorrow to use a friend's computer. The trade helps supplement my benefit payments.'

As Ben wiped the table clean Jenny set out her lunch offering. Ben busied himself with making toast and opening a tin of sardines, whilst Jenny wondered how anyone could live in a space just six feet wide. Over

150

lunch he told of his boat travels – the different view he had of towns and cities, going down the river Severn with a pilot, going aground on the Avon, a body he found in a Birmingham lock. She felt her life had been very dull. When they had finished the food and the wine he took her by the hand and led her over the railway line to the side of the old building. She was suitably surprised. 'It's an old wooden water wheel.' The wood was as white as an old scrubbed wooden kitchen table.

'Yes. When the canal was made they used this as a pumping station to supply the canal with water. Now they only use it on special weekends so it's shut today, but worth seeing.'

'It's part of history but not fossilised, still working. Let's walk down to the river.'

'Not today. I don't like leaving the boat too long. I've had burglars in the past. Let's go back and have a coffee.'

He started stroking her neck as they walked back to the boat but she realised after so long on her own she was not yet ready for any amorous advances. He was attractive, but her mind and body were fixed on one thing only – Lansdown View Guesthouse. If he felt rebuffed he disguised it and happily made coffee and set off towards Dundas. Their pleasant voyage continued and Jenny, not expecting the aqueduct over the Avon, was suitably surprised. Ben moored the boat in the basin and they walked to the aqueduct where it arched gracefully over the river as it flowed rapidly between green willows and fields beneath them.

'Today has been so beautiful. Spring at its best. Thanks for everything.'

'You could stay the night.'

151

'No, I need to get back. Things to arrange. Perhaps we could do this again,' and she smiled up at him as he held her close.

'When I'm back this way again, in a few weeks.'

As they walked back to the boat Jenny telephoned on her mobile for a taxi which would be at a local lay-by in half an hour. They sat at the stern of the boat smoking cigarettes, watching the dusk change the sky, and bats flitting about the trees, then he took her hand and walked her to the lay-by. He kissed her goodnight and murmured 'thanks' in her ear and was gone.

She had had a wonderful day. A different world and new vistas opening up to her, but why hadn't he stayed with her until the taxi came, and why would he have left that morning without her? Probably just a selfish man. In the twilight she saw him walk back and greet two men in dark clothes. Who were they? He hadn't mentioned them. The three of them walked away towards the boat.

The next morning was going to be important to her. A friend she had made on the computer course was coming to help set up her machine. He had all the correct disks and had bought on her behalf a program to help with her bookings. He had recommended a server for emails so her computer could be working by the end of the day and she might understand. Pete, tall with a loping walk and long hair, worked at the college part-time. He was trying to get into graphic design but meanwhile was happy to help his students. Mystified by all that Pete was doing to her blank machine Jenny made coffee and talked to Pyewacket.

'Wouldn't it be easier if we all talked directly to each other without machines, like you and I?' Pye rubbed against her. 'He's doing what's called "booting up". Nothing to do with football. All these odd terms. I think we'll call the computer Bill Gates. I can say to clients, "I'll just ask Bill." Not to be confused with bills. They can be called "Williams" as they are too serious to be "bills". Now I had better go back and be intelligent.' Pyewacket looked deep into her eyes, having understood every word.

'Right,' said Pete with enthusiasm, 'this is your basic Word program. You are used to this from college. Now I'll load the bookings program and run you through it.' Which he did whilst Jenny took notes. She would only know if she understood this once bookings came in. Lastly he connected to the net on her landline with an email address. She would have to advertise this. Now it would be up to her to cope with the system.

She offered to take him out to lunch but as he shut his briefcase he apologised, 'Sorry, I have to be back in college. Perhaps a drink sometime and you can tell me of any hitches. I'm just happy to see computers being used properly. If you start employing staff you may want to get the Sage program, but come back to me with any queries,' and he loped off down the road on his long legs. Before her confidence failed her she practised on the machine for an hour, then her brain turned to pulp, so she shut it down, wondering what kind of logical machine asks you to shut down by instructing it to start.

After a break she thought with forefinger inverted commas, 'Advertising'.

She rang the Tourist Information and gave them her email address, then the university. Feeling it was time to come down to earth she wrote postcards to put in Mr Patel's and the Post Office windows.

'I'm so glad to see you,' said Mr Patel. 'Not lost in Bradford-on-Avon. I would be delighted to send guests to your home. Have you enough bread, sausages, bacon and eggs? It is your festival of Easter, shops may be shut and many people wanting rooms.'

'Easter. Yes. Long weekend, people taking time off. Hadn't thought of that. If I get any guests can I come back to you?'

'Of course. Even if I'm closed.'

'You're so kind, Mr Patel.'

Next she walked up to the Post Office and found Mrs Trubshaw, who was sorting out Easter Eggs.

'Hello, dear, nice to see you again. Fancy any Easter Eggs, two for the price of one?'

'No. Sadly there aren't any children in my life, they've grown up. Although I might buy one for a friend. Yes, I'll take two.' Perhaps Ben would like one when she saw him next, and Mandy might.

'I came to ask if I could put a postcard in your window. My guesthouse is now open.'

'Well done. Going to be the Ritz of Widcombe! I'd be pleased to help.'

Jenny paid for her Easter eggs and as Mrs Trubshaw rang up the till she remarked, 'you were asking at Christmas time about Eleanor Watson. Well she's back. Staying with her mum. Something's not right, but I don't know what. Nosy old Parker that I am!'

'I'll give her a ring. I'm nosy as well.'

'Hello, Eleanor. It's me, Jenny Evans. Mrs Trubshaw said she'd seen you and I wondered how things were. Did you get your money?'

'Oh Jenny! A voice of sanity. My mother is driving

me mad. Can we meet for a drink, or better still a meal? I cannot live on shepherd's pie for the rest of my life.' For the rest of my life, what did she mean?

'Come to the guesthouse and we'll take it from there. It's time I discovered local eating places, if only to advise my future guests.'

An hour later they were sitting in an Italian bistro in the local row of shops. Eleanor, still glamorous in a tailored trouser suit, black hair with grey streaks piled high, looked drawn, lines showing round her eyes. Although Jenny had dressed in her best skirt and blouse she felt dowdy. They had already ordered a carafe of house red and were considering rigatoni and three cheeses or fettucine carbonara.

'Now what's happened? For you to be back in Bath something must have gone wrong.'

'Yes. You remember I told you about my friend Marie?'

'You were thinking of starting up a flower shop together and Bernard's money might help.'

'Well,' Eleanor sighed sadly. 'She used to come round to our house in the evenings and we would talk about gardens, dipping into books, discussing flower arrangements and colours. Ted would be there buried in his newspaper but quietly taking an interest. Unfortunately his interest wasn't in gardens,' she paused, 'but in Marie. I only found out about this last week when I arrived home to Wimbledon to an empty house. Even the dog, Pipper, had gone. And I was very fond of Pipper. Well the house wasn't exactly empty, not quite – he'd left me a bed, the curtains and carpets. There was a note on the bed, which said, "Serves you right!" And perhaps it does.'

155

'You mean he was referring to you and Bernard and he's taken over ten years to react?'

'In our one acrimonious meeting that is what he said.'

'What a cold fish. How could he be so calculating?'

'I don't think he cared until Marie came along. Sudden interested in gardens and flowers, I should have realised. At least she's past "the Cape of Good Hope".'

'What?'

'She's too old to have children. If there were children – that would really upset me.' Jenny noticed there were tears on Eleanor's cheeks and put a comforting hand on her arm. Eleanor continued, 'Now I must be strong, independent and alone. I've always thought he wasn't that important to me, but after twenty-five years you get used to people being there.'

'You mean he took the rubbish out and brought in the coal.' At least Eleanor laughed, but Jenny understood the hurt. She had been there herself.

'There was more to it than that.' Eleanor paused, 'Yes there was much more to it.' She paused, wiping her eyes. 'He's put the house on the market. Didn't ask me, but half the cash will be mine. If I had left Ted and stayed with Bernard life could have been so different.'

'You might have been happier. Perhaps Uncle Bernard would still be alive. Who knows?' Seeing the pain in Eleanor's eyes she quickly went on. 'I would still be stuck in suburbia with Trevor, working for the council and never have met you. We all make decisions that we think are right at the time, and take into consideration everyone we know and love. If it turns out wrong, it turns out wrong, but you still have to say it was the right decision at the time. So what do you intend to do? Ah, here's the food.'

156

Plates of appetising pasta were placed before them and silently they ate for some time enjoying the taste, the wine, and their own thoughts. After a while Eleanor said, 'I would still like to go ahead with the idea of the shop. Like you, be positive. Ted and Marie never knew about Bernard's money, so I have that to start with, and I can live with Mum for very little expense.'

'Somewhat more if you don't want shepherd's pie every day,' giggled Jenny, slightly drunk.

'Have some more wine,' ordered Eleanor, 'and let me plan my future. For a start where are the silk flowers in the guesthouse that you talked about? I could provide them. My first contract?'

'I haven't got that far. Let me think for a minute. To start with flowers in reception and the bar. I know, "Silken Inspirations". For more information contact Eleanor Watson.'

'I like "Silken Inspirations". Whoa, what a name! I know Bath is expensive. Rents and Council Tax. I shall have to look around. Somewhere I could live over the premises would be ideal. "Silken Inspirations", I'll dream of that.'

'No dreaming. Get yourself a business plan and a loan until your ship, or rather your house, comes in. When can you deliver these silk flowers? Apart from the reception and the bar I'll want eleven displays for the bedrooms, then small displays for the landings. You'll need to see the designs of the bedrooms to get the flowers right. Something bronze in the entrance hall and red in the bar.'

'You really are becoming a businesswoman.'

'I've realised you need to play the part – the charming hostess but really the hard woman. When I get guests I'm going to act hospitable. But if they don't pay up – Al Capone, "OK Kid, come up with the goods, or else." Let's order an ice cream.'

They walked back across the dark lamp-lit canal to hear the telephone ringing.

'Hi Jenny.' It was Lyn. 'Your career is about to begin. We're full up. Got room for two Dutch people? They're on their way.'

Jenny grabbed Eleanor's arms. 'You have to stay and help me! My first guests are about to arrive. I don't know what to do. Hard-headed businesswoman, indeed. I'm in a panic.'

'Let's greet them with some coffee or tea. Put the kettle on.'

'You do that. I'll find the towels in the airing cupboard.'

Five minutes later a young couple weighed down by rucksacks stood at the front door. They were both tall and fair-haired, dressed in anoraks, jeans and walking boots and Jenny was relieved to find they both spoke English. She shook them by the hand in greeting and, as they filled in the registration details, told them with pride they were her first guests.

'Would you like a room with a double bed or single beds?'

'Double, please. We are on our, what do you say, we have just got married.'

'Oh, you mean your honeymoon. How lovely. A happy start to a new life together. You've obviously been walking and must be tired. Would you like a cup of tea of coffee?'

'Coffee, thank you.'

After cups of coffee and a rather stilted conversation

about weddings, Jenny said, 'I don't do evening meals, but you must be hungry. Would you like a sandwich? I have some turkey or cheese.'

'Please,' answered the girl, her long blond hair falling over her shoulders. 'We have been walking all day along the Cotswold Way. But the Netherlands is so flat, we're not used to hills. It is beautiful, but our legs are very tired.'

'Right. I suggest I show you your room. You have a relaxing shower and I'll leave a tray outside your door with some soup and sandwiches.' Making appreciative Dutch noises they went upstairs to the first floor double Poppy decorated room.

'What time would you like breakfast? You're my only guests so whenever you like.' They glanced at each other in a way Jenny remembered from years ago.

'Would ten be too late?'

'Not at all. See you then.'

As Jenny returned to the kitchen Eleanor said, 'I feel these sandwiches are going to be a gift.'

'Of course,' said Jenny buttering bread, 'they're on their honeymoon and my first guests.'

'So speaks the hard-nosed businesswoman. I'd better go now. I've enjoyed this evening. The first time I've been able to say that for several days. Tomorrow I shall start on your floral displays before the shops shut down on Good Friday. And I'll be tough enough to send you the bill.'

'I'll enjoy the flowers and be very pleased to pay you. I'm so glad you were here so I didn't go completely to pieces.'

'Now tomorrow. Have you got enough food in for an English breakfast or will it be just Continental?'

'I'll panic again and go and see Mr Patel.'

Mr Patel was very helpful. Sausages, bacon, eggs and tomatoes were no problem.

Before she started cooking Jenny took a deep breath and switched on her computer. At least she had got that right. Were there any emails? Yes, one that requested two-single bedded rooms. She could email or telephone a Miss Sholes in Salisbury. Jenny chose the telephone and booked Miss Sholes and Miss Clark in for four nights from Good Friday. After breakfast shopping would be priority. Although she didn't feel ready to cope with evening meals, snacks were an alternative and she could open the bar. The guesthouse was up and running. It was time to hang up the 'Vacancies' sign.

Chapter 13

Whilst the Dutch couple ate cornflakes gazing into each other's eyes, bacon, sausages and tomatoes were wafting appetising smells from the kitchen. As Jenny cleared the plates she asked them about the Cotswold Way and learnt that it had taken them four days to walk its length. Today they would explore Bath and Jenny gave them some leaflets telling them of her walk earlier in the week.

'Please may we stay until Saturday? Tomorrow we thought of visiting Bristol. We have been told about an old ship there in the harbour.'

'Oh yes – the *Great Britain*. You'll find it very interesting. If you catch the train you can get on the ferry from the railway station to the centre of town. It is a very historic town and there is a Georgian area called Clifton where there is the famous suspension bridge.'

As they rose from the table the girl said, 'It will be good to have a day without those heavy, what do you call them?'

'Rucksacks,' interposed Jenny. 'Have a good day. See you this evening. The front door key is with your bedroom key.'

They left later hand in hand; Jenny tidied their room

and shopped for a long weekend. Maybe Mandy and Kevin would turn up and where was Dean? Communication had never been his strong point. Later she had time to walk by the canal with Pyewacket, no longer on his lead, bounding from garden wall to garden wall. She took her mobile phone with her in case another potential guest might want a room. She was leaning over a black and white wrought iron bridge watching the water, the warmth of the sun on her back, when the phone rang.

'Edith, how nice to hear your voice. Sorry I haven't been in touch. It has been so hectic getting the guest-house ready.'

'So you're open. Good. Have you by any chance got a room over the weekend?'

'Yes. I've only got three rooms taken so far. I only started yesterday. Aren't you having a dirty weekend away with the boyfriend?'

'No. Fortunately not. Tried that. We went to Sidmouth and it was a disaster. I thought a change and some pleasant company might be a tonic. Would tonight be too early?'

'Of course not. It would be great to see you.'

'Right. I shall leave my Special Needs desk in a state of disarray, go home, pack and catch the first train I can.'

'And I'll have a meal ready for you. Probably be spaghetti bolognese.'

Jenny turned to the cat sitting on the lock gate. 'Pye we have to go home and get ready for another guest.'

While the bolognese sauce was simmering Jenny rang Mandy to see how she was. 'Just checking to see if you still have ten fingers and ten toes.' This was her normal phrase when telephoning the children so as not to sound like an interfering parent, or a clucking hen, as Mandy put it.

'The fingers and toes are OK. It's the bit in between. I've had flu and been stuck in bed. I'm up now but so weak. I feel I'm letting Kev down. He's had to do the last job on his own.'

'I've got a double room vacant. Would you like some tender loving care?' She felt it was the least she could do, as they had been so helpful with the decorating.

'I would, but Kev's got to work. I'll see what he says, hang on.' There was a pause, 'Kev says he'll bring me down tonight, if that's all right. Then he can work flat out until Saturday night, his mum and dad will look after him and he'll come down on Sunday.'

'Tell him it's only roast turkey again. By the way is Dean OK?'

'Didn't he ring you? He's in Spain with Cassy, staying with her mother.'

'Has he got a passport?'

'No. Cassy smuggled him in, all six foot of him, in her double bass case. He's grown up now, Mum. Oh, another piece of news: Dad's girlfriend has had a baby boy. Born on April Fools' Day. They're both well. He's called Joshua.'

'How biblical. Let's hope he doesn't break down too many walls. See you this evening.'

She knew she shouldn't have been so abrupt, but the thought of Trevor with a new baby in his arms rankled. She added more mince and tomato paste to the sauce and stirred it too vigorously. Calmed, she sat in her peaceful basement with a cup of tea and rang Lyn to say 'thank you' for sending round the Dutch couple.

163

'That's good. We still have a full house and it's steak and kidney pie tonight, with an omelette as the vegetarian alternative.'

'I've got several rooms taken, but one's for my daughter whose convalescing after flu, and another for a friend needing support. I'm easing my way into this slowly. I've got my feet up and watching the telly.'

'You're being too kind. You wait until Saturday and good luck.'

The Dutch couple returned about five o'clock and went straight upstairs so Jenny continued putting her feet up, Pye content on her lap, until Edith arrived.

Edith, looking old and harassed, grey hair dangling, bundled in through the front door with two large bags. How long will she be staying? wondered Jenny.

'The train was so packed,' grumbled Edith, 'I was squashed up to a tall rugged man for twenty minutes.'

'I don't know how you coped,' answered Jenny. 'Good thing you're not a feminist or you could have sued him.'

'That's an idea. I could have got to know him better.'

Jenny hugged her. 'I'm so glad to see you again. I've missed you and your dry comments. I've had to make them for myself. As you are staying here you have to register.'

'Big Brother?'

'Just the law and fire precautions,' Jenny said as she led her down to the flat. 'For me you are a non-paying guest who can give me support during my first week. And I mean that! I don't want to panic like I did last night. Also Mandy is coming to stay after the flu. I'll make some coffee and explain.'

Half an hour later Edith laughed, 'This is what I need. Stop feeling sorry for myself. Forget about the past few months, meet new people and give you a helping hand.

164

What time's Mandy coming? She should have the first floor room, then I can take her soup at regular intervals.'

'I'm sorry; you'll have to get used to the stairs. Two singles are booked on the first floor, so you're on the second floor in a Honeysuckle single room. I've got to keep the doubles free in case guests want to stay over the holiday. If I'd known you were coming I would have installed a stair lift.'

'I'm not that old,' Edith looked threatening, but ten years younger with the aim of looking after Mandy. 'Now, landlady, show me to my room.'

Carrying a bag each they met the Dutch couple in the hallway leaving for the evening. 'We are going on a "Ghost tour",' the young man explained.

'How exciting,' exclaimed Jenny. 'You must tell us all about it when you return. Would you like sandwiches again?'

'Thank you.'

'I'll leave them in your room.' Sideways out of her mouth she muttered to Edith, 'Remember, sandwiches, Dutch couple, at nine o'clock.'

'Sure, landlady. And double whiskies at ten.'

'Here we are at the Honeysuckle suite. The two misses are booked into the single Poppy rooms.'

'Are they lesbians?'

'Not with single rooms. Sounded more like retired school teachers. But you never know.'

'The room looks good. Clean and bright. I remember what it was like before Christmas.' Edith peered out of the window, 'and a view over towards the canal. TV as well – and satellite. I could stay here all day and you can bring me soup.'

'I know you. You've too much curiosity. You'll be down in the morning.'

'You know what this room lacks?'

'No. What?'

'Kettle. Cups and ways to make tea or coffee. Easier for you. You see it in all guesthouses.'

'I'd never stayed in a hotel or guesthouse until we went to France.' Obviously Jenny was somewhat unnerved, but Edith comforted her and patted her on the arm, 'You weren't to know. It'll save you a lot of time making pots of tea. You'll need several trays, small electric kettles, cups and saucers, and those packets of tea, coffee, sugar and plastic containers of milk you can never open. Convenient but tasteless. But you won't have to run up and down stairs. Think about it.'

'That's the doorbell. Might be Mandy. Come down to the kitchen when you're ready.'

Mandy, with Kev in support, came into the kitchen. Mandy slumped on a chair, pale and quiet. Kev looked washed out as well. Jenny got them some tea; they were too tired to talk. Edith was introduced to them then Jenny dished up the spaghetti for the four of them in the kitchen. There was laboured conversation over the meal then they helped Mandy up to bed where she was tucked up with a hot water bottle and dozed watching television. Kev hovered around then retreated back to Bedminster. Edith and Jenny retired to the kitchen to make nine o'clock sandwiches and find the whisky bottle. After a couple of drinks Edith opened up on her weekend in Sidmouth.

'I realise I've only really known Eddie in a casual way in the evenings. I met him in the pub and that's where he belongs and is good company. But life isn't just made up of evenings. In the mornings he was a right misery. Going on about his arthritis – bit like your sister-in-law, what was her name?

'Sheila. Wonder how she is? Go on.'

'We were in a flat, so I cooked a casserole for lunch. That was wrong. He wanted sausages and chips. It was raining so I got out a book. That was wrong, "Never read a book in me life", he said. I suggested Scrabble, that was wrong. Cards, a game of Whist? That was wrong. His mother said it led to gambling and ruin. So he spent the afternoon watching football on TV with a can of beer in his hand. In the evening he fell asleep in the chair.'

'A proper couch potato, I know the type.'

'Next morning was beautiful. I got up early, he was snoring, and walked along the promenade enjoying the sea and the gulls and got a couple of Sunday papers. He ignored the papers, "load of rubbish", and demanded a cooked breakfast. I refused and he started packing, saying we would be leaving in half an hour. I had to go with him or find a train.'

'What a selfish slob.'

'Outside the "Hail fellow well met" atmosphere of the pub and people, Eddie was nothing.'

'No brain. It can't be all physical appeal, you have to be able to talk to each other.'

'There wasn't a chance for sex. He was asleep! What has depressed me is the fact that the older you get the more difficult it is to find anyone. A lonely old age is hovering on the horizon.' Edith, usually so strong, so down-to-earth, looked old and vulnerable.

Jenny took her hand, 'At least if you are on your own you can decide what you want to read, or walk along a lonely seashore when you like without anyone complaining. Go places, study things and who knows what interesting people you might meet.'

'But you always come home to an empty house.'

'Better than dreading coming home to a house of complaint.' Pyewacket jumped on Jenny's lap, all-knowing green eyes luminous, full of understanding. Jenny looked into the comfort of those eyes, 'The house is never empty if you have a cat.'

'Don't tell me you haven't met some bloke in the four months you've been here. Someone you've fancied?'

Jenny shrugged. 'I don't know when he'll come this way again. His name's Ben and he lives on a canalboat called *Blithe Spirit*. He passes by here from time to time. He has a gypsy look about him, dark curly hair, nice smile and deals in antique books. He's lent me a copy of *Jane Eyre*. He might be back this way in a few days.'

'How romantic. He could sweep you off your feet into the moonlight.'

'Like you, Edith, I'll keep my feet on the ground. Disappointment makes romance a balloon too easily burst.'

The Dutch couple returned at this point. They were introduced to Edith, offered drinks and as they were happy to describe their ghost tour the sandwiches were produced. There was entertaining talk between Edith and the couple about ghosts with Edith finding the right words for the Dutch couple's lack of vocabulary, so Jenny crept away to check on Mandy who was deeply asleep. Turning off the TV she kissed her daughter on the forehead, now cool. Something she hadn't done for some years. She and her daughter had both grown up. They had drawn apart but now circumstances had brought them back together again.

Downstairs the young man was trying to describe to Edith his work in growing bulbs. Edith, having consumed too much whisky, was looking vague so Jenny made some coffee and the couple, mugs in hand, said goodnight.

'Thank you for this evening. Our train to Bristol is leaving about ten. Can we have breakfast at nine o'clock?'

'Of course.'

She helped Edith up the stairs mentioning breakfast would be at nine in the morning, thinking she would see Edith when Edith felt like it.

Jenny spent a quiet day cooking for the weekend and enjoying Mandy's occasional company when she wasn't lying on the sofa in the basement. Edith was sent out to discover Sydney Gardens armed with her camera and at five o'clock the Misses Sholes and Clark arrived by taxi. They wore tailored tweed suits and their grey hair was cut short. Jenny showed them to their rooms looking out over the Abbey and they enthused in cultured tones. When asked if they would like a pot of tea in the dining room they happily accepted. Jenny added Easter biscuits to the tea tray and as she placed it before them tentatively asked if they had any plans for their stay.

'We were wondering if you could recommend a restaurant locally for our evening meal?' Jenny told them of the Italian bistro just down the road.

'And tomorrow we shall explore the town before taking tea with an ex-pupil of ours who lives in the Royal Crescent.' Miss Sholes chuckled. 'No doubt you realised we were school teachers.'

'I did wonder,' stuttered Jenny.

'I taught mathematics, and Mabel geography. So we

won't get lost.' They both smiled over this obviously well-used joke.

'After tea we are going to the Theatre Royal,' added Mabel, 'to see a Noël Coward play.'

'It sounds a lovely day. Especially meeting an old friend. What time would you like breakfast?'

'Oh, perhaps late as we're on holiday. Eight-thirty?'

With relief Jenny retreated to the kitchen.

'School teachers make me feel as if I was ten years old.' Edith looked up from the local paper.

'Discard your gymslip. You're forty something. You're not at school any more. Treat them like anyone else.'

'Breakfast at 8.30. I'll have to get used to getting up early.' Edith tapped her on the shoulder with her newspaper, 'Good Council House office training, up at dawn, now comes into play. I'm going to enjoy satellite telly on my bed for a couple of hours, but remember what I said about the kettles and the coffee.'

In the evening Jenny was just about to dish up shepherd's pie to her non-paying guests when the bell rang. 'Don't panic,' said Edith, 'this your bread and butter. Get used to it.'

It was Eleanor. 'I come bearing gifts.'

'Enter and welcome Bearer of Gifts.'

'As long as they're not Greeks!' warned Edith.

'No, Edith, Eleanor is Bath born and bred. This is my friend Edith, bearer of down-to-earth gifts from Manchester. What have you brought?'

'A floral display in gold, suitable for madam's reception desk.' She unwrapped the display of golden, russet leaves, ears of corn and red rose hips entwined with

170

hops. Edith, Mandy, still in her dressing gown, and Jenny in unison said, 'Oh!'

'That is wonderful,' added Jenny. 'That really shows off the reception area. Makes it warm and welcoming. Thank you so much.'

'Excellent. That's what I hoped. "Silken Inspirations" has made a start.'

'Come in and have a celebratory drink. I'd say stay for a meal but its shepherd's pie, which your mother probably gave you at lunch time.'

'True, but good company will make it a feast.' The four of them sat down to an entertaining meal that even got Mandy laughing. Later Jenny helped her to bed with a hot drink and came downstairs to find Eleanor and Edith with a new bottle of whisky talking about men, and the men were having a hard time. Jenny cleared up the kitchen, not wishing to join in the debate. She still felt anger, or was it jealousy, about Trevor and his new son. Taking men apart wouldn't do her any good even if it relieved Edith and Eleanor's feelings. She turned on 'Bill', the computer, to check her emails and telephoned a Mr Fitzgerald who wanted to stay with his wife and two young daughters on Sunday. She was making out a 'William', as she now called bills, for the Dutch couple when the phone rang. An Australian couple, judging by the accent, wanted to stay on Saturday night. They could take over from the honeymooners. All this was entered on her computer. It would not do during her first week to have double bookings.

Back in the kitchen Edith was saying, 'My first husband, John, wasn't so bad. He was kind and told jokes, made me laugh. I only knew him a year before he was killed.'

171

'How tragic,' said Eleanor, 'what happened?'

'He was in the Army in Germany. No dramatic battle. He just got run down by a tank, silly fool. And I was expecting our Ian. Hard being on your own with a baby, so I rushed into marriage number two far too quickly. Bill was a right swine and when he was drunk used to beat me up. We had another son, Oliver, and Bill packed up drinking for a time until the boys got too lively. He often hit Ian so he screamed, but the first time he hit Oliver I packed his bag and showed him the door. Fortunately he never came back.'

Jenny drew up a chair at the table. 'I never knew you had such a hard time. You're always so practical and calm. It must have been awful, especially with two young children.'

'After that nothing else seems so bad. It was all a long time ago. Social Services were very good. That's why I ended up in Special Needs.'

'And your children?' asked Eleanor.

'The boys are now men. I don't see much of them and they haven't settled down. Who knows one day I could be a grandmother. I think I hear your guests coming in, or burglars.'

Jenny greeted the elderly teachers in the hall, asking if they would like anything: tea, coffee or something from the bar?

'As we're on holiday, Mabel, how about a brandy to finish off our excellent meal?'

'Indeed, Phyllis. An "A plus" idea.'

They settled into the easy chairs in the bay window and Jenny brought them drinks and at the same time the Dutch couple came in and asked for two lagers. She left the four in conversation about Brunel's ship the *Great*

Britain and returned to the kitchen. Eleanor was about to leave. They walked to the front door with Jenny thanking her again for the silk display.

'I can't get over Edith's sad past. I've known her for over ten years and she has never mentioned her first husband.'

'I know we spent time running men down, but perhaps the memory is too poignant for her. She's a feisty lady. Thanks for the evening. Your shepherd's pie bears no resemblance to Mum's. I'll be back bearing more gifts.'

Edith had joined the guests in the dining room and was telling them about the replica of Cabot's ship the *Matthew* that had been built in Bristol to commemorate five hundred years since Cabot discovered Newfoundland. Jenny made some sandwiches in case anyone was hungry and sat down listening with pleasure to the chatter of contented guests. Edith ate most of the sandwiches, forgetting herself, waving her hands in excitement so cheese crumbs scattered the floor, relating a maritime event called the Festival of the Sea when sailing ships again thronged Bristol's wharves. As no one went to bed before eleven o'clock it must have been a successful evening.

On Saturday the Dutch honeymooners thanked Jenny in their broken English and, loaded again with their rucksacks, left hand and hand, for the railway station.

The elderly ladies, chattering excitedly about their day out, wondered if they should take umbrellas as the weather looked showery, then dithered off towards the Roman Baths.

As Mandy had said Jenny hated changing beds, but this would now be her daily task and beds made, carpets vacuumed, Cash and Carry shopping done, she was ready for the Australian couple.

Edith had decided on a shopping spree and Jenny decided to accompany her as far as a toyshop. 'A family with two young girls are staying tomorrow night. They might be bored so I thought a few games in the dining room might be a good idea.' They walked down by the canal and watched with amusement some first-time canal holidaymakers trying to negotiate the locks. There was much shouting and swearing as the boat banged against the stone walls.

'They talk about swearing like a bargee. Now I know why,' commented Edith, 'but it must be fun when you know what you're doing – like your Ben.'

'I did enjoy our day out. I'd like to explore more of the canal.'

'Bit different from the old canal back home in Manchester. The water was black, full of rubbish and the odd dead cat. I was going on last night about life being hard with two youngsters in council flats, but at least weekends we could get out to Ashton Court or Blaise Castle and they could run about in the woods. Did us all good to get out of the flats though. "Colditz", the neighbours called them. The lifts rarely worked and the stairs always smelt of pee. Getting a job with the council meant we could afford to rent a flat nearer the centre of town. It was so peaceful after noisy neighbours.'

'You must had a very difficult time.'

'Prefer to forget it. Now with the flat and a job, which is rewarding, I've put the past behind. I never wanted to marry again. The boys were difficult if men appeared on the scene. They remembered Bill. So I've contented myself with the odd fling.'

174

'Like Charlie.'

'Charlie's advantage was money. We had some good times. That's what I like to remember.'

'That's why you're so positive.'

'I wasn't on Thursday.'

'Everyone can have a down day. You helped me through many down days last year. Don't know how I would have coped without you.'

'Before we both start crying, try that toyshop over there.'

Jenny arrived back at the guesthouse with games of Trivial Pursuit, Happy Families, Snap and playing cards. She stacked these on the bar and found Mandy, dressed in jeans and skinny jersey heating up baked beans and grating cheese. After this snack Jenny suggested a stroll by the canal and arm in arm, Pyewacket bounding around them, they walked slowly up to the next lock.

'Somebody's waving to you, Mum.'

Jenny waved back. 'It's Ben.'

He jumped off the boat holding a central mooring line and was introduced to Mandy.

'You got home OK on Tuesday?'

'Yes and thanks for the day.'

'Sorry I can't stop. I've an appointment tomorrow in Bristol and the lock's set right. See you on my way back to Bradford-on-Avon. Have some turkey sandwiches ready.' With that he jumped back on the stern of the boat. Jenny shut the gates behind him.

He handed her a windlass, 'Can you open the paddles for me. It'll save me time.' Jenny went to the other end of the lock and turned the handle, listening to the clinking sound of cogs turning, then the rush of water, which had become a background sound at the guesthouse. Mandy watching, cuddling Pyewacket in her arms, noticed how young her mother looked.

Ben chugged off to the next lock. 'He's a bit of a hunk,' said Mandy with a note of surprise in her voice.

'Yes, I shall have to look out for him in a few days' time.'

'What's all this about turkey sandwiches?'

'Just a joke. I shared my snack with him on Boxing Day. That's how we met.'

Edith was sitting out in the garden when they returned, with some interesting bags from a successful shopping expedition. Jenny found chairs in the garage and the three of them sat enjoying the spring sunshine. Mandy was looking less pale and a smile had returned to her eyes.

'I don't think we should go back to Bristol for a few days, Edith. We should stay here to keep an eye on Mum. I have just been introduced to Ben, he might lead her astray.'

'Good. High time she was led astray.' Jenny, who had found some secateurs, was cutting back some of the rambling roses and told them to mind their own business. When Jenny went to answer the doorbell Edith called, 'If that's the Australians I'm betting they're called Bruce and Sheila.'

On returning some ten minutes later Jenny said, 'No they weren't Bruce and Sheila. A Mr and Mrs Jones from Milton Keynes. Young couple touring the West Country. They've taken the Rose double and have gone straight out again into town and won't be back till late. The bell again. Could this be Bruce and Sheila?'

A tall, tanned middle-aged man and a petite dark-

176

haired woman greeted Jenny. His manner was larger than life as he said, 'G'day' and took the cases up the stairs two at a time. The wife didn't speak. Jenny wondered if she was allowed to get a word in against the loud Australian voice. She showed him where he could leave the hire car beside the garage and when she asked if they would like a pot of tea they decided to stay in the garden with Edith and Mandy. The canal was a new experience for the Australians and every time a boat chugged by the man would jump up to watch the locking procedure. His wife sat quietly smiling at him. Over the tea with Easter biscuits the wife told them she was originally from Italy. Her lilting Italian accent added colour, as she related how they had come to Europe to find their roots and perhaps members of their families. They had spent two weeks in Italy, had seen where she had been born in Turino and met some of her cousins. She remembered very little of Italy as, with her parents, five brothers and sisters, she had emigrated to Australia as a young child.

'My first real memory is the boat. We had such fun, then Sydney was so different. Learning a new language. The food. Now Don is looking for his roots near Bath.'

'You're too right I am. My folks emigrated in the Fifties. Apparently you paid ten pounds, got on a boat and six weeks later made yourself a new life.

'I was born out there and listened to the folks talking about England, but it was so good in Oz – the weather, the food, the homes – they stayed. Dad had worked on a farm over here and life hadn't been easy. Up at dawn for the milking. Mum got ill during the bad winter in '47, so Australia's sun suited. Maria and I are looking for a village near here called Westwood. It's in Wiltshire. D'yer know of it?'

Jenny and the others looked blank. 'I've only lived here since Christmas. I'll go and get the map book out of the car.'

They all peered over the gazetteer, got confused over grid references but found the village near Bradford-on-Avon.

'That's great. Thanks so much little lady. Tomorrow we'll go see what we can find out.'

'Please take the map.'

'You can try looking for your family on the gravestones,' suggested Mandy.

'It's Easter Sunday so you may even find the vicar there,' said Edith.

'After Mass we will discover Westwood,' said Maria firmly. 'Now you have refreshed us we will walk round Bath. Why is a town called after something you wash in?'

'I gather a ride on the open-topped bus tells you all you need to know.'

As Jenny carried in the cooked breakfasts next morning Misses Sholes and Clark were advising the Joneses from Milton Keynes to visit Wells Cathedral and Cheddar Gorge. The young couple looked rather alarmed. Perhaps they too had Jenny's conditioned fear of teachers, so she interjected to the elderly ladies, 'How was your theatre visit?'

'Oh, we did enjoy it. Noël Coward's *Hay Fever*. We did laugh. The bit at the end when the couple creep away and the family don't notice because they're arguing. Hilarious.' The young couple looked relieved.

Don and Maria came in, obviously after Mass, Maria carrying a prayer book, and both tucked into cereal whilst Don studied the map.

Soon the guests had departed, the Joneses making for Land's End, the teachers to morning service at the Abbey and the Australians to discover their relatives. Jenny set to on the turkey dinner for her own family and the day passed peacefully, Mandy and Kevin happy to be together again.

Peace was over when the Fitzgeralds arrived. The parents, in smart clothes, looked worn. The two girls in frilly frocks were sulky. Jenny suggested a pot of tea and soft drinks before they found their rooms. Jenny, as she left the room, heard the smallest child shout, 'I hate Easter biscuits. I want to go to McDonalds!'

'Later, darling,' soothed the father.

Some time afterwards Jenny came to clear away the tray and found Mrs Fitzgerald alone with her feet up smoking a cigarette. She looked more relaxed.

'Hope you don't mind me smoking.'

'Not at all. You look as through you've had a busy day.'

'We've been to see my mother-in-law in a home up on Lansdown. The poor lady has Alzheimer's. She doesn't make much sense. We find it distressing when we can remember what a lively person she was. The children don't understand and get bored. My husband has just taken them over to the play park. I think I can hear them coming back.'

The children rushed back in through the front door. Jenny, trying to think of something friendly to say, said, 'What pretty dresses.'

'They're all right for Grandma but we're *not* wearing them to McDonalds. Come on Suzie,' and they were off up the stairs.

'Rest over,' said Mrs Fitzgerald and heaved herself out of the chair.

'I'll help you with the cases,' offered Jenny. Fifteen minutes later the four of them clattered down the stairs looking far more casual and heading for town.

Jenny settled down to her evening routine with 'Bill', answering emails and doing accounts. There were two telephone reservations so the following week would be busy. Edith came up from the basement where she had been watching television with Mandy and Kevin. 'Those two lovebirds are making me feel like a gooseberry, or is it raspberry? Do you think it's time to open the bar?'

'Good idea. Double whisky coming up.'

The first to return were the two old ladies who had enjoyed visiting Victoria Park. Seeing the games on the bar their eyes lit up.

'A game of Scrabble, Mabel?'

'Certainly, Phyllis. Would you care to join us Mrs . . .?

'The name's Edith. You'll have to remind me of the rules,' and they were content for an hour.

The family came in replete and Jenny produced another pot of tea and cokes for the girls. Jenny indicated to the girls that there were card games on the bar and the two decided to play Beggar my Neighbour. The parents gave Jenny a grateful look and settled down, Mrs with an Aga Saga and Mr with the *Observer*. Jenny went to make some sandwiches then returned to provide whisky and brandy for the Scrabble players. The children were laying out a rather fractious game of Pelmanism, normal bed-time long past, and to keep the peace she asked if she could help them. They played a tense game with Jenny looking on as umpire. There were groans when a move went wrong and whoops when a pair was won. In the end the parents came over to watch and the younger daughter eventually won by two pairs. 'Julia always wins,' grumbled Suzie. 'She can remember things.'

Mother quietly said 'Bed-time now,' and father shepherded them from the room but reminded them to say 'Goodnight' to the other guests.

'Thank you,' said Mrs Fitzgerald. 'You were very kind to them. You have no idea what bliss it will be to watch TV in bed. I think *Midsomer Murders* is on tonight.'

'You'll be asleep before the first adverts,' and the Scrabble ladies wished her goodnight.

'Nice kids,' said Edith.

'You wouldn't have thought so at five o'clock.' She explained the situation and said, 'It only goes to show your first impressions may be wrong.'

'As I found out to my cost,' said Edith thinking of Eddie, and returned to the game. It finished just as the Australians returned. Edith hadn't done badly as they all had close scores but the maths teacher won. 'It's because I think mathematically,' she said with a chuckle.

Don and Maria were so excited. 'I've met up with two cousins,' Don exclaimed. 'Elizabeth and Henry.'

'They are all so alike. Same hair and build. You can see they're related.'

'We went to the church and the vicar was just leaving. I said I was looking for the Hayman family and the vicar said, "Where do you want to start, there are so many of them? Try the pub." And there they were. My father's brother's son,' he gesticulated in the air working it out, 'my cousin, was so welcoming. He works on the same farm my dad worked on. He's asked us to stay on Tuesday. Introduce us to the family.'

'That's marvellous,' said Jenny, 'to rediscover a family after forty years.'

'Did you father never keep in touch?' asked Edith.

'Couldn't really. Reading and writing wasn't his strong point. The farming was more important so he

181

never went to school much. In Australia he couldn't keep away from the land and ended up working in a market garden. It was in his blood. Today's been so amazing I'm buying everyone a drink.'

With drinks all round talk went on for some time about families and their ancestry. Edith talked about her ancestors working in the mills and Phyllis confessed that her great-great-grandmother had been hanged for poisoning a husband for the insurance money.

Jenny hovered at a distance, again enjoying guests happily talking together. She hoped it would always be like this, but perhaps she would remember these more vividly because they were the first – like your first day at school or a new job.

Next morning Jenny was swirling clean white clothes over the tables when Suzie and Julia came in dressed in jeans and T-shirts.

'You're up early.'

'Mummy and Daddy said if we were good we could go to Longleat on the way home. See the lions and wolves.'

'I've heard you have to be careful of the monkeys. They rip off windscreen wipers on the cars.'

'Great!'

'Well as you are here and being good, I'll put a word in for you, if you help put out the knives and forks. Which is your left hand? Good. Put the forks on the left and the knives on the right.'

As the three of them worked, metal cutlery clattering, Julia said, 'We had to go and see Grandma yesterday. It was awful. D'you know she has a moustache.'

'And there was an awful smell,' added Suzie.

'It seems awful to you, because you're young. It's sad

really. That old lady was young once. Just like you.' The table laying stopped.

'She couldn't!'

'She was. Pretty like you two. If she's your grandma, probably very like you. When she was older she must have met a handsome young man and he would have been your grandfather.'

'No. He was old with crumpled skin.'

'Not always. Once he was young like you.'

Suzie started placing knives and forks thoughtfully, 'They was never like us.'

'Well if you can try and think of your grandma in a different way perhaps the next visit won't be so bad.'

Jenny gave them plates to put around while they assimilated this information. 'You can be waitresses for the cereals whilst I get the bacon grilling.'

When the parents arrived their daughters brought cereals to the table and Jenny whispered, 'They have been helping me lay the tables. They can have a job here as a waitress any day.'

The Misses Sholes and Clark, now Mabel and Phyllis, were going on a boat trip after breakfast, and the Australians were exploring Bradford-on-Avon. They would be back in the evening. Meanwhile Jenny bade goodbye to the Fitzgerald family, who were returning via Longleat, and the little girls kissed her goodbye, which touched her.

Kevin and Mandy spent the morning putting up the more suitable of Uncle Bernard's pictures on the stairwell walls, and Jenny was pleased when Dean rang from Spain, apparently sitting on Cassy's mother's veranda. Edith was more serious, trying to get her mind back into Council House mode for the following day, but wished to take them out to lunch and suggested Eleanor came with them.

183

After a loud long phone call to Eleanor's mother this was arranged and the five of them enjoyed a lunch outside a pub by the water. Jenny's eyes kept on looking down the river as the boats passed by until Mandy nudged her. 'He won't be back for a couple of days.'

By four o'clock her non-paying guests had left, Kevin and Mandy giving Edith a lift home.

'You know what your most important task is tomorrow?' reminded Edith.

'Buying kettles, cups and saucers for the bedrooms.'

Mandy and Kevin were in agreement.

'It has been so good to have them,' Jenny said to Eleanor on the way back to Lansdown View Guesthouse. 'The part of my past life I want to remember. And they put up the pictures.'

'I enjoyed Edith's company. She's been through the mill and come out the other side still thinking the right way up.'

'Yes. She's been a good friend to me,' and she told Eleanor of their trip to Paris. 'I've travelled so little. It was a great confidence-builder.'

'Now the Easter break is over,' Eleanor said, 'I shall be getting on with your flower displays and visiting estate agents with a view to finding a shop.'

'You may find Mr Slocombe helpful. From his manner with me I think he may have a finger in an estate agent's pie.'

The elderly ladies returned at dusk having enjoyed their river trip and with a brandy each settled down to another evening of Scrabble. The Australians bounced in later, impressed by the history of Bradford-on-Avon and its ancient Saxon church. 'Gee, there's so much history.' They drank cans of lager whilst the teachers filled in gaps in their knowledge on the history and geography of Wiltshire whether the Australians wanted it or not.

They all departed in the morning, Don and Maria excited to be staying with Don's cousin and promising the teachers they would visit Stonehenge. They were all grateful for Jenny's hospitality and after they had gone she felt the need to unwind despite the washing and vacuuming that needed to be done, so she wandered by the canal.

She had only been in business five days but she wanted to assess how successful she had been. She had enjoyed herself. It was exciting. What would the next client be like? The guests had all been pleasant and got on well together – but this would not always be the case. Tea-making in the rooms was essential but she would also offer tea and coffee downstairs for those who wanted to be sociable, for which she must charge. It was a pity there wasn't a separate lounge. Could she turn an upstairs room into a lounge? No, she wouldn't make enough money. Not that she had done that this weekend with Edith and Mandy as non-paying guests, Eleanor being around and the bottles of whisky consumed, but it had been fun. She didn't think Liz would be very impressed with the figures for the first week. The feeling she had had through winter, of battling through an impenetrable forest of workmen and bureaucracy, had been worth it. Now she was in pastoral downland, with blue sky overhead, and a bright horizon.

She returned to her work with vigour and had time to go into Bath to the catering company and buy small kettles and unopenable cartons of milk. New guests would be arriving in the evening and she would be ready for them, and Ben might turn up tomorrow.

Chapter 14

Jenny attended to the needs of three sets of dull middle-aged tourists on Wednesday morning. The women with colourless frizzy hair all wore beige or olive green, and the men mild checked shirts. They talked in dull voices of the weather and traffic problems. Jenny was relieved to see them depart, as she wanted to get on with her back garden. She had an ulterior motive; she wanted to see if Ben passed by.

After loading up her car with plants from a garden centre she spent the day weeding and planting. The phone rang three times with bookings, and the doorbell twice, so with an email booking she would be full for the first time. Although she was pleased about this and turned the sign to 'No Vacancies' she hoped it would not interfere with a meeting with Ben. Now she wished she had told Ben where she lived, and would have liked to walk up the locks, but couldn't until her six sets of customers had arrived, and that could be at any time. The last two to arrive were sales representatives who grumbled about parking and traffic hold-ups. She charmingly showed them to their rooms, realising this type of client would be part of her bread and butter, and having checked they had front door keys told them she would be out for an hour.

She made her way up the towpath and there under the trees she found *Blithe Spirit* moored, with Ben taking his ease in the dusk with a cigarette to keep off the midges and a can of beer.

'Hi,' he smiled, 'I was hoping you'd turn up.'

'I couldn't get away. I run a guesthouse and had to wait for all the guests to arrive. Now I'm free for an hour.'

'So that's what you do. Come aboard.'

He gave her his hand and she clambered on deck. He didn't let go of her hand and kissed her for a long time. 'I hadn't realised how disappointed I would be when I didn't see you at the lock. Which was unreasonable. Why should you be there? Now here you are, and I'm very pleased you've come.'

Jenny laughed, 'I spent all afternoon in the garden hoping you would pass by, but guests got in the way. I'm pleased to see you too.' He pulled her inside the cabin and the kissing continued. As he touched her she could feel urges stirring within her she hadn't felt for a long time but she knew she had to get back to the guesthouse. She pushed him away saying, 'Sorry. I feel like you do but I have to get back.'

'No, your guests can wait,' and he swept her off her small feet to the bed.

She felt feelings of desire and passion long denied her, and later lay satiated and fulfilled, murmuring words of love in his ear. She wanted to stay here all night but the guesthouse, her dream, now her conscience, said 'you have to get back home'. Languidly she dressed, and kissed Ben, who smiled up at her, 'Thank you. That was beautiful.'

187

'I expect you say that to some girl at every mooring.'

'No I definitely don't. If you can get away tomorrow I shall stay here until lunchtime.' He pulled her on top of him, 'You're wonderful. Tomorrow?'

She left swiftly, pulling her clothes straight. It had been a great passionate experience, just what she needed. Someone to make her feel special, young and beautiful, and she would see him again tomorrow. She ran back down the path and let herself in through the kitchen. There was no one demanding a drink and she had no idea who was in or out, but they were all adults and responsible for themselves. She poured herself a stiff whisky and thought back over the last few hours. The evening light in the sky, Ben kissing her, his unmade bed, their lovemaking and her reluctant parting. Had she needed to come back, could she have stayed there? As she heard a key in the lock, conversation, the reps returned and coming into the bar she thought she had made the right decision. They both asked for whiskies and she left them discussing the commercial world of clothing.

In the comfortable shell of her flat Jenny stared at her reflection as she brushed her teeth. She had just made love to a man who wasn't her husband. Because of her parents' puritan attitude Trevor was the only man she had had a chance to know in a carnal way. Her father used to pace up and down outside their front door if Jenny wasn't back home by 10.30. He would have been delighted to have invented the chastity belt. Opportunity had never come her way, unless she had wished to lie in the undergrowth of the local churchyard, as some of her school friends did. She had just become a new emancipated woman, but with that came the thought, what if I'm pregnant? She rummaged through the collection of pills she had removed from the suburban semi. Were there any contraceptive pills left? She found some, probably long after their sell-by date, but took one. She must find herself a doctor. To be a single parent mother in her forties would seem foolish.

She set the alarm for six in the morning. Breakfast would be for twelve people. She needed her entire mind engaged into 'breakfast'. She found herself using Liz's commas to say 'breakfast ' with a slight swivel of the hips. By seven the sausages were grilled and keeping warm, tables laid with sterile plastic jam pots and butter. Toast ready in the toasters and bacon under the grill. She was pleasant and charming to her guests, but her mind was elsewhere, two locks up the canal.

The reps were given their 'Williams' and mentioned they would stay again when they were in the area. Rooms would be vacant so she consulted 'Bill' to find out about further enquiries. There were two for later in the week. Deciding to take her mobile phone with her, in case there were more bookings, with sandwiches and a bottle of wine she set off swiftly to see Ben.

He was not in sight but the door was ajar and she found him still in bed.

'Why get up when we shall be back here in a few minutes?' he asked. 'Make us a cup of coffee then come back here and let me strip your clothes off.' Jenny's thoughts had been in the same vein and within minutes they were curled together in his bed, the coffee getting cold.

Some time later as they dressed Ben said, 'If we went on up to Bathampton could you get back?'

'Of course. I'll get a taxi. I've got my mobile in case

189

someone rings with a booking. I was full last night but hope more guests turn up this evening. I suppose it will always be like this, as I need to make the money. Like you and your books.'

'Yes. I ought to be at Dundas again this evening.' Jenny remembered the aqueduct and the two men in dark coats.

Content in each other's company, Ben at the tiller, Jenny at his side, they chugged through the outskirts of Bath whilst munching her sandwiches and drinking the wine. White fluffy cumulus clouds in a vivid blue sky raced overhead, and the song of birds made their music. Jenny could not remember the last time she had felt so happy.

They were nearing Bathampton when her phone rang and brought her down to earth. It was the Tourist Information Office. A coach company's bookings had gone wrong. For how many people could she provide beds?

'Five doubles, and I don't do evening meals.' She wanted to keep the singles for passing trade.

'OK, thanks,' said the singsong voice, 'they're American so no problem with the language. They'll be with you at six o'clock. Send the bill to the tour company.'

Jenny put the phone down. She was shaking and could feel the sweat on her forehead, 'Don't panic. It's all right I can cope.'

Ben took her in his arms, 'Of course you can, my darling.'

'I've got all the beds to change. Must get to the Cash and Carry – need sausages, eggs, bread and milk. I shouldn't have come.'

'You are allowed to have your own life as well. We're

just coming to Bathampton. I'll moor and we can go into the pub, have a drink and you can ring for a taxi. Relax.'

'Oh. I recognise this. This is where we first met. Bath's not far away.'

'No. It's our Christmas sandwich place. Travelling by boat can be deceptive. You'll be back at the guesthouse in no time. And now I know where you live.'

Ben, seeming concerned by her anxiety, moored quickly. Jenny rang for a taxi, and they sat outside the pub with a coffee as he wanted to keep an eye on the boat.

As he stirred the sugar in his drink Ben asked, 'Look, I know you want to make a go of your place, but is there any chance of you taking a few days off and I could take you up towards Calne? You're such good company and so ... Well, the lovemaking and everything.'

She held his hand, 'I would love that too. Perhaps before the late May holiday it will be quiet. After all the work of getting the place open I need a break. I'll find a date before the end of May. But call in for a sandwich anytime and I'll help you through the locks.' She heard a taxi toot and left with a passionate kiss. In the back of the cab she realised she had left her knapsack behind. In a few days he might be back down the canal and return it to her.

She dealt with the Cash and Carry and changed the beds. Would anyone notice the vacuuming hadn't been done? At six o'clock a coach pulled up outside, leaving its warning lights flashing whilst bags were unloaded and traffic built up behind it. Ten people, all talking at once, congregated in her hall. A tall middle-aged man in a loud shirt and straw trilby hat became their spokesman, and politely apologised for their sudden arrival, due to some

191

booking error. They all registered whilst Jenny made polite noises and wondered where Nantucket and Chattanooga were.

'Although it's late for afternoon tea would you like pots of tea or coffee and something really English like crumpets?' There were murmurs of approval and when she had handed out the keys, explaining there wasn't a lift or a porter, set to with the toaster, crumpets and fruitcake she had fortunately bought. Uncle Bernard's willow pattern was coming into its own. It transpired that the group had spent two nights in London and were visiting Bath for one night before going on to Stratford-upon-Avon, the Lake District and then Scotland. Thinking the Americans would miss most of England's most picturesque parts and Wales, Jenny gave them maps of Bath and places where they could find an evening meal. She mentioned the canal and Sydney Gardens if they wanted an attractive walk into the centre of the city. They left satisfied and she breathed a sigh of relief. They were amused when she had said the house was about two hundred years old – built when their country, America, was just beginning.

She cleared the crockery away and Pyewacket bounced up in the kitchen wanting to be fed. Strictly speaking the cat wasn't allowed in the kitchen but as no one was around she gave Pye his meal. 'How can anyone know about Britain,' she asked the cat, 'if they stay one night in a few pretty places?' What about the wild places in Cornwall or the industrial Midlands and the poverty-stricken north? They will go away with a very false impression, but that happens all the time. She paused, thinking – after all, what do I really know about Ben? Maybe the boat and the beautiful scenery are just a background to what? Not like Trev. We know all about him. No veneer there. Pye meowed in agreement.

Later in the evening all the guests returned and Jenny took mental notes of the places where they had eaten. Most of the guests went straight upstairs, jetlag still a problem, but one elderly man and his wife stayed up for a nightcap of Bourbon. Jenny was enchanted as they talked about their life on the prairies of America. They had just retired and wanted to see the land of their ancestors who had left England in the nineteenth century when the Enclosure Act meant they lost their farm. The wife talked of a journal she had found that her ancestors had written about their new life in America. The hard work, lack of food, illness, children born and short lived, the fear of Indians, the menace of the ranchers. The stories delighted Jenny and she was impressed by the strength the couple had derived from their past. This is what she liked about the guesthouse. The histories and colours of other people's lives embroidered together.

With another Bourbon the farmer said, 'I can't get over how small everything is over here, and how close together the towns are. Something I'm really looking forward to seeing is the sea. We are staying on the coast in Scotland somewhere. We've never seen the sea.'

They bid each other goodnight and Jenny set the alarm again for six o'clock. The Americans were appreciative of their English breakfast, then the coach sped them away on the tourist trail of the Roman Baths and the Royal Crescent whilst Jenny sent the account to the tour company.

Jenny made sure 'Bill' and the Tourist Office knew she

would be closed for five days before the late May bank holiday that used to be called Whitsuntide. She was now getting used to the early morning routine, and the lull in the middle of the day when she often went to see Lyn. They swapped anecdotes of guests and Lyn gave her a warning of a rep that turned out to be a 'flasher'. She also gave advice that if guests arrived late and there was the occasional need to be sociable with drinks and sandwiches, this should be added to the bill. In the back of her mind Jenny realised evening meals were something she would have to face.

A visit to Liz, the accountant, was now advisable. Liz, elegant as ever, was wearing flowing garments to obscure her rather prominent bump. Yes, she said, a baby was due in six weeks. Brian was delighted and after she went back to work he was going to be a househusband.

'He never was at home in the Council Office,' said Jenny. 'Yes, he will make a good father and enjoy bringing up a child.'

'Actually it's two children. We had to have IVF treatment and this is the result. Because I earn more than he does, this seemed the best idea. Now about your account. You didn't get off to a very good start.'

'No. I had my daughter and a friend staying. They needed a bit of support and we had fun.'

'Business is not about having fun. Business is about making money.'

'I know that. It's just so difficult when the guests are so interesting. I know that was not good business but I'm doing better now. I have in my mind doing evening meals, but it will take some time to organise this. Finding a chef, food outlets.'

Jenny didn't like to say she had been thinking of Ben

and little else. He might pass by tomorrow. He had returned her haversack and for two hours they had lived in another world. In a couple of weeks they would spend five days together.

Liz was saying, 'Make a note of everything you spend. Equipment, telephones, overalls, anything on which we can get tax back. Are you taking this in? You seem at bit vague?'

'Oh yes. Write everything down. Find a chef. Drift along canal. No. Sorry. That's later – having a few days off.'

'You haven't got time for a break. I despair of you ever making a profit.'

'There's more to life than making money. You will find motherhood will change your view of many things. There will be so little time for yourself you'll take every opportunity you can to do your own thing. Hope the birth goes well. It'll be so exciting. I'll send you a business plan of my ideas for evening meals.'

As Jenny drove home she thought – Liz may say, 'running a business is about making money', but for me the business has given me an aim in life and I want to enjoy it. If I had wanted to make money, I would have sold the guesthouse and saved myself the work and worry of the last four months. But in creating Lansdown View I have met interesting people, Ben included, and expanded my horizons in ways I would never have expected.

'Mrs Evans. I asked you for a pot of tea ten minutes ago.'

Jenny came to. Ben had just chugged passed and she was daydreaming.

'Sorry, Mrs Barnes. The tea and crumpets will be with you shortly.' She must pull herself together. She was behaving like a sixteen-year-old in love for the first time, and resenting the time she had to spend waiting for her guests to arrive.

When they had last met Ben had said he would be back this way in a few days, but she knew he wouldn't wait near the lock. It was a pity he wouldn't leave his boat for any length of time otherwise they could make love in her flat, but she couldn't persuade him. It was so frustrating! Maybe, with a bit of luck, the four guests she was expecting would arrive early. As afternoon turned into evening and dusk descended the fussy Mrs Barnes returned from her walk into town at nine o'clock and wanted sandwiches, then complained the cheese was hard. Then a gormless couple who had gone out for a meal rang the bell, rather the worse for drink, forgetting they had a key. Later Mrs Barnes came down in her dressing gown complaining about the noise the drunken gormless couple were making. Were they having a furious row or making violent love? Jenny wondered as she knocked on their door and asked them to keep the noise down. The door didn't open but the noise ceased.

'All quiet now, Mrs Barnes.'

'Well, I wouldn't want them to murder each other,' explained Mrs Barnes, 'think of all the bloodstained sheets you'd have to wash.' Jenny noticed Mrs Barnes was holding a paperback with a rather gory cover and wondered if the lady's imagination had run away with her. To her ears it sounded as if the TV was on too loud. The last of the four turned out to be a Japanese couple backpacking round Europe and their train didn't arrive in Bath until 10.30. It was too late to find Ben and she lay on her bed crying tears of frustrated rage.

When the last of her guests had left the next morning, these being the Japanese who did not come down to breakfast until 10.30, Jenny set out up the canal to what she thought of as their mooring, but there was no sign of Ben. He too had his business to run, Jenny convinced herself, as she moped home, and took out her misery on the dirty washing.

A few days later at breakfast Jenny overheard a conversation between two of her guests, Mrs Hamilton and her daughter, a tall, pasty-faced plump girl wearing a boring grey suit, with dark hair in a ponytail. Mrs Hamilton herself had unnaturally blond hair and was elegantly dressed. The girl looked miserable.

'You must make a good impression, darling. Remember to tell them you're a Queen's Guide and have Grade Eight piano. I really think I ought to go with you.'

'No.'

'And you mustn't look so surly.'

'That's how I feel.'

'Remember Daddy is expecting the best out of you.'

Jenny wondered what the problem was but it was none of her business.

An hour later she started on the vacuuming, thinking everyone was out, so just opened the door of the Hamiltons' room. The sulky girl was lying on the bed crying.

'Sorry,' said Jenny, 'I'll do the room later. You OK?'

'I don't want to go to Bath bloody University,' shouted the girl. Then she subsided, embarrassed, 'Sorry, it's not your problem,' and she dried her eyes.

'Why don't you want to go?'

'Mummy's making me. So she can hold up her head at

197

the Bridge Club and the WI and show off about her wonderful children. "John's a barrister now and Olivia's off to University, though sadly not Oxford",' she mimicked. 'I want to be a gardener, but she says that's dirty work for men in grubby trousers.'

'Many women are gardeners these days. They're on TV all the time.'

'But it's not the right status for Mummy. "My daughter's a gardener," would not go down well in her cosy little set in Chalfont St Michael.'

'Where is your mum?'

'Out visiting an old friend from boarding school days.' So there was time to talk.

'Why can't you go to horticultural college? You're eighteen and can do what you like.'

Olivia sat up on the bed looking more animated, 'If I go to Bath they will pay for everything. If I go to a horticultural college they won't. I don't want to start out in life with a debt of thousands of pounds – it's blackmail really. They'd disown me if I didn't have a degree. They have to have status. What would you do?' What an odd question, Jenny thought, to put to the landlady.

'Well, I don't know. I've never lived in the circles you move in. I'd probably get a job in a garden nursery. What subject are you hoping to study?'

'Biology. Then Mummy hopes I'd do research. She doesn't realise you need a First to do research. Am I likely to get a First?'

'Doesn't biology fit in with horticulture? Do the course then find a job in the gardening world.'

'That would be three years away.'

'It's not that long. You'd have a good time, make new friends and get away from dominating parents.'

'Yes, they're control freaks.'

'What do your friends or boyfriend think?'

'I've never had a boyfriend. Too much Guides and piano. All to impress, not what I wanted.'

'What time's your interview?'

'Twelve.'

'Better wash your face and do your hair. Shall I find out which bus you need, or get you a taxi?'

'Get a taxi and put it on the bill.'

It was possible that this was the first decision Olivia had ever made for herself, Jenny thought. Money may give you material things; no doubt there was a pony in the paddock and the latest stereo in her bedroom, but no real freedom to make your own life. A bit like life in suburbia but for different reasons.

Mrs Hamilton returned in the early afternoon and Jenny made her a pot of tea and asked if she would like a snack.

'No thank you. I have just had the most superb salmon mousse with an old friend. She lives up on Lansdown in the most beautiful house with amazing views over the city.' Mrs Hamilton could get a job writing adverts for an Estate Agent, thought Jenny, if she ever demeaned herself to get a job. She went on gushing, making sure Jenny knew her husband worked in the City and her son was a barrister, when Olivia returned looking happier.

'I got in,' she announced with some pride.

Mrs Hamilton arose and gave her a cool kiss. Jenny asked if they would like more tea and the mother said no, they had to get back to Chalfont St Michael, but Olivia said, 'Yes please. I'm so hungry.'

'You have to watch your figure, darling. Besides I'll be late for my bridge club.'

Jenny ignored this and made a sandwich for Olivia and stayed to ask her what the university was like.

'It's great. The biology labs have so much equipment, and the sports facilities are good. They train champions there.'

'You know you've never liked sport, darling. Besides it would interfere with your studies. Now we must be going.'

At reception Jenny handed her the bill.

'What's this about a taxi?'

'The buses don't go that way,' lied Jenny.

'Good luck with your exams,' Jenny smiled at Olivia, 'I hope you get what you want.'

The early spring bank holiday was a busy time and the house was full every night for a week. Jenny worked hard and found her afternoons, when she could relax, were necessary for her to keep going. At this time she tended her garden, put geraniums in terracotta pots outside the front door and was content with the 'No Vacancies' sign in the window. Eleanor was a frequent visitor with her silk flower displays that now decorated every room and Jenny treated her to lunch at the Italian down the road.

'How's your mysterious bargee?' Eleanor asked.

'Still being mysterious but he is gorgeous. Mandy called him a hunk. I missed him the last time he passed. If he turns up again I'm going away with him for a few days. The canal is so beautiful and peaceful.'

'And the sex?'

'Yes. With Trev's attentions being elsewhere I've missed that. I'm looking forward to a few days away. A passionate dalliance on the canal. And you. Have you found anyone?'

'No. But I'm working on the estate agent. We have been to see several shops, but either the rent is too high, or the premises too dilapidated. I'll probably go for the latter and get in contractors, but the site has to be right. The sale of the house is going through so I'll have money. Mum's getting worse, so absent-minded. She put coffee and tea in a drink today. I should try and find her a home, bearing in mind the waiting lists.'

'Old age is not easy to deal with. I can remember putting my parents in a home ten years ago. My mum kept on asking when she could go home, but they couldn't look after each other. Dad had had a stroke and Mum dementia. Trev was a great support in those days. Helped me clear out their house and the sale paid for their care. We used to visit them once a week. It was always so sad. In thirty years' time we'll be like that.'

'Not me. I'll take up hang gliding, then let go.'

On Wednesday afternoon after the early bank holiday there was a bang on Jenny's kitchen door.

'You said you'd help with the locks,' Ben ordered. 'Come on, I'm going down to the river.' Jenny dropped the knife she was drying and followed him out to the canal. She was so happy to see him and kissed him before he had time to give her a windlass. Half of her was worrying had she locked the back door, would any guests arrive, where was Pyewacket, but the other half was so pleased to see Ben. He hadn't forgotten her. With fervour she opened the lock paddles, opened and closed the gates until they arrived on the Avon. Ben moored on the river and gave Jenny his firm hand as she boarded the boat.

'Welcome aboard, cabin boy. Where were you last week?'

201

'I was working. I saw you go by but guests got difficult. I had a terrible day.'

'At least I found you again. I expect, cabin boy, you have to be back at work soon, but I have brought wine and hope we can enjoy this in my bed.'

They kissed as he unbuttoned her shirt and she closed the curtains.

An hour later, love satiated, at peace with the world, knowing she would see Ben again for their few days together, Jenny wandered back up the towpath. Pyewacket bounced out of the bushes as she neared home, hungry for his tea and Jenny felt the world was hers. In two weeks she would be away on *Blithe Spirit* with her lover.

Chapter 15

The next two weeks passed in a dream of work – breakfasts, bed-making, vacuuming, shopping and making sandwiches. Except for one incident that would give Jenny palpations to her dying day. A cheerful couple with a toddler were staying for two nights, so for the first time the cot was erected in the parents' bedroom. He was a bouncy child, called Charlie, who smiled and laughed. His parents gave him tea in the dining room, Jenny having cooked up a few baked beans and bacon. The young boy enjoyed his food with gusto and smeared most of it over his face and the table. Then the parents took him to the play park and Jenny could see them through the window pushing him to and fro on the swing, and then helping him over the climbing frame. It was family picture. She wished she had a camera. They swung him, one, two, three, jump back to the guesthouse then asked for some warm milk for his drink.

'Charlie's asleep now.' The father asked, 'We have a baby alarm. Could you cope if we went out for an hour? We don't get much time out on our own.'

'Of course. I'll keep an eye on him.'

All was quiet; other guests came in, enjoyed drinks

and the couple returned two hours later. They too bought drinks and chatted to other guests before they went to bed. Jenny, having a full house, set her alarm for six.

In the early morning the alarm rang and as she slowly became awake, which usually involved smoking a cigarette and arranging her thoughts for the day, she heard a rattling upstairs. Was somebody trying to get in, or go out? She headed up the stairs. Charlie was there, standing on a chair, trying to open the front door. It clicked and the door opened. '*Play park,*' he said.

'No darling. The play park is asleep. We'll have to wait for the park keeper to come and wake it up. I'll take you back to bed and your parents. Now, one, two, three, jump up the stairs.' Charlie settled down in his cot. The parents roused themselves, a look of alarm on their faces, but Jenny calmly said, 'Charlie was wandering around. I'm just putting him back in his bed. Could you lock your door?' She left swiftly and was sick in her own toilet. What if he had got out on that busy main road? Guests had the right to come and go, but she would have to raise the lock on the front door, put up more signs and add 'lock your door' to her spiel for welcoming guests.

When the family came down to breakfast she took the parents aside and told them what had happened. The parents were dumbfounded.

'We know he's boisterous and can climb, but to get out of his cot and find the key ...'

'That's why the chair was moved – so he could reach the door handle,' exclaimed the wife.

'He's a bright boy. You're going to have your hands full for a few years. I'm just so relieved he's all right. I must re-think my security. Put railings and a gate in the front.'

'Could you get the locks put higher up the door? It could apply to your kitchen as well with a garden outside and the canal beyond.'

'You're right. But I do lock the kitchen at night. Don't want hungry guests helping themselves to breakfast early.'

As they left for a day out Charlie, strapped into his buggy, gave Jenny a big smile. She asked what he would like for tea, 'Fish fingers,' he said with a grin. She agreed – she had always been a sucker for young children.

A few days later Jenny closed Lansdown View for a few days. She had given the key to Tom who had agreed to feed Pyewacket. Standing by the lock with two carrier bags, one of clothes and one of food and bottles of wine, she was going to forget hard work, telephones and being polite to guests for a few days and enjoy romance and exploration. She felt like the heroine in *Frenchman's Creek* waiting for her lover and adventure in his sailing ship, though admittedly a narrowboat was not as exciting. Ben greeted her with a kiss and a windlass and she spent the next hour opening and shutting locks but at the top of the flight Ben took her hand and guided her to the bow of the boat, where there was a chair and a glass of wine.

'Relax and watch the world go by,' which she did. Houses appeared to slide by and hills came into view. Yellow irises and kingcups added colour to the rushes along the banks and ducks quacked by with their ducklings. With a cigarette and the wine Jenny relaxed and let the tensions of the last few weeks wash away from her. The sun shone out of a pale blue sky and swallows swooped over the water, sipping it as they passed. A heron standing still by the reeds flapped off at their approach and she saw the bright turquoise of a kingfisher as it flashed by.

She rushed back through the boat, banging her hips on cupboards in the narrow space, to tell Ben about the bird. He laughed and pulled her to him as he steered.

'It's good to hear you talk about these things. It makes me realise I take them for granted. Why don't you make us some sandwiches, I'm hungry, then you can sit in the bow and continue with your kingfisher watch.'

'I'd rather sit back here with you.'

'OK, if you don't mind the noise of the engine and the fumes.'

'I just want to be with you,' and she hugged him so his steering went off course into the bank.

Ben laughed, 'perhaps we should moor now we're in the bank, then we could really be together.' He banged the mooring pins in with a mallet, whilst Jenny took off her clothes and snuggled down in his bed in anticipation.

Later they sat together at peace in each other's company watching the world go by until they came to Dundas aqueduct.

'We'll stop here for the night. I've got to meet some clients at seven. They're an odd couple and perhaps would be suspicious of a stranger. Whilst I see them would you mind going for a stroll over the aqueduct? You haven't crossed it yet, and it's very impressive. Then we can have a romantic meal for two and go to bed.'

Jenny remembered the two men from her last visit. She wondered why she would be considered as suspicious, but agreed to a walk. It was still daylight and she would enjoy a stroll. The boat itself became claustrophobic after a few hours. She walked slowly beside the canal as it bridged the Avon and leaning her arms on the Bath stone parapet, still warm from the sun, watched the river flow below. The three arches of the bridge, cream in the evening light, were beautiful. A few birds were singing, midges swirled in frenzied circles in the air and bats were flying erratically to catch them. On the other side of the aqueduct the path and canal went into woodland and it was darker. The sounds within the trees frightened her – branches cracking, bird calls, snufflings. She returned slowly and a barn owl, white-faced with black eyes, flapped over the aqueduct. Its wild call startled her and she ran back to the boat, not caring about the mysterious men. She saw their dark rather threatening outlines disappear along the towpath in the gathering twilight. Why did they seem so sinister she asked herself? Not wishing to put a blight on the evening she put them out of her mind. Ben was whistling as he put a meal together and she was welcomed by the smell of frying onions.

'Did your meeting go well?'

'Sure.'

'Did they buy any books?'

He looked as if he didn't understand her for a second. 'No but they are considering a couple.'

On the table were lighted candles and an uncorked bottle of Claret. She was told to sit and enjoy the wine whilst he produced an excellent risotto, followed by fresh grapes and Stilton cheese.

'That was wonderful,' sighed Jenny. 'It makes a change for someone else to do the cooking. I imagined you lived on sardines or beans on toast. Obviously that's not the case.' Over their quiet and seductive meal they had swapped stories on their own lives. Jenny's upbringing and married life seemed so dull in comparison to Ben's. His father had been in the Diplomatic Corps and he had spent his early years in foreign embassies with education at boarding school. At university he had dropped out and ended up travelling the canals.

'My family don't want to know me now. Especially as I never married in the right circles and provided them with grandchildren. But I'm happy doing what I want to do.'

'Like me. I've stopped being the devoted wife and have the freedom to do as I want. Nine months ago I was at my wit's end. Now I am confident on my own and able to make my own decisions. I feel better, stronger and younger.' She talked more about her plans for the guesthouse.

The food, wine and fresh air had made her sleepy and soon Jenny was wandering off to bed discarding her clothing as she went. Ben was not far behind, assisting with the odd button.

Sunlight reflected the ripples of the water on the pine roof of the cabin. Jenny slipped out of bed, dressed and walked out along the aqueduct. The music of the dawn chorus was orchestrated to the mist rising off the river below her. A deer was grazing in a field and rabbits hopped by the hedges. She strolled over the aqueduct to the woods and now saw bluebells under the trees and a wren darting into the undergrowth. Heading back to the boat a buzzard wheeled in lazy circles overhead and a fox was trotting across the pasture. Why couldn't life always be this peaceful, she asked herself? But she knew deep down inside herself, as she saw the fox stalk a rabbit, that all life hunts on smaller prey just to survive.

By the time Ben awoke she had tidied up the supper and put what breakfast she could find on the table. Yes, she thought, he's like Trev in the mornings. Don't talk to him. She made a cup of coffee and sat at the bow as the sun warmed her. She smoked a cigarette thinking of her early morning walk and listened to a cuckoo calling.

Ben only wanted coffee and grumpily rejected her suggestion of boiled eggs or toast. To lighten the mood she asked where they would stop today.

'We can stop at Avoncliff for lunch. Its pretty there; you'll like that, and get to Bradford-on-Avon about three o'clock.'

'Tea and cucumber sandwiches?' she asked flippantly, trying to bring a smile to his face.

'Don't be silly. These are important new clients I have to see. Friends of the people I saw last night.'

'I hope they're not as creepy.'

'Just people,' he snapped. 'Stop letting your imagination run away with you.'

'I'll look forward to Avoncliff and lunch,' she replied stiffly. Ben was in no frame of mind to talk to her and best left on his own. She didn't know him well enough to anticipate his moods, nor could she know what the sinister men said to him last night. She didn't imagine ancient books caused this tension, but possibly large sums of money were involved. She took her coffee and cigarettes and again sat in the bow on kingfisher watch. As she flicked the third cigarette butt over the bow she realised the atmosphere had got to her. At Avoncliff there was another smaller aqueduct over the Avon. They moored overlooking the river and the Crossed Guns pub, the clunk of mallet on mooring pin having become a familiar sound. Whilst they ate some sandwiches Jenny tried to talk of their picturesque surroundings but had little response.

'Sorry. I'm not very good company today.'

'Not the day for a dalliance in the rushes,' she joked.

'No. We must get on, but I'll let you steer the boat for a bit.' At least her erratic passage up the canal brought a smile to his lips. As they stood side by side at the tiller Ben said, 'I'll moor the far side of the tithe barn at Bradford-on-Avon, so I can walk into the town and we can do the next lock either tonight or tomorrow.' It was beginning to drizzle, but Jenny didn't care. She noticed the old jumbled roofs of the old town, the river flowing past gardens of graceful houses to join the valley of the canal, then the old Norman tithe barn and its ancient gables and great wooden doors. As instructed she jumped off the boat and held the mooring rope. Beyond the quay was a pub, the dark archway of the road bridge and the next lock. Ben tied professional knots on the bollards and then said, 'I'll get off into town. The sooner I'm gone the sooner I'll be back.' Then he added, 'Please don't start looking through the books. I know exactly where they are and it gets difficult if they get moved.'

Jenny laughed, 'Like my old boss who used to take files for a meeting and never put them back.'

'Exactly. You don't mind being left alone for a while?'

'Of course not,' and she kissed him, her hands caressing his curly dark hair and the stubble on his chin. 'But I shall miss you,' and he walked off into the rain carrying a briefcase.

Jenny watched Ben walk towards the road, ready to wave to him, but he didn't look back. Then, feeling drowsy, she curled up on the bed and slept. She awoke to rain drumming on the metal roof. She had thought of walking to the tithe barn and exploring, but the rain was too heavy. She made a cup of coffee and watched the raindrops creating circles on the murky water of the canal. She felt cold and damp. She had no extra clothing but surely Ben would have thick jerseys for cold weather. She started looking through likely cupboards and eventually lifted up the lids from the seats in the living area under which were storage spaces. There were no thick jerseys but piles of leather-bound books, dark brown with age, some embossed in gold-lettered titles.

Oh, she thought, these are the books he was talking about. They are beautiful. I know he said don't move them but I wonder what they are about? She picked up a volume and opened it, expecting paper or parchment stained brown with age. But no! Inside was a plastic bag of fine white powder.

'What's this?' she asked herself. 'Surely not icing sugar. Bloody hell. No, it can't be!'

She sat down hard, feeling a cold sweat on her body. Her hands were shaking as she picked up another book. The same white powder. Her mouth had gone dry as she spoke to the air – it seemed to steady her, talking, as though she, at least, was real.

'I've seen enough TV news cuts to know this is hard drugs. How did Ben come by these? He must be selling them. Those two men last night. This is terrible. Awful. How could anyone as kind and gentle as he seems to be get involved? Does he take them himself?' Now she felt angry, frightened, and started pacing the cramped space.

'This boat is a sham. The man himself is a sham. He's lied to me. His whole life is a lie. He duped me into coming away for a few innocent days of fun when all the time he's running a drugs racket. The bastard! And what a fool I've been.'

She stood stock still, her thoughts in panic. 'I'm here on his boat alone with these drugs. No one's going to believe I knew nothing about them. Should I wait till he comes back and confront him? No. Call the police? Why involve myself, it's nothing to do with me. I'd best get out of here as fast as I can.'

She stuffed all her clothes in her bag, looked around to make sure she had left nothing. There was an old jacket hanging on the back of a door. She took it. At least it would keep off the rain. She left slamming the door behind her.

When she got to the road bridge she paused to check on her bearings. Yes, standing on the bridge looking down at the canal the road to town was to the right. She looked at the quay, *Blithe Spirit* looking forlorn in the rain. She sighed, thinking of the two days when she had been happy and loved. She must remember the good times. As she turned to find her way into town she saw two burly men clamber on the boat and knock on the door. They had the look of policemen, but could be crooks. One of them she thought was carrying a gun. She waited, watching, unable to move. When the door didn't open one man put his practised shoulder to it and went inside. The other talked on his mobile phone. A van and several cars swerved onto the towpath and skidded to a halt beside the boat. Jenny had to stay. Several men, some in police uniform, alighted from the vehicles to assist the first intruders. A raid. And Jenny knew what they would find. She had left the books on the table.

The rain was seeping down her neck. She was shivering either from cold or fear. It was time to leave. Jogging, she set off to town and the railway station. She paced the platform for half an hour and the thought came to her. If she had stayed on the boat she would now be in handcuffs, shoved in the back of a van. Police swearing, treating her like dirt. It was a scary.

To the comforting rhythm of the train Jenny stared through rain-splattered windows, retracing her two-day journey along the river valley. Seeing the canal again, the aqueducts, meadows and woods, her eyes moistened. As salt tears ran down her cheeks reflecting the raindrops on the windows outside, she thought how different it could have been. If he had been honest, perhaps they could have fallen in love, she could have sold the guesthouse, become a water gypsy and travelled the canals. But not with a drug peddler who did so much damage to other people's lives.

Lansdown View had never looked so welcoming and the purring cat was a bonus. After a stiff whisky she went to the fridge to find some cheese for a snack. Beside the cheese were some turkey slices. 'Today's your lucky day, Pye,' she said as she cut the meat up in a bowl. 'I don't think I'll be eating turkey sandwiches ever again.'

As she lay in bed that night, another whisky beside her, she fondled the cat's ears and thought – I must treasure the good memories. Although it was a pleasure, Ben wasn't as good at making love as Trev. Until this experience I never knew how lucky I was. I suppose that's why other women find Trev irresistible.

Chapter 16

Jenny didn't sleep well. She had bad dreams. Sometimes she and Ben were locked in a dark cell. In other nightmares they were rushing through woods with police and bloodhounds on their trail. As the dawn came she slept more peacefully, then remembering Tom would be round to feed Pyewacket, dressed and knocked on their door to retrieve the key.

Tom and Dorothy were surprised to see her.

'You're back early.'

'Yes. I did enjoy the boat for two days then we had a disagreement and I came home on the train. Was the cat all right?'

'Presumably. He ate his food. How far did you get?'

'Bradford-on-Avon.'

'Did you see any sign of this bloke who got nabbed for drugs?' asked Tom. 'It was on the news this morning. They found half a million pounds' worth.'

'That's a lot of money. No. No excitements like that,' Jenny stuttered. 'Just beautiful scenery and then a stupid argument.'

'Well perhaps you'll see him again soon. He's bound

to chug by. Here's your key. Pop in for a cuppa some-time when you're not busy.'

Jenny made her way to Mr Patel's, noticing Mrs Barrett's curtains twitch at number five. She realised she would have to improve her ability to lie to get through this situation. At Mr Patel's she bought eggs, bread, milk and the local paper. With a cigarette to calm her nerves she thought she would scan through the paper to see if there was any mention of Ben. She didn't have to scan far. It was the main headline. '£500,000 heroin hoard found on canal boat.' A man had been arrested and would appear in court today. No names as yet, and no accomplices mentioned. When his name came out things could be tricky. She would be like Manuel in *Fawlty Towers* and 'know nothing'. In the meantime she would be her new strong self and get on with life. She had two days of freedom; she would make use of it and not brood on the past.

Remembering the two old school teachers – that seemed like years ago, yet was only Easter – she decided to explore the local countryside and go to Wells. She needed to take her mind off yesterday's awful events, and the poor old rusty car could do with an outing to charge up the battery. Although she had always lived within the same area she had never been to Wells. It was a revelation. The beauty of the cathedral with its sweep-ing arches, the carvings, the worn stone steps up to the Chapter House. She sat in main aisle listening to the choristers practising for Evensong then lit a candle for Ben. Her parents would have chided her that it smacked of papacy but it gave her comfort. Afterwards she indulged herself in a cream tea and wandered down the main street, hopping over the water as it left the well, giving the city its name. Jenny smiled as she realised she had come from one watery place to another.

She took the old teachers' advice and drove back via Cheddar Gorge. This was awesome. The dark cliffs overhanging, threatening. Half way the car engine was overheating so she stopped in a lay-by. The silence was ominous. What a mysterious place. Dark and menacing. Then there was an eerie sound. A stone cracked off the cliff and bounced down, stone upon stone, to the road below. Jenny had had enough of this place and prayed her car would start. It did, and she spent the journey home debating on what newer car she could afford and also realised she had seen more of her native home countryside in a few days than she had seen in forty years. 'That's freedom for you' she thought.

Being out exploring she was unaware of local news. She didn't want to know. But the phone kept on ringing. She ignored it whilst she found her slippers and fed the cat. In the end she had to pick up the damned instrument.

'Hello. It's Mandy. Are you all right?'

Jenny had to improve her lying technique. 'I'm fine. Been to Wells for the day. Why do you ask?'

'That hunk Ben. They had it on the news today. He's a bad lot. Drugs. You're not involved are you?'

'No Mandy. Yes, I've been out on his boat but I don't know anything about this. As I said, I've been out all day. I'm perfectly OK.'

Next it was Lyn. Jenny said the same thing, then, 'The doorbell's going. Talk to you soon.'

Eleanor was at the door. 'They haven't locked you up. God, I was worried about you!'

'Come in. Why is everyone so concerned?'

'Look at the evening paper. "Local Romeo – big time drugs pusher".'

'I'm not surprised. "Girl in every port and a port in every girl."'

'I don't mean that. What about the drugs? His name's here and the name of the boat, *Blithe Spirit*".'

Jenny couldn't deal with Eleanor's green-eyed stare. She just burst into tears. Eleanor took her by the arm back into the house. Best keep what Jenny had to say in private. Still sobbing, Jenny told her the whole story, whilst Eleanor clasped her arms around her.

'It OK. I believe you. I won't say a word. I can't imagine you having anything to do with it. You just fell for an attractive man, as we all do. Could it be he took you along as, say, camouflage? A couple look less suspicious than a man on his own.'

'Maybe. But he was always so kind. Gentlemanly.'

'Partly it's the upbringing – public school and good manners. And he liked you. An amoral person can separate the two and never see they've done anything wrong, because they don't live their lives by your rules.'

'Who told you that?'

'A long-lost lover. He was a doctor of philosophy, and manipulated ideas to fit in with his way of life. But it is true. You have rules for yourself, like – I will not kill, I will not steal. But can you impose them on other people?'

'You have to, somehow. Otherwise there would be chaos, violence, and war. Are we getting out of our depth?' wondered Jenny.

'Come on, I'll take you out for a meal. You're thinking too much and don't want to stay in all night answering the phone.'

217

'I'll have to eventually. But not now.'

Arm in arm them went to the local Italian who gave them a free bottle of the house red for all the trade Jenny had sent their way. Deliberately Eleanor talked of other things, which included a shop she might buy in Weston, a district of Bath near the hospital.

'Hospitals are always good for trade – flowers for the sick, dying and new babies – and I can live over the premises. I'll have to get a small van for deliveries but as I can't drive myself, find an aggressive young man who can cope with Bath traffic.'

In turn Jenny talked about her plans for evening meals. After the catastrophe of her two days away, work was the alternative to take her mind into new ideas. The evening meals now were a challenge she must overcome.

They parted, Jenny feeling more positive but then she had to face her answer phone. It had to be done; friends could be worried for no reason. The first call was from Edith whom she rang and they arranged to meet the next day after work for a meal.

The other calls were asking for accommodation that she was happy to arrange.

She was back in business again and Lansdown View would be one of the best guesthouses in Bath.

She spent the next morning browsing through cookery books, realising her cooking ability extended little beyond the Sunday roast, casseroles, shepherd's pie and spaghetti bolognese. She had never had the money or the time to explore culinary delights and imagined Trev would not have appreciated them if she had. She would have to consult her guesthouse expert and went round to see Lyn. Lyn was busy in the kitchen preparing vegetables. 'I hope you don't mind if I keep slicing these onions. Ken's gone to see his mum today so I'm on my own. Chicken casserole for ten. Then I've got the desserts to do. What happened on your canal trip? Did you suspect anything about him?'

'No. The canal was beautiful. The only suspicious thing was he was never happy to leave the boat with no one aboard.'

'Now we know he had half a million pounds stashed away in antique books that's no surprise.'

'No. More like common sense. We had an argument, something very trivial, and I left before any police appeared. I want to forget the whole thing. I've come here to ask your advice about meals.' Lyn fortunately wasn't nosy but liked giving advice.

'Make us both a coffee and get that file off the shelf. That's where I keep my menus. It's divided up into hors-d'oeuvres, main meals, vegetarian options and desserts. I try to plan meals in a fortnightly cycle, then if someone does stay here for two weeks they don't get the same thing twice, and you can plan the shopping more easily. It looks posh if you type out the menus and serve the veg separately, then you can charge more.'

'What's tuna niçoise? I can't even pronounce it.'

'That's dead easy. Bed of lettuce, new potatoes and salad. Then tuna out of a tin with pitted olives. Keep the dressing, out of a bottle, separate. Look, I know what I'm cooking for the next few days. Borrow the file and come and help me peel the potatoes.' Lyn not only liked giving advice, she was also bossy.

As they stood side by side at the sink Lyn remarked, 'You know you'll have to employ someone. Either a cook or a waitress. You can't do it all on your own. And make sure you have an evening off each week.'

Jenny walked home thoughtfully. Evening meals would be far more complicated than a fry-up for breakfast. Now she was looking forward to her meal with Edith, whom she could talk to openly about her fling on the boat.

The two friends found a quiet restaurant in Christmas Steps, a picturesque medieval street, and over steak and chips Edith said, 'You had a lucky escape from the hunk. If you had been a few minutes later I'd be visiting you in prison, standing you bail, rather than sitting here.'

'Thanks for the thought. I was very lucky. I just cannot get over how such a charming man could be so rotten, selling drugs to people.'

'Do you think he used drugs himself?'

'Not obviously, but it may be why he dropped out of college and his family disowned him. And by what it said in the papers I wasn't the first of his conquests. "Local Romeo" indeed.'

'It said in today's *Evening Post* a passer-by saw a woman on board and the police would like to question this woman. You didn't leave your knickers in the bed?'

'No I did not. Any description?'

'No.' Jenny's bravado collapsed and she glanced around the restaurant at the thought of the cops bursting through the door at any minute.

'That's frightening. Don't think I could cope with the police. I'll just keep quiet. It wouldn't be good for business if I got my name in the papers, and possible accusations.'

'I think you're right. If they have no leads on you, hopefully they'll never find you. And you can't prove you knew nothing.'

'You would have thought if he were selling drugs he would seem a lot better off. The boat had seen better days and his clothes were so scruffy.'

'He could have led a double life and has money in a Swiss bank and a villa in the south of France. Or someone blackmailed him into doing these things. A run-down boat isn't going to attract attention. It could have been camouflage.'

'Yes. Eleanor said I might have been camouflage too.'

'You won't be the first woman to have had the wool pulled over her eyes by a gigolo, thinking it was true love. Talking of which, do you remember Bartholomew Prendergast who lectured the art appreciation course?'

'Big flamboyant man.'

'He asked me out for a drink the other night. He's quite a card. Do you think love is lurking there?' And their conversation moved on to other topics.

The following evening, having gleaned all the information she could from Lyn's file, Jenny walked round to Rosebank to return it. A familiar tall thin figure was walking towards her. It was Jake Fowler. They stopped to exchange pleasantries and Jenny asked how the business was going.

'Oh. Fine. I just feel a bit cheesed off, as a mate of mine from uni has asked me to go on an archaeological dig in Ireland over the summer. I'd love to go but can't really because of Zak. He can't run the business on his own.'

'I'm sorry. A missed opportunity for you,' and she went on her way.

Having spent an entertaining half hour with Lyn and Ken, Jenny was walking home when a thought struck her. She hurried home and telephoned Jake.

'I've just had an idea. If you went on the dig in Ireland would Zak be capable of working in the guesthouse kitchen? I'm thinking of doing evening meals and need some help. He's given me tips and recipes in the past and you've said he's a good cook. Of course he'd have to do the Hygiene Certificate, could he manage that?'

'He's got that. After he left school with no exams he got a job in a big hotel kitchen but he couldn't cope with the stress – all the different courses, people shouting – but your guesthouse might be quite different. With just a few guests and one type of meal. Let me talk to him, think about the business as well, then come back to you.'

Jenny couldn't settle to anything for the rest of the evening. The business would be up and running again tomorrow and this was her last quiet evening until the end of summer. Jake rang back about eleven o'clock.

'Zak thinks it a great idea, and so do I. My mate says the dig starts towards the end of June. This means we can finish our current jobs and close the business down from July to October. The accountants won't like it, but tough, it's our lives. I'll feel happier too knowing he is seeing you every day. If he's on his own he forgets to take his tablets that keep him calm. Could you make sure he takes them?'

'That's fine. I'll take care of him. On the days he isn't here I'll ring him and remind him about the tablets. The end of June gives me time to plan the meals and get the necessary food and equipment.'

'Zak says he'll come round over the weekend to talk to you.'

Now Jenny was excited. A new beginning; something to achieve after the disaster of Ben.

Chapter 17

Zak turned up on Saturday morning full of ideas and recipes. He was no longer the silent young man of last December who let Jake do all the talking. They spent a happy hour with Jenny making lists of food, saucepans and kitchen utensils. Zak could obviously read but his writing ability was limited. He wouldn't be able to write a list of what he'd used and Jenny would have to take that into account.

Later guests started arriving and she was back into the routine. One of the clothing reps returned, which pleased her. She remembered his name, which pleased him. Later on another small grey-suited man booked in. She remembered his face but not his name. She assumed he came to Bath on business. In fact, looking at 'Bill's' records, he had been three times before. A Mr Smith from Stafford. An unmemorable name from an unmemorable town. The man only spoke when necessary. He had grey hair, greyish wrinkled skin, and in fact he was as grey as his suit. Jenny suddenly felt sorry for him. He went up to his room and did not come down again until breakfast the next day. In an effort to make him smile she exclaimed what a beautiful day it was, but he just agreed. Would he like a morning paper? No, he had his book. Jenny noticed it was a Thomas Hardy. Not the most cheerful of authors. He had cereal and toast – no robust breakfast for Mr Smith.

Jenny was getting used to foreign visitors, especially from the States. She told them the places to visit and thought she should get commission from the open-top bus companies. Some time in the future she would go on a bus herself. Perhaps when Edith was in town and they could have a laugh. The younger Americans liked to make sure you knew their worth. One man, standing big and strong as though he was about to hit a baseball bat across the dining room said, 'I'm big in water in Seattle.' Had he come to see the local water company? Another made it known he was at a business meeting in the Caribbean last week, then talked about airports and jetlag. Jenny knew if they were that important they would be at the four-star hotel up the road. How different from the elderly farming couple from the Prairies, who had come on the double booked coach tour, and dreamed of seeing the sea.

She found people visiting the university more entertaining. Many of the men, mostly lecturers, were first recognised by their beards. One of them said to her at breakfast, 'I was able to lie in bed for an extra five minutes today because I don't shave. Over my life I have calculated I have been able to spend an extra two months in bed by being a bearded wonder.' He had a merry twinkle in his eye and lectured on chaos theory.

Two other visitors to return were Mr and Mrs Fitzgerald. They were wearing black and without the children. Realising what must have happened Jenny gave her condolences, and asked if they would like a pot of tea.

'Any chance of anything stronger? We've just come from the wake,' explained Mr Fitzgerald. 'A sad occasion, but to use the hackneyed phrase "a merciful release". Life had become a torment to her.'

'One good thing about today,' added his wife, 'as it so often is at funerals, was seeing so many of her old friends and relatives. Listening them to talk about her life – she had been a journalist – made us remember how she used to be. It helps put things in proportion.'

When Jenny returned with the drinks she asked after Julia and Suzie.

'My sister has come to look after them whilst we're away,' Mrs Fitzgerald told her. 'They're sad of course, but didn't know her that well. After we saw her at Easter they were much more curious about her and their grandfather. I had to find old photos of their wedding and the family growing up. It was something you said – about old people being young once.'

'I'm sorry if I interfered. We were just chatting as they helped me lay the tables.'

'No, no. I think it was helpful in getting them to understand. Thank you for being so kind to them.'

Over the next two Saturdays Zak would turn up in the kitchen and they practised making casseroles, so as to get into a routine, used to working together and seeing how long the preparation and cooking took. They made enough for fifteen people then Jake was invited to a meal to give his opinion. The rest of the meals they froze for future use. The meals met with Jake's approval and whilst they ate he told them with great enthusiasm about Ireland in prehistoric times. Jenny had heard of Stonehenge but knew nothing about barrows, Iron Age camps and dolmens. She found it difficult to grasp that these monuments were built three thousand years ago.

'I'll have to show you. Let's get in the van and go for a drive.'

'I can't. Customers start arriving about three o'clock. Anyway what can you show us round here?'

'Plenty. Tomorrow morning after breakfast. Have a pub lunch and be back in time for tea.'

'Better still we can take my new, well, newer, car. So far I've only driven it to the Cash and Carry.' She was very pleased with her new small shiny metallic blue Ford.

The next morning she stacked the dishes as fast as she could and picked the two young men up by 10.30. Jake directed her through small Cotswold stone villages and told her to park beside a stream. As she got out of the car, pleased with its performance, she felt the difference of the countryside from the town. There was the scent of new-cut hay, flowers in the hedgerows, fluffy down from the willows blowing in the wind. A sign directed them to Stoney Littleton Long Barrow. They crossed the stream and clambered up the boundary of a muddy field. Jenny wondered why Jake was carrying a torch. At the brow of the hill they came upon a grassy mound and round the far side was an entrance like a cave. Jake went inside, bending low, and switched on his torch. The interior was built of stone with alcoves. Dark and mysterious. What had happened here three thousand years ago? How long was three thousand years?

'This,' said Jake solemnly, 'is where the Ancient Britons buried their dead. Only the important people.'

'Why?'

'To show they were powerful. Think how different it

was. Few people. Only the crops and animals that you cared for to keep you alive. The cold of winter with fire the only heat and light.'

'I don't like it much,' said Zak, 'it's spooky.' He went back out into the sunlight. Jenny bumped her head on the stonework and she too was glad to be in the open. As they walked back down the hill Jake described how the people had lived here so long ago. She could feel his enthusiasm, his sense of history and thought how dull he must find plumbing. The next village to which he directed her was called Stanton Drew. Here they found two circles of standing stones. Jenny didn't find this creepy, she just wondered why. Why put up these big heavy stones? It must have been important to go to that much trouble. Jake said experts thought it would have been for religious reasons.

'Like building Wells Cathedral. To worship God or their gods.'

'Exactly.'

'I never knew anything about ancient history before. Do you to know, I've learnt more in the last nine months about art, history, people and now cooking than I learnt in eleven years at school.'

'It's like scales dropping from your eyes.'

'The world is opening up. It was always there, but I never saw it.'

They had a quick ploughman's lunch in a local pub and made for home.

'Thanks so much for showing us these places. We won't have any time for exploration next weekend. Will we Zak?'

'No. Cooking for twelve, or more, I hope.'

*

227

The first evening went well as there were only three couples wanting an evening meal. They had prawn cocktail, beef casserole and trifle, followed by cheese, biscuits and coffee. There were no hiccups, and Jenny mentioned to the guests they were their first evening customers and was asked to give their compliments to the chef. 'I'm not a chef,' Zak said slowly, 'I'm a plumber.' They both laughed and toasted themselves with a glass of wine. Zak couldn't drive and said the walk home would calm him down.

The next night the roast potatoes for eight got burnt, but there were some croquette potatoes in the freezer so that was taken care of. 'We can have soup for a starter tomorrow,' planned Jenny, 'use up the unburnt pieces of the spuds.'

'Yeah. Onion soup would be good, with a few herbs, potatoes to thicken. Who's going to know? Go well with the salmon salad to follow.'

On Thursday and Sunday evenings there were no meals, to give themselves a break, although Jenny still had to man the bar. Each night she dropped into bed exhausted. After two weeks they were getting into a routine and Jenny realised the figures were up, even taking into account the extra spending and Zak's pay.

Dean came home for the vacation broken hearted, as Cassy had gone to Spain with his best mate. He found himself a job in Sainsbury's stacking shelves but was taking up one of the bedrooms, which meant less money coming in. She was out in the garden one afternoon dead-heading the roses and mentioned this to Tom who was tending his sweet peas. 'Our students are away for the summer. He could stay with us if he can afford the rent.'

This situation worked out well and Dean helped out in the guesthouse some evenings so Jenny got time off to see Eleanor for a meal, or Lyn for more advice. Occasionally Dean went to see his father and came back one evening saying, 'Josh is a nice baby. I didn't think I would like babies but I do like bouncing him up and down. He laughs so much.'

'What does he look like, your half brother?'

'He has ginger hair, like Dad, and it's curly. And brown eyes with green flecks in them. Dad is very good with him, better than Sharon. She goes out most evenings when Dad's home. I don't think being a mother agrees with her.'

'Trev was very good with you when you were small. We had some fun times, which you won't remember.' She found the old photo albums and they spent a happy half-hour leafing through the pictures. Dean and Mandy burying Trev in the sand at Weston-super-Mare. Dean and Trev on the dodgems at the local fair. Mandy in her ballet tutu. Jenny remembered the display as the little girls pranced around like a herd of elephants. Trev had to go outside because he laughed so much.

'Shame it all went wrong,' sighed Jenny. 'Perhaps it's middle age. Knowing you're not young any more.'

'Well Josh seems to have given Dad a new lease of life, even if Sharon doesn't like it. She seems to spend a lot of money on clothes.'

'Which probably explains why Trev hasn't paid me back yet for my half of the house. I expect it will sort out eventually.'

This conversation got Jenny thinking about the divorce, having given it little thought over the last few months. She tried to contact Mr Figgis, whom she had consulted in the dark days of last autumn, only to be told he had left the firm in the New Year. Hence the lack of progress. Exasperated by the firm's inefficiency she went to see Mr Slocombe, of Slocombe and Slocombe, who smoothly set the divorce procedure in motion again. He may be smooth as a snake, thought Jenny, but he knows what he's doing.

So July ran into August. Jenny realised that Zak, despite his pills, had bad days when he was very slow and forgetful. She had to take over then, but Dean, aware of the situation, often helped out. The worst occasion was when Zak put sugar, instead of salt, and a tin of strawberries, thinking they were tomatoes, in a beef casserole. Zak fell about laughing at the expression on her face when she tasted it. She told him to go home and lie down and resorted to a humble cottage pie, much to the guests' disgust. Two of them left to find the Indian restaurant in the main street. The next day she and Zak chuckled about it together.

She wished she had time to keep a diary about the unusual things that happened, like the evening there was frantic banging on the kitchen door. Jenny opened it to a girl in her twenties drenched from the rain that had been falling all day.

'Can I have a room for the night?' She had no luggage, not even a handbag, and was a sorry sight.

'Come in,' invited Jenny, concerned about her plight. She was obviously crying. 'Have you got any money?'

'Oh God. I left everything on the boat. I just couldn't take any more. He's been shouting at me for three days.'

'Who?'

'My fiancé, Pete. Well he isn't now. I threw my ring in the water. "Wind that paddle, push that gate, pull that rope. No, you're doing it all wrong." Last night we came adrift. It was my fault because I hadn't tied the rope properly onto a bollard. I need to be in a proper room, with a shower and then a bed. Not some narrow bunk. I never knew how awful Pete was.'

Dean was standing in the doorway enjoying the drama; fortunately it was not a meals night. Jenny glanced at him smiling, 'My son will make you a hot drink whilst I will make sure your fiancé, or ex fiancé, is all right with the boat. Locks are difficult to manage on your own.'

She found Ben's old jacket. Although it was too big, and brought back upsetting memories, it had its uses. She encountered a very angry young man in a waxed jacket, wet hair plastered over his forehead, drifting in the middle of a full lock wondering what to do. She opened the gates for him and took a mooring line as he chugged out. Maybe the fact that he hadn't tied the boat up meant he knew little about what he was doing. He probably wasn't angry, but frightened. She had watched enough boaters negotiating these locks to know the signs of panic.

'Can we have a word?' said Jenny, feeling in a situation of power. The young man found the back mooring line and, glowering, stood beside her.

'I have a very upset young lady in my guesthouse. She wants to stay the night but has no money. She say's you've been shouting at her. Could you give me her handbag so she can pay, or alternatively I'll help you up the next two locks and find out what the problem is? I gather your engagement ring is in the canal.'

The young man looked crestfallen. 'I'm not like this

usually. I don't know what to do if things go wrong. Yes, please help.'

'Two more locks to do. Where's the windlass?'

'She threw it on the bank somewhere.' The young man went in search.

'Right, Pete, I think that's the name. I'll open the next gate and we'll take it from there.' There were other boats around to help and they had moored within forty minutes.

'What you do now is up to you. But I'd appreciate money for the night, her handbag and some dry clothes.' These were found and Pete thanked her.

'I don't know what came over her. The way she behaved!'

'And the way you behaved! Perhaps a night to think things over? You know where the guesthouse is.' She stomped back to the guesthouse, tired and cold. Why should she have made it her problem?

Dean let his mother in, to drip water over the clean kitchen floor. He had obviously looked after the young lady very well. She had now showered, warmed up and was wearing one of Jenny's dressing gowns, whilst clothes were slopping around in the dryer. Chestnut hair curled around her oval face, no longer the waif from the storm but a beautiful woman. Dean was quite smitten. Handing the young lady her belongings from the boat she said, 'Here's your handbag and some clothes. Pete's up at the top lock, thinking. One of the Honeysuckle rooms is free. You can have that. Dean can check you in, and take your card or cheque. Now I am very chilled, getting the boat through the locks you couldn't handle, and I'm going to shower and get warm.'

When she returned to the kitchen in her second best

dressing gown she found Dean making sandwiches and soup. Sheepishly he said, 'Tessa's so hungry. You don't mind do you?'

'Tessa is it? No. As long as she remembers to pay.'

'Why were you so cross with her?'

'She just abandoned her boyfriend at a lock. He didn't know enough to get out of the situation and shouted at her, because he panicked. If they are going to make a go of life together she shouldn't walk out on such a problem. Should've tried to help. Perhaps a night apart will help them decide what they really want out of life. Can I have some soup too?'

'Sure. I'll just take this up.'

'Just knock on the door and leave it outside.' Dean looked disappointed.

When he returned he picked up her wet coat from the floor and hung it over the sink to drip. 'This coat's far too big for you.'

'It belonged to a man friend of mine.'

'Is this the hunk Mandy told me about?'

'Yes. That's why I know about locks. Sadly he turned out to be a crook but the coat's useful.' Sensibly Dean didn't ask any more but warmed up the soup.

Jenny was busy grilling bacon the next morning when she heard rustling outside the back door, followed by a timid knock. Making sure the grill was turned off she opened the door to a bank of flowers behind which stood the young man she had met last evening, now with groomed fair hair and clean jeans.

'These are for Tessa.'

'Well, come in.'

'No. I was hoping you might give them to her. She has to make up her own mind. I'll wait on the boat.'

Jenny was left holding several bouquets. What should she do? She dashed upstairs and put two outside Tessa's door. The rest were left on a table set for one. Continuing to cook breakfasts the look of curiosity on guests' faces amused her. Would a romantic drama unfold? Were the other residents eating their meal more slowly to see what would happen? Tessa, holding two bunches of flowers, came into the room and gasped at the other bunches on the table. She read the cards and sat down dazed. Jenny offered her tea or coffee.

'No ... No thank you. I have to go.'

'Pete's up at the top lock.' Tessa gathered up the flowers and Jenny ushered her out though the kitchen. Did the guests sigh with delight as Tessa, leaving a trail of petals, ran off up to the canal? Jenny hoped the couple would resolve their problems but realised she would never know.

Another story with no ending.

Mr Smith from Stafford returned, for the fifth time Jenny noted from 'Bill's' records.

'Nice to see you again, Mr Smith. What brings you to Bath so frequently?'

'I'm an inspector for the ... er ... Tax Office.' He was lying, and being diffident, not good at it.

'Will you be going out this evening, Mr Smith, dining here, or would you like a snack in your room?'

'No thanks. I'll just be up in my room. I can have tea there and I like reading.'

'Enjoy your evening. I'll see you in the morning.' She tried to smile but his sad eyes made this impossible.

Next morning guests drifted in, crunched on their cornflakes, enjoyed bacon and eggs, businessmen rustled their *Financial Times* and couples, knowing each other too well, said nothing, but there was no sign of Mr Smith.

Jenny waited until the other guests had left, then knocked on Mr Smith's door. 'Your breakfast's ready,' she called, but there was no response. He must be ill, she thought, and ran downstairs to get the master key. When she opened the door there was a peculiar smell in the room. Once she had opened the curtains she saw Mr Smith lying on his bed fully clothed. There was no need to touch his cold cheek to know he was dead. Beside his bed were a small empty whisky flask and a brown pharmaceutical bottle she could not identify. There was an envelope addressed 'To whom this may concern' which she left in its place and, not wishing to stay in the room, locked the door and went downstairs to phone the police.

Within ten minutes she could hear sirens wailing and a police car and ambulance were parked outside. She showed the police his room and busied herself in the kitchen but realised she couldn't stop shaking and sat in reception with a cigarette until the police came back down to question her. The policeman identified himself as Detective Sergeant Gray and noticing she was trembling, gently asked about Mr Smith, but there was little she could tell him. He showed her the letter. It read:

'Since my wife died I have found life unbearably lonely and have now found out I have cancer. There is no point in carrying on, so I shall poison myself with formaldehyde, which I use in my work as an embalmer. I have no family so there is no one to contact. My will is kept at my bank. I apologise to Mrs Evans for putting her in this situation.'

Jenny found she was crying. 'This is so sad. To feel that desperate. The poor man.'

'Miserable job too. Must have affected his mind over the years. Do you know where he worked? It was probably for an undertaker. They use formaldehyde.'

'No. He said he worked for the Tax Office, but it wasn't convincing.'

'I'll check with undertakers, and contact Stafford Police. You'll have his home address in your register?' Jenny showed the detective sergeant her records.

'There'll have to be a post-mortem. Better not touch his bedroom until that's done just in case there was foul play.' Jenny nodded, too upset to reply, and watched the ambulance men carrying the covered stretcher down the stairs and place the master key on the reception counter.

'We'll be in touch,' said Detective Sergeant Gray, then paused. 'Would you like a neighbour to be with you until you get over the shock?'

'No thanks. I'll be all right.'

But she wasn't all right and couldn't settle to work so she strolled up the canal, thinking of Mr Smith, and comparing his despair with her own after Trevor had left. Then another thought occurred to her. Mr Smith's suicide would be in the newspapers, maybe on the radio. The publicity wouldn't do her business any good. Who would want to stay in a guesthouse where people killed themselves? The thought jolted her back to the nitty gritty of coping with today. How would she put such a sad event to the other guests when they returned and to people making bookings? But before getting back to work she must tell Tom and Dorothy. Seeing police and the ambulance outside the house would worry them.

With looks of concern they welcomed her into their

home, made her sit down and gave her a cup of sweet tea for the shock whilst she told them what had happened.

'How tragic for the man to be so alone,' said Dorothy, 'to have no one to love.'

'You mean that if I kicked the bucket you could go and annoy the rest of the family.'

'Don't make jokes at a time like this,' reprimanded his wife. Talking to the old couple calmed Jenny. She mentioned that the tragedy might affect the reputation of the guesthouse but Tom patted her on the shoulder saying people had very short memories. 'You're the only one who will remember every time you go into the room. Perhaps it would be a good idea to change the decoration.' Jenny thanked them and returned home to talk on the telephone to Lyn.

'Tom's right. Might be difficult for a few days but the only person it will affect is you. I can remember we had to call an ambulance when a guest got food poisoning. We'd had grilled sardines that night. I haven't been able to touch them since. It turned out he had had a dodgy beefburger in town at lunchtime. It took a lot of explaining to the other guests. It might mean your numbers are down for a few days, that's all. Enjoy the rest.'

That evening one couple returned and collected their bags saying they had found more suitable accommodation. The rest of the guests were sympathetic, but business was quiet for a few days, and Jenny tried not to let the image of Mr Smith's sad mournful face fill her dreams.

Chapter 18

Towards the end of September Zak became depressed and couldn't concentrate on what he was doing. Jenny was mystified, as the evening meals had become a great success, and Zak enjoyed the cooking. One afternoon as they were slicing runner beans she asked him what was wrong.

'Next week Jake'll be back,' he stammered, cutting his finger on his knife, so Jenny had to find the blue tape. 'When he comes back I'll have to go back to plumbing.'

'I thought you liked plumbing?'

'It's OK. There ain't many jobs I can do, but I can help Jake. I like helping Jake – but I loves cooking.' He sighed. 'I don't want to leave.'

Jenny laid her hand on his arm, 'You must talk to Jake about it. Find out what you both want out of life. Don't worry. Your beef Burgundy tonight is going to be brilliant.'

And it was. Jenny was left wondering what to do. Should she be looking for another chef? It was up to the brothers, she could not interfere, she had far too much respect for them.

On the morning after Jake's return the brothers called

on Jenny. Jake was full of his archaeology trip and excited about their dig of an Ancient Bronze Age village. He showed them photos of stone foundations set in misty hills and bronze implements and jewellery that he called artefacts. Zak sat there in depressed silence.

'Now it's back to the grindstone, or should I say quern?' and he chuckled at his joke, the other two remaining silent, not understanding its meaning.

'But Jake, I dusn't want to go back to plumbing. I likes working here.'

'We have to Zak. We need the money and there's that big contract I arranged in June, putting in heating in a new block of flats over Twerton way.'

'Then I'm letting Jenny down.'

'Don't think that,' interrupted Jenny, 'I can get an agency chef in at short notice, though I doubt if they will be able to do what we have done in the last three months.'

'Good, because we need to do that contract, otherwise we'll be broke.'

'Perhaps,' suggested Jenny, 'it'll give you time to think about what *you* want from life, Jake. I know there are bits of the plumbing business you hate, like the accounts and ordering stuff. Can you get a job in archaeology now you have experience?'

'They don't pay well enough. I'll have to think, but we do have to start this job next Monday, then let's see what happens.'

So it was left that Zak would leave on Saturday and Jenny would find a temporary chef. As she rang the agency she thought, so much for not interfering, but she had to speak up for Zak as he couldn't defend himself.

*

The agency charged so much for chefs Jenny could only afford to keep him on for one week, and put an advertisement in the local paper. The agency chef rather fancied himself as he had worked in big hotels and knew the business. He wanted to cook exotic dishes in the nouvelle cuisine style, the ingredients of which Jenny thought too expensive, so there was a conflict of wills for the week. He took a dim view of doing all the preparation himself, and the washing up, as he was used to underlings doing this for him, so Jenny was lumbered with more work.

Two young men applied for the job advertised in the local paper. Jenny chose the more prepossessing but he turned out to be all talk, and she wondered if his qualifications were genuine once he had burnt the sauce, and his pastry for the steak and kidney pie was like leather, bringing complaints from the guests. He lasted two weeks and in desperation she returned to the agency who agreed to send along a new chef on Monday.

On Sunday it would be the day before the anniversary of Uncle Bernard's death and Jenny had arranged to spend the day with Eleanor as they both had memories to share. After breakfast and once the guests had departed for the day she drove to Eleanor's new home, a flat above the flower shop she had leased at Weston that Jenny had yet to see. Each week Eleanor sent flowers to the guesthouse – small flowers that Jenny put in vases on the dining tables. They were delivered in a small white van with 'Silken Inspirations' written on the side. The attractive young driver had blond curly hair, broad shoulders and a pleasant smile. Jenny herself would have fancied him if she were twenty years younger, and thought Eleanor had employed him for the same reasons. With pride Eleanor showed Jenny the flat above the shop. It was newly decorated with pine floors, bright rugs and leather sofas. Bernard's portrait of her was on the wall and Jenny insisted she must come to the guesthouse to choose more. The shop itself was a delight of perfume and colour. Jenny was fascinated and wanted to know more about the flowers and from where they came. It was a new world to her.

They decided to lunch at a pub on the top of Lansdown then walk across the racecourse. Jenny had never driven up Lansdown's steep hill and admired the beautiful Georgian terraces and elegant houses. Over lunch, Jenny only having a cheese omelette as she was rather tired of thinking about meals, Eleanor tucking into a juicy steak from which Jenny pinched several chips, they chatted over their memories of Bernard. Jenny related some of his seafaring stories and talked about watching him make the model ship. Then, changing the subject slightly, she said, 'I remember you saying something about making love in the afternoon when anyone might knock on the door added to the excitement. I found the same on the boat with Ben. Not knowing what might happen must keep the adrenaline going.'

'Yes. I shall always remember those afternoons with pleasure, despite all the unhappiness that came later.'

'Perhaps you'll have some luck with your handsome delivery man.'

Eleanor laughed, 'I thought so too. That's why I employed him. Only to find out he is having an affair with another equally handsome man. So no luck there,' and they both laughed at the mistake.

'But there is a rather charming man in his fifties,'

Eleanor added, 'who comes in a couple of times a week to buy flowers for his mother who he says is in hospital. As she's been in the hospital for over two months I hope it may be just an excuse for him coming into the shop to chat. Have you got over Ben yet?'

'I still dream of the happy moments, but there weren't that many of them. I've been too busy with the evening meals to think about anything else. I was enjoying this until October,' and she went on to tell Eleanor about her chef problem.

As they walked over the grassy racecourse towards woods, leaves glowing gold and brown in the sunshine, Jenny said, 'I've been so involved with the guesthouse I hadn't realised autumn is here. Am I getting *too* involved?'

'Just at present because of your chef problems. But think of the situation you were in during October last year.'

'Yes, I was at rock bottom. Even tried to commit suicide with a bottle of aspirins and whisky but fell asleep instead. I was appalled at what I'd done and was determined to climb out of that hole. Sadly its thanks to Uncle that I could.'

'And think what you have done since then. Do you remember the panic you had on that first evening? I've seen you change from being timid and unsure of yourself into a confident woman.'

'Thanks. You too are standing on your own two feet, no longer dependent on Ted.'

'If you had forgotten it's autumn perhaps you need to take more time off. Make sure you have time for your-self and keep things in proportion.'

'You're right. Keep the no-meals days, Thursdays and

Sundays, for myself. Go and see Mandy. I haven't seen her for months. Visit places of interest. I have yet to see the Holborne Museum and it's only along the road. You as well – never do the accounts on Sundays, nor go and see your mother.'

Pleased with their new resolutions they walked on, enjoying the scenery and the rest of the warm afternoon.

By five o'clock Jenny had to be back at Lansdown View to greet four new guests, but afterwards walked up the canal, with Pyewacket brushing her legs because she had forgotten to feed him. She looked across the canal now noticing the foliage on the far bank and the ducks quacking in the water. She picked the cat up – 'It's nearly a year since I came here after visiting Mr Slocombe. Do you enjoy being here, Pye? You like sitting on the reception desk and being stroked by the guests. I've changed in that year, come out of the dark wood and found a hilltop where I'm in the sunshine, but I'm glad you're the same. Still the familiar old wise cat.' The direction of her thoughts changed. 'I wonder how Trev is now? Has he changed with Joshua and Sharon to look after? What we would make of each other if we ever met again? Now I'll get your tea.'

A very dramatic young man called Louis who, from his accent, was perhaps French, came from the agency on Monday. True, he had the ability to cook, but each evening became a drama – would the meat be over-cooked, the sponge pudding go flat? One evening he was nearly in tears after he had forgotten to put the cumin in a curry. He sat at the table with his head in his hands, 'I am an artist, Mrs Evans. It has to be perfect.'

'Tastes all right to me,' she replied taking a teaspoon-ful from the saucepan.

'You have no soul.'

'Let's just get on with it. It's nearly seven o'clock and there are the starters to do.'

'How can I reveal my talent in this atmosphere?'

Jenny's nerves were frazzled but she kept calm. Did he have a drink problem, as she noticed the cooking sherry bottle was empty most evenings.

It was at this time that Mrs Hamilton, who had come in the spring with her reluctant daughter, Olivia, for an interview at the university, returned with her husband but without her daughter. She was as elegant and as gushing as ever, her husband tall and silent, in a grey suit.

'We've come down to see darling Olivia. See how she's settling in. We're taking her out to dinner this evening.'

I expect Olivia will enjoy an evening with the Grand Inquisition, thought Jenny. She was clearing up the guesthouse meal, the excitable Louis having flounced off home, when she heard the Hamilton family return. She went into the bar to ask if they would like a drink and stopped in surprise. Where had the mousy Olivia gone? Here was tall slim girl in jeans and a designer top with shiny long dark hair and lovely skin. Her father was talking, laughing with her, and obviously adored her. Mr Hamilton ordered a whisky for himself and a sherry for his wife. Olivia wanted a lager but her mother interrupted,

'A mineral water, darling, we don't want you turning into a drunkard,' but Mr Hamilton requested a pint of Fosters. Jenny asked how she was getting on, and the girl talked of her room in hall and the friends she had made. She now sounded an adult, no longer a child.

Perhaps the problem lay in the fact the father loved the daughter dearly, and the mother, jealous, had tried to dominate the two of them. Jenny wondered where it would take them. Would Olivia go off the rails with her newfound freedom, or outmanoeuvre her parents to get what she wanted? She would never know. She found this a frustrating part of the job – being in the middle of a story and never knowing the ending.

The last straw with Louis came on Saturday, Bonfire Night. Every time a firework went off he put his hands over his ears.

'I cannot stand the noise. How can I think? I will go mad.'

'Don't be silly. Its just people enjoying themselves. Have you done the desserts yet?'

'The desserts? To hell with your desserts,' and he threw the dishes to the floor. 'And your casserole is nothing but dog's turds.' The big saucepan sailed across the kitchen. Jenny dived under the kitchen table; she knew the next thing to go would be hot soup. She peered out from under the table and saw with relief he was getting his coat.

'My genius is not appreciated in this foul hole.'

'I hope the fireworks frighten you to death,' she shouted in anger as the door slammed.

What should she do now? Eight guests would soon want a meal.

Grabbing her purse, she rushed out to the Chinese takeaway and bought fried and boiled rice and twelve varying dishes. Where could she get a dessert? Perhaps the Italian would sell her a gateau? This done, she wondered, as she hurried back, could she clear the kitchen floor so she could walk without slipping on the wrecked meal? Working frantically for a quarter of an hour it was workable. Combing her hair and smoothing her clothes, she went in to the waiting guests and said there had been a problem in the kitchen and would the guests like a free drink before she served up the evening meal that would be various Chinese dishes. No one refused, so with all the haste she could muster, she dished the food up in individual dishes, so all the guests had a taste of everything. Afterwards they complemented her on the meal and she wondered if they knew what had happened. After all, the row had been noisy, or should she do Chinese takeaway meals more often?

Delayed reaction set in so she smoked a cigarette and enjoyed a double whisky to keep her going as she worked until midnight to clean the kitchen, vowing to do the cooking herself until she heard from the Fowler Brothers.

Chapter 19

Monday turned out to be hell. She smiled cynically at her euphoria when Zak was working with her. Firstly she had to replace the china Louis had broken, then devise a menu she could cook and serve on her own. This meant a visit to the Cash and Carry to buy as many already prepared items and frozen vegetables as she could find. For the first evening she decided on individual cottage pies that she could keep warm whilst doing the vegetables. Melon for a starter she could do beforehand, and the cheesecakes could be defrosted when she got home. Peeling potatoes for twelve was taking her an age when the agency rang asking if she would like Louis, such a good chef, to return.

She told them what she thought of Louis in strong terms. In fact she was downright rude, but felt better for it.

Everything was under control by 6.30, when she realised the tables had to be laid. On returning to the kitchen Pyewacket was sitting on the kitchen table looking smug, not done in catering kitchens, and was hurled down the stairs into the basement. She hoped the health and hygiene inspectors were not amongst the

247

guests. The melon was on the tables when the first guests sauntered in, one couple asking for sherry, the man saying, 'You do know my wife's a vegetarian?' Jenny took a deep breath and said she hoped an omelette would be acceptable. Heading for the kitchen she heard the woman say, 'These guesthouses have no imagination.' They have, thought Jenny, in ways that would frighten you.

She had cleared the melon dishes and was placing the pies and vegetables on tables when another guest asked, 'May I have a bottle of wine?'

'You'll have to wait until I have served the food.' The man looked affronted.

'Sorry, I shouldn't have spoken like that. The chef walked out on Saturday. I'm having to do all this on my own.'

'Oh dear. Of course I'll wait.'

When the final dish, cheese omelette, had been set before the vegetarian she went over to the man, dining on his own, and asked which wine he would like and he selected a bottle of claret. Another couple requested white wine and she took another bottle out to the kitchen. Slumping in a chair with a cigarette and a glass she thought – now I know why the cooking sherry went down so fast. When she could no longer hear the clink of cutlery it was time to collect the dinner plates and she was surprised to see the guests had already stacked these. 'Thank you for being so helpful,' she said, 'I hope you all like trifle.'

'Could I possibly have fresh fruit?' asked the vegetarian. Only if you say 'please' thought Jenny but went to look. She usually had fruit on the bar with the cereals at breakfast. When teas and coffees had been sorted she had intended to eat herself, but was beyond food and stuffed it in the fridge. Once the dishwasher was on its first run it was time to return to the bar. She hoped everyone had gone out or up to their rooms, but the single man was sitting on a stool at the bar with his bottle of claret.

'Can I help you with the dishes?' he enquired.

'No thanks. I have a machine to do that.'

'Then please come and join me in a glass of wine.' Half an hour's relaxation with a drink and a cigarette was inviting so she perched on a stool beside him. He introduced himself as Michael and said he was structural engineer who came to Bath on business every month. He kept on putting his hand on her arm and stroking it so she was relieved when a couple came back from a stroll in Sydney Gardens and she could serve them drinks. The dishwasher had finished so she hid in the kitchen restacking it. The last thing she wanted tonight was some lecherous man on his own making advances. It had happened before and she was glad there was a strong lock on the basement flat. She was a fool to have accepted the drink.

At 10.30 she closed the bar, said goodnight to her guests and sought refuge in her flat. Pyewacket nearly tripped her up demanding his belated tea. 'Oh, Pye,' she said as she forked out his food, 'it's been an awful day. I've been on my feet since six this morning. I forgot the menus. I forgot to get out of my working clothes. What can they have thought of me?' Her shirt was splattered in gravy and her oldest jeans had split at the knee. 'Then I forgot to feed you. Tomorrow at six it will begin all over again.'

There was a knock on her flat door. She felt like ignoring it, probably the lecherous Michael, but in case it was an emergency she had better answer it. It was Michael, swaying slightly. Obviously the claret had gone to his head.

'I came to kiss you goodnight.'

'No you didn't. Now turn right round and go to your room.'

'Won't you come with me, tuck me in bed?' She shut the door firmly in his face.

On Tuesday breakfast went well and the vegetarian was happy with her poached eggs. Michael looked somewhat the worse for wear as he paid the bill and asked if she had any aspirins. Typing the menu for salmon with hollandaise sauce, new potatoes and peas, the thought of scraping new potatoes made her drive to Sainsbury's and buy new potatoes with herbs and butter off the shelf. There were firms who prepared potatoes and chips for caterers. Perhaps Lyn would know, and it would be good to talk over her problems with someone.

Lyn gave her the telephone number of a firm that prepared potatoes then said, 'In the short term what you need is a waiter or waitress. Don't you have students living next door? Ask them. The money would come in handy with this student debt problem.'

'You are so clever. Never thought of that. I'll go and ask Tom and Dorothy. By the way I nearly got seduced last night. He's a structural engineer and is threatening to come again in a month's time.'

'What's his name? I'll see if he's on our blacklist.' Lyn went away for some moments, 'Oh yes. He's been here a couple of times. Seems charming until he's had a few drinks. He got on very well with Busty Bertha at "Mon Repos" until they fell out.'

'You have a blacklist?'

'Yes. People you don't want back. Usually bad payers but also people like your engineer. You'd better start one.'

'Thanks. I will. I have several names I'd like to put on it.'

Tom and Dorothy were as welcoming as they always were, wanting to give her tea and home-made cake, but she said there was no time and explained the situation.

'Well, we don't really see that much of the students, except when they pay the rent. Better if you put a big advert in the hall so they notice it. It being next door, it might appeal.'

'Especially if you said there was a free dinner,' added Dorothy.

Jenny went home and typed out on 'Bill', in bold and a large font, 'Wanted: waiter or waitress, 6 pm to 9 pm, minimum wage, free dinner. Apply after 8 pm, next door at the Lansdown View Guesthouse', then returned with this to her neighbours.

Dinner that night proceeded more smoothly and even the vegetarian opted for the salmon. Jenny was just clearing away the coffee cups when the doorbell rang and three students, two girls and a boy that she recognised from next door, stood there. Over a glass of wine in the kitchen Jenny told them of the work they would have to do. One girl decided she wasn't interested if she had to help out in the kitchen, but the other two wanted to know more, looked at the dining room and decided to share the work between them. The girl, Emily, agreed to do Monday and Friday, the boy, Paul, Tuesday, Wednesday and Saturday. The agreement had to do with when they saw their boyfriend and girlfriend. Paul said he would

251

start tomorrow, the curry being an incentive. 'Make sure you look smart,' was Jenny's parting remark.

Paul turned up in a newly ironed shirt and his best jeans and set to with a will to lay the tables. The meal went very well, the guests, some of whom knew about the absence of a chef, looked pleased, and Paul enjoyed his meal. Emily was equally as well turned out and efficient so Jenny's life returned to equilibrium.

November turned to December before the Fowler Brothers came to see her on a Sunday morning. Was their contract on the Twerton flats over?

'Would you like to come out to lunch?' asked Jake. As her idea of keeping Sunday to herself had gone awry the idea was appealing, but, as she didn't know what they had decided, could she stand the suspense?

'I would love to. Only on condition you tell me your decision now.'

'I'm afraid the decision is no,' said Jake seriously.

'Oh. Oh dear.' Tears were pricking her eyes and she felt she was about to make a fool of herself.

'It's *NO* to the plumbing trade!' he shouted, and they were all laughing and hugging each other.

They piled into Jenny's shiny blue Ford and made for The George at Norton St Philip. Jake recounted the story of their last two months as Jenny drove up the steep hill to Odd Down. They had a contract to put in the central heating for a four-storey block of flats, twenty flats in all. Due to some computer error the developers had omitted to tell the Fowlers there were actually two blocks, so twice as much work and money. They had worked all the hours they could, long into the evenings, to get the work done. Getting enough piping and radiators at short notice had been a problem and working round the painters, plasterers, bathroom and window fitters who were also employed at the same time.

'The foreman had got all his timing wrong so everyone was making the best of it. Zak got quite freaked out by all the people,' commented Jake.

'Too many cooks and not enough Indians,' said Zak from the back of the car.

'I think you mean "Too many chiefs and not enough Indians",' Jake said to his brother.

'Or "Too many cooks spoil the broth",' said Jenny. 'But I prefer what you said.'

'So the job,' continued Jake, 'took much longer than we expected but we've got enough money to relax a bit. Think of ourselves. Meanwhile I'd looked round the employment agencies and found nothing to suit a plumbing archaeologist so I got in touch with the Archaeology Department at Bath University. I know one of the lecturers there. He told me one of their lab technicians was taking maternity leave. If I was interested, go and see the technician boss, which I did, and took the job. The pay isn't great, but the job is just up my street. I start in January and can hopefully go on the dig again in Ireland in the summer. Turn left here. In the meantime a plumbing mate could do with some help up until Christmas, so Zak is free as a bird.'

'You do want me back, Jenny?'

'Of course I do, more than ever, and on better money. When can you start?'

'Tomorrow? I've been thinking of some great new ideas.'

'Good. There are a couple of people I'd like you to meet. Two students I've employed as waiters. They're very easy-going. I think you'll like them.'

'Now tell us how the guesthouse has been?' asked Jake, 'Oh, we're here. Tell us later.'

'I know this place,' exclaimed Jenny, 'Uncle Bernard painted it. There's a picture on the stairs. It's a lovely building.'

'It's quite famous. Been a pub for six centuries. Come and have a closer look.'

They walked past the half-timbered front, the upper storeys leaning over them, into the cobbled courtyard with a wooden gallery on one side. It was a building from another time and Jenny enthused about its age, 'but it's not nearly as old as those other places you showed us, Jake.'

'Not by two to three thousand years. Let's find lunch.'

Over the meal, before a roaring log fire, she told them about the terrible chefs and how Louis had thrown food all over the kitchen. She made it sound funny and they all laughed.

'Now you know what to do, Zak, if Jenny gets out of order. Throw soup at her, so she hides under the table.'

The meal felt like a celebration, and afterwards they went for a walk at Tucking Mill by a fishing lake where the mist rose gently over the still waters in the cold winter air.

'You know, it must be a year since we three met and you did the plumbing. The house was so cold and damp.'

'It's been quite a year for all of us. New directions for everyone, and all for the better.'

'You can say that again,' echoed Zak.

When Emily arrived the next evening Jenny drew her on one side before introducing her to Zak, so Emily knew why she was employing a short, plump, monosyllabic, brain-damaged plumber to do the cooking. Emily accepted this – and after she had laid the tables was asking Zak in a friendly manner what he was cooking. For the first time since July Jenny was wondering what to do with the evening, though she would be chatting to the guests and dealing with the drinks. Perhaps it was time she looked at the accounts, neglected since October. She knew at the end of September that the introduction of meals had meant she was in profit but now the amount was much higher. She checked the figures; yes they seemed to be correct. With Zak, Emily and Paul's wages to now consider the profit would fall but it would be worth it, not to be working a sixteen-hour day.

It was time to contact Liz again, who was now back at work, the twins being about five months old, and get her view of the situation. Liz suggested Jenny came to their house near St Andrews Park, Bristol, as Liz often worked from home now and Jenny could stay to lunch and see the babies. Jenny happily agreed so on the next Thursday she drove into Bristol and found St Andrews Park just off Gloucester Road. Liz, dressed in her standard smart trouser suit, showed Jenny up to her first-floor office in a comfortable Victorian semi overlooking the park. 'Computers have made all the difference to working at home. At the touch of a button I have all the information I need about any client here or in the office. How are you getting on with your computer?'

'Fine. It's easier that I expected. I call it Bill after Bill Gates, and we get on very well. I have a college friend who helps me out if things go wrong.'

'Brian's out with the twins so let's have a look at these accounts before we get interrupted.'

Jenny produced her files and Liz, businesslike as ever,

studied them in silence. Jenny felt very small, the way she did when visiting the doctor. Eventually Liz leant back in her chair and smiled. 'I'm impressed. Frankly when you started I felt you were floundering and could possibly go bankrupt, having spent so much on refurbishment. But you've managed to build up a clientele surprisingly fast and the evening meals have helped a great deal. You must have acquired a good reputation very quickly. Do many people return for a second time?'

'The business people do. Her thoughts turned to Mr Smith, but she said nothing. Tourists are a one-off, but several guests have come on other's recommendation. There is limited parking for two cars at the back of the property – that helps. I wanted to ask you about employing other people. Is there anything extra I need to do – insurance, tax, that kind of thing?' She went on to explain the circumstances.

Liz laughed. 'You wouldn't learn that on hotel management courses. To find a good cook first seek out your local plumber. Have you tried proper chefs?'

'Yes. I tried three. The last one threw the food at me. Zak and I work as a team. He can't stand lots of people and stressful places so we are both well suited.'

'He'll need Conditions of Employment, backdated to July, and the waiters. Regarding employing these people,' Liz did some quick sums on her calculator, 'you won't make so much profit, but it won't put you in the red, and you won't die of exhaustion either.'

They then discussed making her car part of the business, and opening a new savings account for building repairs and redecoration.

'Finally,' Liz said, 'it's time you started paying yourself a salary. You appear to have been living on nothing since Easter. What do you do for money?'

'I take it out of Uncle Bernard's estate money. I haven't had time to spend money. A few meals out, personal things, not much else.'

'Better to pay yourself something. Keep the estate intact. I expect you haven't been buying National Insurance stamps – that will affect your pension. You must get these things sorted. I see Brian returning. Better go and warm up the quiche.'

They greeted Brian at the door and Liz turned from efficient businesswoman to loving mother. She unzipped the babies from their woolly winter garments. 'This is James,' a dark-haired little boy was handed to Jenny, 'and this is Emma,' who was identical. Jenny just hoped she wouldn't drop two babies but managed to carry them to what was called the playroom, but had obviously been the kitchen-diner. Jenny put them down on the sofa and sat between them as they clutched at her fingers and smiled at her with dark eyes. Now there was time to say hello to Brian. He flopped down in an armchair, looking so different in a polo neck jersey and cord trousers.

'I've been up since six o'clock, I'm shattered.'

Jenny smiled at him, 'If that's shattered, it looks well on you. Both you and Liz are looking great. I think parenthood suits you.'

'I long for the old nine to five, dull, boring existence of the Council Offices.' He slid out of the chair and kneeling in front of the twins tickled their tummies, making them giggle, 'instead of looking after these two rascals.'

'They are gorgeous,' said Jenny, 'you're very lucky.'

'And lucky to have Liz who is happy to go out to work and provide lunch. I'll put these two in their cots while we eat.'

'I'll give you a hand.' With a baby each they found their cots and tucked them in. 'Now this wasn't something I ever expected to be doing whilst we sat at opposite desks in the Council House.'

Over lunch Jenny entertained them with stories of the guesthouse then asked if Brian ever heard gossip about the office. Brian reported that the new boss set targets for everyone. 'The phone has to be answered within two rings and you have to give your name. Made for stress. And, surprise, surprise, Mr Has Been won first prize for his dahlias at the local flower show.'

'I'm glad he has an interest to keep him out of Mrs Has Been's way. She always sounded a dragon when she rang up. I like to imagine him snug in a garden shed with a cuppa or perhaps a secret bottle of whisky.'

'How's Edith?' And so the conversation went on until Liz, feeling out of it, asked if Jenny had any plans for the future of the guesthouse.

'I can't see any way to solve the problem but it would be lovely to have a lounge where people could take their drinks, relax, read or play cards. On nights when a few guests do this, it gets very cramped.'

'Could you put up a conservatory in the garden?' suggested Brian.

'That's an idea, but on the other hand they like sitting in the garden on warm evenings.'

'Compromise. It would need structural work, but move the kitchen into some of the garden.'

'It would be expensive,' said Liz thoughtfully, 'and wouldn't increase profits.'

'Well, I like to keep thinking the place can be improved.'

After lunch the three of them fed the twins and played

with them until it was time for Jenny to return at five o'clock for her evening guests.

The following Sunday Jenny invited herself to lunch with Mandy and Kevin, not having seen them for several months. Lunch was a takeaway, Mandy saying she was too tired to cook, and over sweet and sour pork and chicken chow mein they exchanged news, Jenny having so much to tell them of Zak and the chefs.

'Are you two coming over for Christmas like you did last year?'

'Actually, Mum,' said Mandy, hesitantly, 'we thought we, and Dean, would stay here for Christmas day. Well, not exactly here. We're going to Kev's mum and dad for lunch and then over to Dad's for tea.' Jenny tried to conceal her disappointment. Christmas by herself, but wasn't that what she wanted a year ago?

'You see Dad's on his own now with Josh. Of course. You don't know! Sharon's left him. She had been seeing this other bloke since June, she hated looking after Josh, babies were not her scene, and in November she calmly announced she was off to Australia with this man. One day she was there, the next she was gone, and Dad was lumbered. He's paying a fortune in day nursery care. The poor little chap isn't even a year old and he doesn't know what's going on. A one-parent family in reverse. So we thought we would go over and watch Josh open his presents. He really is a dear little thing, curly auburn hair and big hazel eyes.'

'Besides,' said Kevin beaming from ear to ear, 'we can get in a bit of practice.'

'Practice?'

259

'That's another bit of news, Mum, I'm expecting a baby in June.'

'Oh, Mandy, how lovely.' Jenny gave her daughter a hug. 'And well done, Kev,' who was also enveloped in another hug. 'Oh, that's made my day. It's made my Christmas. A new baby in June.'

'We'll come and see you on Boxing Day,' said Kevin as though it was the consolation prize.

'Only if Mandy feels like it. We can't having you get too tired.'

'Mandy's as strong as an ox. She can wallpaper a room quicker than I can.'

Jenny went home in a state of excitement. She was going to be a grandmother, despite the fact that she felt she was far too young to be a granny. Her state of excitement lasted for several days. She was excited about everything. Christmas, carols, decorations, food and presents. She bought presents for everyone, including Josh – a woolly tiger with floppy legs. She got Paul to put a Christmas tree in a pot, and he and Emily decorated it before leaving at the end of term. She asked Edith and Eleanor for Christmas day. Edith was pleased to be invited. Although she had two sons she had no part in their lives and Christmas was a lonely time for her. Eleanor's admirer had now become a friend but he was busy with his mother on Christmas day so she was happy to come.

It had been planned to shut the guesthouse for a few days from Friday to Wednesday, so Zak could have some time off. Then a young couple, Mr and Mrs Thomas, from the flats along the road, came to the reception desk one evening and asked if Jenny had room for Mr Thomas's parents, his brother, wife and two young children. They would only need beds, nothing else. It was just that in their small flat they had no room to sleep all their relatives. 'No room at the inn' came to Jenny's mind and the idea of a family staying in the house appealed. It wouldn't affect Zak, so she agreed.

All the shopping had been done: food ready, beds made and Jenny sat peacefully listening to carols waiting for her guests. The Thomas family seemed to fill the hall. A tall elderly grandfather with a fine white beard, and grand-mother with grey hair done up in a bun. They introduced their son and daughter-in-law, Philip and Jane Thomas. They were an attractive couple in their thirties with two excited children called Mark and Annie, who shyly clung to their parents' arms when Jenny said hello to them.

'Have you got your stockings ready for Father Christmas?' They nodded.

'Luckily there's a chimney in your room so he can leave his sleigh on the roof and climb down.' They looked at her with wide eyes.

'Bother,' said Grandfather, 'I forgot to bring Father Christmas mince pies to say "thank you".'

'I've some to spare,' reassured Jenny, and armed with mince pies she showed them their rooms. Half an hour later they all went out again and Jenny awaited Edith who arrived hot and bothered having battled with trains and their random service.

'I must admit,' Edith said as Jenny handed her a mug of coffee, 'I didn't get up early. Yesterday, the office stayed in the pub far too long, and then Bartholemew took me out for a meal, so I didn't get to bed very early.'

'I hope you enjoyed yourself.'

'I did. Bart is good company, in an aesthetic sort of way.'

'You can pretend you're a nun. Wear sweeping black

robes.' Edith smiled into her mug of coffee and said no more.

Jenny spent some time fiddling around in the kitchen with vegetables and stuffing and when she returned to the dining room suggesting a drink, found Edith deep in a travel brochure.

A whisky in hand Edith asked, 'Last year we went to Paris and enjoyed it. How about Amsterdam next year?'

'Edith, what a great idea. Rembrandt, Van Gogh, canals. When?'

'So it doesn't affect your guesthouse too much, in February or early March. I haven't been away since I went to Devon with Eddie. That was months ago and I need a break.'

'You don't think Bartholemew will whisk you off to Venice or Rome for some art appreciation?'

'No. I like the idea, but odds of a hundred to one. So I shall plan for myself and I thought you might like to tag along?'

'Sure. The dates suit me. The guesthouse is doing well now, so there is some leeway.'

They had supper planning their holiday then Jane and Philip Thomas, returned, as Mark and Annie needed their beds. Once the children were settled Jane and Philip came down stairs.

'Would you like a drink of some kind, or if you have a baby alarm, Mrs Thomas, would you like to go out again? We can babysit.'

'We would quite like to go to Midnight Mass at the Abbey. We don't get much time to ourselves.'

'If Mark and Annie are asleep, leave us the alarm and go for a stroll about the town before the service. Do you know the way?' Jenny showed Philip the map whilst Jane went to find their coats.

'They like milk if they wake up,' she said winding a scarf round her neck.

'Between us we must have at least thirty years' experience of looking after the under-tens. I'm sure we can cope,' said Edith with confidence, and the young couple left.

'If I was their age and had two hours at my disposal the last place I would go is church,' declared Edith.

'Something I've learnt over the past nine months,' said Jenny, 'is you regard everyone as an alien. British and foreigners alike, none of them ever think like we do.'

'Everyone in the world is mad, 'cept thee and me. And I'm a bit worried about thee,' quoted Edith.

A few minutes later the baby alarm came into voice. 'Has he been yet?'

'No.'

'Let's see how far we can jump down the stairs till he comes.'

'No, we're s'posed to be asleep.'

'Action stations,' said Jenny, and they bolted up the stairs.

'Where's Mummy?' demanded Mark, standing on the landing.

'She's gone to church to welcome the little baby Jesus,' said Jenny gently.

Edith added, 'When baby Jesus has arrived she'll come back, and she'll be very tired and want to see you asleep. Father Christmas won't come and fill your stockings unless you're sleeping.'

'Told you,' said Annie to Mark.

Much to Jenny's surprise Edith took them by the hand.

'You talk funny,' said Mark, 'you don't speak like we do.'

'No. That's because I come from Manchester.'

Guiding them back to their room she said, 'If you lie down I'll tell you a story.' The children went with Edith, and Jenny crept downstairs and waited, listening. 'Once upon a time there was a little lamb who lived near Bethlehem with his mummy. One night the shepherds who looked after him ...'

Fifteen minutes later Edith entered the dining room and was handed a large whisky.

'Did you tell them a nice story?'

'Yeah. Jack the Ripper and the three kings.'

'"Once upon a time there was a little lamb".' She held up the baby alarm. 'It was lovely, and they're asleep.'

'I still remember my Chapel upbringing.'

'I wasn't going to have guests over Christmas but I liked the thought of having children around.'

'Your turn to tell them a story tomorrow.'

'Dracula meets Father Christmas.'

'Now that is over the top.' They finished their night-caps and went to bed.

Jenny was busy stuffing a turkey when Mark and Annie came shyly to the kitchen door.

'Hello. Happy Christmas. Are you hungry?' They nodded. 'Would you like some cornflakes?' They nodded again. The grandparents had said don't bother with food, but surely a bowl of cornflakes wouldn't matter. The children sat at the kitchen table and as they ate Jenny asked, 'Did Father Christmas come?'

'Yes,' whispered Mark. 'He brought me a car, felt pens and some Lego.'

'And satsumas,' added Annie, 'which we've eaten. I got some clothes for my Barbie doll, felt pens and some marbles.'

'Did Father Christmas eat the mince pies?'

'Yes he did. I think it's odd,' said Mark thoughtfully, 'he didn't leave any sooty footprints on the carpet.'

'I've just had the chimney swept,' said Jenny seriously, 'so its very clean. Do you want any toast, I'm having some?'

'No thanks. Can we have some milk, please?'

'Of course. I've got some paper here. Why don't you find your felt pens and we can see how well they work.'

For the next half hour Jenny ate her toast and watched the children happily drawing, until their parents summoned them back upstairs to get dressed.

Philip Thomas paused, 'This is an awful cheek, but I don't suppose we could borrow a couple of chairs for the festivities? My sister-in-law is short on chairs.'

Laughing Jenny told him to help himself and was amused to see the family walking along the road with chairs held aloft as though defending the women and children from attacking warriors.

Whilst the turkey was slowly roasting Jenny and Edith wandered round Sydney Gardens and then had the meal ready as Eleanor arrived. It was so civilised – three middle-aged women having Christmas dinner together – and how dull. The second bottle of wine provoked more lively conversation, mostly about men, and some wicked comments from Edith about goings-on in the office, then they played Newmarket with much laughter until Tom and Dorothy arrived for a cup of tea and Christmas cake which turned into an old-fashioned parlour game that Tom and Dorothy had played in their youth.

'This game is called Subject and Object,' said Tom. 'I'm the subject, Dot is the object. We'll go outside the door and decide who or what we are, then you have to guess. We can only answer "yes" or "no".' They left the room but soon returned.

'Are you animal?' asked Eleanor.

'No.'

'Are you vegetable?' asked Edith

'Yes.'

'Can we eat you?'

'Yes.'

'Anything to do with Christmas?'

'Yes.'

'Stuffing?'

'No.'

'Do you contain fruit?'

'Yes.'

'Christmas Cake!'

'Yes.'

'And Dot's the icing.'

'Yes.'

'Too easy,' said Edith, 'try this one. Come on outside the door, Jenny.'

And so the game continued with Edith being a potato and Jenny a potato peeler, and Eleanor and Dorothy being an oyster and a pearl. This turned to other games and much hilarity, slightly interrupted by the return of the Thomas family who joined in after the two tired children were asleep. Jenny went to bed content – it hadn't been the dull day it could have been.

When Jenny arose next morning and peered out of her basement window she smiled to see Mark kicking a new football at his father under a sign in the play park saying 'No Ball Games'. The whole family were going out to the Mendips so the children could run free.

'And guess where we're going to afterwards?' announced Mark.

'Back to your auntie's house?'

'No.'

'Swimming in the Roman Baths.'

'Of course not,' Annie answered with scorn, 'we're going to the pantomime,' she started dancing around, 'at a proper theatre.'

'How lovely. You must tell me all about it when you come back.'

Edith looked at Jenny with understanding, 'You really love having children around, don't you?'

'Yes I loved watching Mandy and Dean grow up. Didn't you with your boys?'

'No. I was happier once they'd left school and I was no longer being summoned to the headmaster or forking out for uniform and school trips.'

'No sign of them settling down?'

'I'd be the last to know.'

Mandy, Kevin and Dean turned up at lunchtime and tucked into cold turkey, jacket potatoes and salad.

'I get these cravings for jam doughnuts,' longed Mandy.

'You'll have to wait till the bakers open,' Kevin was quite stern, 'and eat healthy things, drink lots of milk. My baby's got to be big and strong.'

Edith twigged that Mandy was expecting and gave her congratulations, 'You're making your mother broody,' she warned.

'How did yesterday go with Trev and Josh?' asked Jenny.

'It was so funny,' said Dean, 'Josh tore all the wrapping paper off the presents then sat in a large box and played with the paper.'

'He did like a big plastic car someone gave him,' said Kevin, 'he pushed it then crawled after it. And he liked the furry tiger. He went to bed with that.'

'I'm glad the day went well. How was Trev?'

'Doing his best,' reported Mandy, 'but not very well. He knows he owes you for half the house. Your new solicitor has made that clear, but he has no way of paying it. The solicitor has also given him your address but he doesn't know you own Lansdown View.'

'Keep that quiet. I don't want him sponging off me, but I'll ask Mr Slocombe to go easy on the money and concentrate on the divorce.'

'Once a divorce gets in the hands of solicitors it tends to get nasty,' commented Edith. 'It bumps up their fees. Perhaps Muslims, or is it Hindus, have a better idea. They just say, that is the men, "I divorce thee", three times and it's all over.'

'Good thing we never got married,' said Mandy. Then tentatively to Jenny, 'Would you like to see some photos of Josh? Kev took them on his digital camera then printed them off. He's so cute and he *is* our half brother.'

'Yes, I'd like to see what he looks like. I hope he reminds me of you two and not the faithless Sharon.'

Mandy showed her a few photos of a bright-looking baby crawling after a red car; in one he was looking at the camera, smiling with large hazel eyes. Curly auburn hair tumbled over his brow. He looked strong, healthy and full of life.

As they cleared away lunch Kevin asked Dean, 'Do yer fancy going to the rugby?'

'No, too cold. Challenge you to a game of Pontoon. So the five of them sat down with amassed small change with Pyewacket looking on and batting the pennies to make his presence felt. The women were soon bankrupt and enjoyed the indulgence of chocolates, alcohol and bad television whilst Dean and Kevin battled it out. As Dean threw another empty can of Fosters in the bin he suggested they stayed the night and Jenny was happy to agree. The top two rooms were free.

She was busy making sandwiches when the Thomas family cheerfully returned from the theatre, including the couple from the flats.

'Is it possible to have a drink?' asked Mr Thomas, 'or would it infringe your licence?'

'Have it on the house.' She opened the bar then asked, 'Did you enjoy the pantomime?'

'There was this giant,' whispered Annie. 'He was huge and kept saying,' she jumped up and trying to put on a growling voice, said, '"Fee, fi, fo, fum, I smell the blood of an Englishman."'

'Then there was this horse, I think it was two people in a costume, but it was very funny,' said Mark, 'then we kept on having to shout out, "Look behind you," whenever the giant came on.'

The whole family were all chatting and chuckling about the evening and Jenny took the sandwiches down to the couch potatoes in the basement. Later she heard 'goodnights', and father chasing the squealing children up to bed with cries of 'Fee, fi, fo, fum, I smell the blood of an Englishman. Be he alive or be he dead, I'll grind his bones to make my bread.'

The next morning the family opted for breakfast as they had a long journey ahead of them, and Jenny was sorry to see them leave. She wished all guests were that easy-going. Edith came down looking dismal, but not too dismal for eggs and bacon.

'The thought of the office tomorrow. I've been there too long. It always seems to be the way that interesting people, like you and Brian, move on and the dull, unimaginative people remain and get duller. I'm even having to watch *EastEnders*, so I can understand what they're talking about.'

'Do you enjoy *EastEnders*?'

'No. Too much violence. Reminds me of husband number two.'

'Has he got a name?'

'D'yer know, I've forgotten. Oh yes, Ron. It would be nice to take early retirement, but I can't afford it.'

'Could you change tack and get a clerical job in one of these special needs schools?'

'No, I've tried. Too old. It's cheaper to employ younger people. I shall bide my time for two years, then freedom, as far as my cash will allow.'

'Blow it on a cruise and find a rich sugar daddy,' Jenny suggested.

Edith laughed, 'No, I'll probably enrol at the Open University and see what their summer schools have to offer.'

Jenny, carrying one of Edith's bags, walked with her to the station and waved her off, looking forward to a break in Amsterdam in a few weeks' time.

The young ones drifted down at lunchtime, consumed coffee and toast, and despondently left to take up the life again that they had had three days ago.

Chapter 20

New Year's Eve was a night Jenny preferred to ignore. She found it depressing, the thought of another year gone, rather than something to celebrate with forced jollity and revelry, so she would be happy to relax in the basement with a bottle of wine, some cigarettes and an old film on the television. The weather had been freezing for several days so her flat would feel extra cosy.

There were only six guests on this Saturday night so Zak and she had soon finished serving dinner and the guests had gone out – two to the theatre and four friends to a party. At eight o'clock she told Zak he could go, as the brothers were going to the local pub to see in the New Year.

She was piling the dinner plates back on the shelf when the back door crashed open with a rush of cold air. She whirled round and saw Ben standing in the doorway, dressed in prison denims. For a moment she thought the loving Ben had returned to her, something she had imagined, until she saw the look in his eyes. Pure hatred.

'How did you get here?' she stuttered.

'I had to be taken to the BRI for treatment they couldn't do at Horfield. It's not difficult to hit a warder over the head when you have to go to the bog. Walked out, knocked a cyclist off his bike and rode to Bath. They keep you fit in prison.' He walked slowly towards her, 'I've dreamed of this moment for six bloody months. What I'd do to the woman who shopped me.'

She backed away, 'But I didn't! I wouldn't do that. I swear I didn't. I loved you.'

'You did, you bitch. You left the books where the cops could find them and I'm going to make sure you'll never give evidence against me ever.'

'I didn't. I just ran. I didn't want to be found with drugs.'

'You did, you cow, and now you're going to pay,' and he hit her hard across the face several times.

'I've never talked to the police. They know nothing about me.' But he wasn't listening.

'Have you any idea what hell it is in there?' and he punched her in the stomach so she doubled over in pain.

'Honestly Ben, I did nothing. I loved you. We were having a beautiful time.'

He pushed her against the table. 'You set me up, played the tart for me,' and he put his hands round her neck and pressed hard. 'I've been longing to do this for months.' She tried to scream but his hands were over her windpipe.

Jenny brought her knee up as hard as she could into his crotch so he staggered backward with a groan and she made for the door. In the garden he tried to grab her. She dodged round one of the picnic tables and ran out on the canal path. He caught her again and tried to punch her in the face. She sunk her teeth in his arm very hard. He swore in pain, holding his arm. She tried to run again but the frosty grass was slippery and her feet wouldn't grip.

She felt his strong hands on her ankle and she fell again. This time there was no solid ground but the crack of ice, the shock of cold stinking water and profound darkness. She screamed, her head went under, and she kicked herself back to the surface. It was such an effort to move in the freezing black foul water.

In the darkness her hearing became more acute to the sound of scuffling on the path, a voice shouting, 'You f***ing bastard,' then an odd metallic clanging sound. She was feeling weaker as the cold penetrated her body and her movements were getting sluggish. Then there was a blaze of light and footsteps. A familiar voice was calling her name but she hadn't the strength to call back. She kept on swallowing the disgusting water and her efforts to stay afloat were getting feeble. Drowning might be easier; she could no longer feel the cold. Then a silhouette appeared at the edge of the lock, 'I've found her, Zak. There's a ladder here. I'll go down.'

Jake clambered down and she heard him exclaim, 'Christ!' as he launched into the icy water that cracked as he swam towards her. Then she was grabbed under the arms as her head sank once more into the murky water. He swam with her back to the ladder and pushed her against it. Treading water, he managed to get her hands on the rungs, 'Try and grip.' He directed her feet to the lower rungs. Where are my shoes? she vaguely wondered. With Jake pushing she climbed to the next rung, and the next, then felt warm hands wrap themselves round her wrists and she was out on the frozen grass, Jake dripping beside her. She was crying hysterically and the foul water was pouring out of her mouth. 'Be sick as much as you can,' ordered Jake. All she could do was lie on the frozen ground shaking uncontrollably.

'Zak, that bugger's coming round again.' She looked up and in the headlights of Jake's van had the satisfaction of seeing Zak pick up a frying pan and deliberately hit Ben on the back of the head, so he slumped onto the gravel path.

The brothers helped her to her feet, when she was promptly sick again and then propped between the two of them they helped her back to the kitchen as sirens announced the arrival of the police. Two constables clapped handcuffs on Ben and unceremoniously dragged him off to their car. A plain-clothes officer arrived whom Jenny recognised as Detective Sergeant Gray, the man who had investigated Mr Smith's suicide.

'You have quite an exciting time in your guesthouse, Mrs Evans,' he said with a twinkle in his eye. 'I glad you're all right. I gather you knew this man.'

'Yes. He's Ben Robinson, an escaped prisoner from Horfield.'

'And are these the two men who came to the rescue?'

'We're Jake and Zak Fowler. Zak works from Mrs Evans.'

'Well, I think questions like why you know an escaped prisoner from Horfield can wait till the morning. Best if you both get out of your wet clothes and get warm. If you give me your address Mr Fowler I'll come and get a statement in the morning. You OK to drive home, or would you like a PC to drive you?'

'I'll be all right,' Jake shivered. 'It's not far.'

'Shouldn't Jenny go to hospital?' asked Zak. It was the first time he had spoken.

'It being the busiest night of the year Mrs Evans will probably be better off in her own bed rather than waiting

274

in Casualty. Better get checked out in the morning, though, after swallowing all that canal water. A police-woman can help you while you get cleaned up, but could you find someone to stay with you overnight?'

'I'll try. And thank you, thank you everyone.'

Jake propelled Zak towards the door, 'Happy New Year, everyone,' he said with a raised eyebrow.

'I've got to find my frying pan,' Jenny heard Zak saying as he crossed the garden.

'In the morning will do,' answered Jake.

The policeman took his leave and left a gentle police-woman to help Jenny down to her flat. The policewoman ran a warm bath, peeled her wet clothes off her and helped her into the soothing water. 'Put the clothes in the bin,' ordered Jenny. Fifteen minutes later Jenny, feeling better mentally, but aching in every joint, got herself out of the bath whilst the policewoman found her a nightie and dressing gown. Then she looked with horror at her face in the mirror.

'Not a pretty sight,' said the policewoman and went off to find the antiseptic cream.

Over a cup of tea that made Jenny vomit again the policewoman asked her for the name of friends who might stay with her. 'Try Eleanor first. Then Lyn.'

Jenny found her address book and the policewoman talked to Eleanor. 'She asks if she can bring a man friend. Might be reassuring in the circumstances.'

'Yes, of course.'

'They'll be here in half an hour.'

'I wonder if they would like a double, or two singles?' said Jenny.

'Like that, is it?' and their laughter relieved the tension although it made Jenny's ribs hurt.

Eleanor arrived full of concern, made even worse when she saw Jenny's face, then introduced Clive. He stayed in the background whilst the policewoman explained the situation to Eleanor then she left with more thanks from Jenny.

'Now,' said Eleanor, 'do you want to go to bed or stay up for a bit?'

'I'd just like to sit here quietly and pretend nothing has happened. I won't be able to sleep. Put the telly on if you like and get yourselves a drink.'

'Do you want to talk about it? I gather it was Ben.'

'Yes it was, and I don't want to talk about it yet. I can hear someone ringing the reception bell.'

'I'll go,' said Clive. He was soon back. 'Two somewhat outraged guests wanting a drink. They were even more outraged when I told them what had happened, but I don't know how to open the bar.'

'Keys in the kitchen?' asked Eleanor. Jenny nodded. 'I'll sort it out – and breakfast as well.'

Clive, a tall slim middle-aged man with greying hair, settled down again, 'I must say this New Year is a bit different. I was looking forward to meeting you, but not like this.'

'Nor me. If you want a bed the two rooms on the top floor are free.'

'No. I'm happy here. And if you've gone to bed I might watch an old horror movie after twelve. No point in sleeping with all the fireworks going off. Tomorrow, if you're agreeable, I could take you to Casualty while Eleanor does the breakfasts.'

Jenny was shut in her own little world as the midnight explosions brought in the New Year and Eleanor made her a hot water bottle and tucked her in to bed. Lying there, the horror of it all came back to Jenny – the hate in Ben's eyes, the pain he inflicted on her, the fear as she tried to fight him off on the canal path and the final terror of the icy water. Eleanor held her in her arms as she cried herself to sleep.

At eight Eleanor roused them both. She had slept beside Jenny in her clothes that were decidedly rumpled, dark hair awry, but did her best to make herself respectable for the guests. She helped Jenny dress in loose comfortable clothes and Clive assisted her upstairs to the car. At the hospital while they were waiting, Clive tried to make her smile by looking through the piles of magazines trying to find the oldest. After an hour he had come across *Woman and Home*, August 1977, then they were called to the doctor. Clive helped her into a chair then retired in emabarrassment when he was called Mr Evans. Jenny explained what had happened, to the amazement of the doctor. He checked she had been sick several times then thought the water would not be a problem, but prescribed antibiotics as a precaution and gave her a tetanus injection. He got her to lie down on the couch and felt her ribs and limbs and declared there were no breakages. He examined all the bruising especially round her neck and stomach and wrote out another prescription for painkillers and anti-bruising cream.

'I take it you have told the police?'

'Yes, they are coming to take a statement this morning.'

'Basically physical healing will just take time. Psychologically things might take longer. If you find you can't sleep go and see your doctor, or you may require counselling. I think you're lucky to be alive, five minutes longer, who knows. You have very good friends.'

Painfully she walked back to Clive, who made her sit

277

whilst he went to the pharmacy, then he got her home and back into bed as fast as he could. She looked so pale he was quite worried.

Eleanor greeted her with, 'Mandy and Dean are coming over.'

'Did you ring them?'

'No. I'll get you some tea. The guests have all left. The four friends looked rather hungover and didn't want breakfast. Anyone due here tonight?'

'I can't remember.'

'Don't worry. I'll change the beds anyway and stay as long as you need me.'

Her next visitor was Detective Sergeant Gray and his female sidekick.

'I've just left the Fowlers. They're both fine. Lucky Zak stayed behind to make sure you were all right.'

'Why?'

'He saw this man hanging around when he put out the rubbish and didn't like the look of him. He left and came back in through the front door. Heard you shouting, phoned his brother then waylaid Robinson with a frying pan. Not an easy task for someone as short as he is.'

'What a wonderful pair they are,' said Jenny thoughtfully.

'Now I'm sorry to put you through this but tell me all about Ben Robinson.'

He sat quietly whilst the constable took notes and Jenny haltingly, with a few tears, told them about the affair from start to finish.

'So it was you who left the books with the drugs on the table.'

'Yes. But I didn't tell anyone. I don't know how the

police knew.'

'It was the two at Dundas that you saw. They were undercover men. They wondered who you were. Pity you didn't come forward sooner.'

'I wasn't involved. I was scared that I would be. It seemed better to keep quiet. Afterwards I felt he'd taken me along as camouflage.'

'That's what his girlfriends down on the Avon thought as well.'

'He was a busy bee.'

'Wasp more like.' The police took their leave and Jenny slept, exhausted by the interrogation. As she was stirring Mandy came in with a cup of tea.

'How are you feeling?'

'A little better. It was a relief telling the policeman everything.'

'The hunk turned out to be a right bastard.'

'How did you know there was anything wrong?'

'Dad rang us. He heard on the local news that a woman running a guesthouse had been attacked and he was worried.'

'Oh,' Jenny was too surprised to say anything else.

'Dean and I are going to stay here and run things until you're on your feet again and the bruises have gone down. We don't want you frightening the guests.'

'Thanks. Everyone is being so kind. I shall never know how to thank the Fowlers.'

'The phone's been ringing all day, people wanting to know how you are, and Tom has brought you a bunch of early daffodils. He said it was a sign of spring and life goes forward. And we've sent the press away with a flea in their ear. Four guests have arrived and we have told them there will only Continental breakfasts and we'll charge them less. Zak's apparently rather shaken, so Jake is keeping him at home for a week to keep an eye on him. His new job starts at the beginning of term. So everything is under control.'

Jenny lay back content to let her daughter take over. Eleanor came in to say she was going home with Clive, but would return tomorrow, so the three of them, Jenny, Mandy and Dean, settled down.

To think, mused Jenny, when I first came here I thought I had finished with children and was going to run my life without them. Now they are children no more and looking after me. How stupid I was.

She slept badly, reliving her ordeal in nightmares then waking up in a cold sweat. She thought about reading herself to sleep but this only made her head ache and she dozed until it was light then made herself a cup of tea. A long soak eased her aching limbs then she dressed, which took forever, then climbed the stairs thinking this must be how very old people feel all the time.

Mandy persuaded her to eat some toast then she enjoyed the new experience of watching Dean vacuuming and washing the kitchen floor. Dramatically he put his hand to his brow and with a theatrical sigh said, 'A woman's work is never done.'

'Don't make me laugh. It hurts.'

This was how Detective Segeant Gray found them when he came with the statement for her to sign. When she had read it through and signed it Jenny asked, 'What do you think he did with all the money he must have made? He didn't seem to spend money on himself and that boat had seen better days. Is it hidden away in a Swiss bank?'

Dean, who was secretly enjoying the intrigue,

suggested, 'Maybe he's put it in the Left Luggage at Paddington Station and the ticket's in his coat which is hanging on your back door.'

'Oh yes, sergeant, please do take his coat. I nicked it when I left as it was raining so hard.'

'You've been watching too much television, young man,' said the policeman severely, 'but I'll take the coat and see what forensics come up with. What we're wondering is whether he was being blackmailed or threatened by someone higher up the drugs chain. That's why we had undercover men working on the case. His father is quite an important diplomat. By the way, Robinson is an alias. Its supposition, but perhaps his family would be harmed or disgraced if he didn't do what he was told. He had used drugs in the past and got mixed up with criminals. That's why he was thrown out of Oxford. When I interviewed him he seemed frightened of something, but isn't telling. It's up to him now; no one else can help him. Thanks for your assistance. I hope I won't be seeing you again, until you're asked to be a witness.'

'Witness?'

'Of the attack.'

Jenny felt a sense of panic, but said quietly, 'Yes, of course.'

When the sergeant had gone, she bust into tears and Dean took her in his arms to comfort her and rocked her to and fro. 'You'll be all right, Mum,' he kept murmuring in her ear. He found her some kitchen roll.

As she dried her eyes she saw Tom and Dorothy's daffodils on the table, took a deep breath and said, 'Tom's right. Spring is coming and I must look forward. Be positive. "Onwards and upwards" as the saying goes.'

As the week continued Jenny recovered, helped by visits from Eleanor and Lyn and her children's cheerful company. Dean had to return to Plymouth to finish projects he had neglected the previous term but Kevin stayed for the weekend. The Fowler Brothers turned up in the kitchen on Sunday morning, unusually shy in her company.

'I don't know how to thank you,' stammered Jenny. 'I would probably be dead if you hadn't stayed, Zak, and you hadn't fished me out of the water, Jake.' She too was lost for words. She gave them both a big hug then not really knowing what to say or do made some coffee and told them about Ben.

After a pause Jake said, 'I start my new job tomorrow. Is it all right with you for Zak to come back?'

Jenny turned to Zak, 'Do you want to come back?'

'Oh yes! If you feel OK.'

'I'll be fine. Mandy and Kevin, who have been fantastic, are going back to Bristol tonight. There are only four guests so we won't be busy. Did you get the frying pan back?'

'No, we think it went in the canal.'

'I'll get a new one when I go shopping. Better still, Zak, why don't you come with me to the Cash and Carry?'

Chapter 21

So, with much willpower on Jenny's part, life returned to normal. Zak came in early to help out with the cleaning as Jenny found too much exertion painful but the guests were happy and the meals as good as ever. The frozen conditions continued, cold clear blue skies overhead, freezing branches and leaves decorated with glittering white crystals and the ducks slipping on the ice in the canal, wondering where their water had gone, which amused Jenny. She took pleasure in feeding them and the garden birds. Ordinary tasks took her mind off that terrible night.

One morning as she was throwing out some stale bread and cake she heard an anxious yell, 'Oh Tom!' from next door. She looked over the wall to see Dorothy bending over Tom prone on the grass. She dropped the bread and as fast as she could manage with the still present pain, went round to their garden gate.

'What happened?'

'I was in the kitchen and heard him call out. Then I found him on the grass. He was moving flower pots.'

'Between us can we get him inside out of the cold?' With difficulty they got him on their bed.

'You keep him warm. I'll ring for an ambulance.'

'Do you think he's had a stroke?' Dorothy's face was covered with tears. 'He should never have gone out in that cold.'

'I don't know if it's a stroke, Dorothy. I'll get help as quick as I can.' She found the phone and dialled 999 wondering why her fingers wouldn't work properly in an emergency.

'Do you know First Aid?' asked Dorothy.

'No. Wish I'd learnt it now. He's still breathing. And I can feel a slight pulse in his neck.' The two women sat by the bed until the green-clothed paramedics arrived and soon whisked Tom away, asking for the ladies to follow with an overnight bag for Tom.

'Can you do that,' asked Jenny, 'while I telephone Zak and get the car started?' Then she was driving to the hospital while Dorothy sat mute, worrying. The sun became dim as fog drifted over the city, the weather on the change. They waited in Accident and Emergency in stressed silence for over an hour. Jenny noticed other people, pale and strained, waiting for news, and a child crying in pain waiting, waiting.

A solemn-faced doctor took them into a small room and told them Tom had died from a second heart attack. He said the usual sympathetic clichés but Dorothy was in a state of shock and did not hear them.

'Are you their daughter?' asked the doctor.

'No, a neighbour. I'll take her home with me and look after her until her family hopefully can help.'

Drizzle covered the windscreen as they drove home, as if in mourning for an old friend. Back in her cosy basement Jenny made Dorothy some hot sweet tea and rang the son, Neil, that she had meet at Christmas over a year ago. He was at work but would get away as soon as he could. Dorothy seemed locked away in her own world of grief and there was little Jenny could do, so she went upstairs to tell Zak. He was upset, as he had often chatted to Tom over the garden wall. Jenny, hoping the evening meal wouldn't be a disaster, returned to Dorothy, now quietly crying. Jenny sat next to her on the sofa, her arm around her and the two of them wept together until the son arrived. Neil looked stressed but calm and took his mother back to her home. Jenny said she would call in later with a meal if they wanted it and offered to tell the students. Paul was the only one in, getting ready for his evening stint at the guesthouse.

'I can't believe it. I was talking to him this morning. Poor Dorothy. I'll tell the others. It's going to be a miserable night.' The three of them tried to be cheerful for the sake of the guests, but their heart wasn't in it. Jenny noticed the daffodils on the table had wilted as though the hope of spring had gone.

Neil took gentle care of Dorothy and arranged the funeral in four days' time. Jenny offered to do a buffet lunch for the mourners to which he eagerly agreed. Just a few members of the family, he said. Jenny knew how well liked and respected Tom had been and doubled the numbers.

Under grey skies with a chill wind that crept into the bones Jenny and Zak gathered with the students to attend Tom's cremation. Dorothy arrived with her son and his wife. She leaned heavily on Neil's arm and sobbed through the moving service.

Jenny did her best handing out food at the buffet. She noticed Mrs Barrett eating her fill, and Mr Patel talking shop business to Mrs Trubshaw from the Post Office.

Funerals often brought people together; they were sad, concerned and polite, with grievances put aside.

Later in the day as Jenny and Zak were clearing up, Neil came round to express his thanks and to say he was taking Dorothy home with him for a few weeks.

'She needs a rest and time to think about life without Dad. What she wants to do. Thanks for all you've done.'

'Tom and Dorothy have been good friends to us. Wish her well,' and Zak nodded.

January turned to February, snowdrops appeared in gardens and hedgerows.

Jenny's aches and pains receded, and a few days away with Edith in Amsterdam set her well back on the road to recovery. They enjoyed the brown cafés, trips on the canals and the Van Gogh museum. How that man suffered, thought Jenny, and then painted such wonderful pictures. Again her view of the world had been widened and she felt more confident because of this.

After a month Dorothy returned looking well but older. She came to see Jenny and announced, 'My son and I have decided it's time for me to move. My balance has never been very good and I fall a lot. Tom used to pick me up. But now he's not here to do that. Neil has found me a nice flat. There's a warden to look after me, and long red strings to pull if I feel ill. He's only down the road and there is a lovely view over the park.'

'That sounds like a good idea, and you'll enjoy being near your son.'

'In a way I'm looking forward to a change, as much as I can look forward to anything without Tom,' and her tears started to flow, 'and I shall miss the old house, the students and friends. But it's for the best.' Jenny held Dorothy's hand until she had composed herself. Dorothy had always been one who thought of others, 'And are you better after that dreadful attack?'

'I'm fine, but I don't sleep well.'

'Now I must go and start sorting out all my furniture and belongings. Not looking forward to that. Too many memories.'

'I'll give you a hand when I can. At least I can take your rubbish to the tip, and if you feel unwell at night just bang on the wall. They're not that thick.'

A few days later she was taking some of Tom's clothes to the Oxfam Shop when a thought occurred to her that she tried to reject. It didn't seem right to make capital out of a friend's death. But the idea kept on coming back to her, interfering with her already disturbed sleep.

If I talk to Dorothy now, she thought, estate agents won't have to be involved. That'll save her some money. I'll do it in the morning.

Jenny was tongue-tied as Dorothy plied her with tea and shortbread. 'I was thinking, wondering if, would you be upset if ...'

'If you bought the house. I was hoping you might suggest it. You've made a success of Lansdown View but you're pushed for space.'

'Exactly. It would be so much better if there were a lounge and a larger dining area. There could be twelve more guests and better reception rooms.'

'I would like to think of you turning this house into Lansdown View. Happy guests, good food, perhaps enjoying Tom's garden,' mused Dorothy.

'It would be lovely to sit out there in the evening. But

I'm getting ahead of myself. I don't know if I can afford it – Liz, my accountant, can advise me on that. I just wanted to make sure you didn't mind.'

'No, I don't mind, but you won't get rid of my students till after their exams.'

'Nothing will happen that fast. Besides I don't want to lose my waiters.'

Jenny made the flippant comment to keep the mood light, but both she and Dorothy knew when the time came for parting there would be sadness.

Chapter 22

Jenny had a spring in her step as she left Mr Slocombe's office. The sale of Dorothy's house had been agreed, the mortgage settled and her divorce had become absolute. She was free, free as a bird. She thought back to her first visit to Slocombe and Slocombe in her shabby grey suit, and how anxious she was about the refurbishment and the fear of failure. Well she hadn't and here she was, dressed smartly, highlights back in her short fair hair, ready to run an even better guesthouse.

Her mind was full of plans for the guesthouse extension. There was three months before the students left so there was adequate time. Jake had found her a good plumber; Kevin had agreed to do the decorating on his own, Mandy having stopped work with the baby due in June. As she turned the key in the lock she was thinking of the best way to incorporate a new lounge and dining room when Zak came out into the hall, potato peeler in hand, but looking perturbed, and told her there was a man to see her.

'I didn't know what to do with him. He's got a baby with him. He said, as its a nice day he'd wait in the garden.'

It couldn't be! Not today of all days when she was free. She rushed into the kitchen and peered through the window. It was. She slumped down at the table and lit a cigarette. Zak, with an enquiring look, produced the cooking sherry and a glass.

'Good idea. Thanks.'

Zak went back to his peeling with the comment, 'He's a bouncy little boy.' Literally, thought Jenny, as she watched him fall off the seat of the picnic table and pick himself up, laughing.

She stubbed out the cigarette, took her sherry in one swig and went into the daffodil-scented garden.

'Hello ex-husband.'

'Hello ex-wife.' Trev looks very different, she thought. He's much thinner. Jeans and a well-worn jersey suit him. His hair, curly ginger, was growing over his collar, hadn't seen a barber for months, and his aggressive moustache had gone.

What do you say to a husband who walked out on you a year and a half ago? She had no idea. Her brain would have to rethink many things, so she turned to the child.

'You must be Josh.' Josh stopped staggering around on unsteady feet, smiled at her and nodded. Jenny noticed the bag of toys on the handle of his buggy. 'What have you got in that bag?' Trevor unhooked it and Josh carried it over to Jenny.

'Oh look. A car. Can you say car?'

He took it out and pushed it along the wooden seat of the picnic table. 'Brrumm,' he said.

'Talking isn't his thing yet,' said Trevor. 'He's great at toddling around and climbing. I have to watch him like a hawk. You see, no one's ever bothered to speak to him. Sharon wasn't interested and child minders don't have time. He can say "Dad", and "Bye Bye". Never learnt to say "Mum", she wasn't there long enough.'

'Sorry it didn't work out.'

'What she wanted was status. A house, baby in designer clothes. Didn't realise it meant hard work. She would never get up in the night to feed him. Housework and washing were a closed book to her. Takeaways all the time.

'When I said the money from the sale of her flat had to go on paying off your half of the mortgage she spent it on a car. Not an ordinary car she could put Josh in, but a two-seater sports car to impress people. Which she did and he's welcome to her.'

Trevor was angry – he'd been made to look a fool. Having got over her shock at seeing him, Jenny remembered and smiled to herself – Trev feeling sorry for himself.

On seeing his father's anger Josh stopped playing with his car and came up to Jenny who set him on her knee. To change the mood she asked Josh, 'Do you like ducks? They go "quack quack".' Josh didn't seem to understand. 'I'll go and get some bread then we'll go and see them. Have you got any reins, Trev?'

'No.'

'Then strap him in his buggy. Don't want him falling in the canal.'

'No. Not after your experience. I'm glad you're all right. Mandy said he was a convict. How did you get mixed up with him?'

'Not enough experience of life, Trev. After all, the only man I've ever really known was you.' The pair of them laughed and Josh relaxed. 'I think that's broken the ice,' she said and they both understood the two contexts.

As Jenny pushed the garden gate open she asked,

'What brought you here today, Trevor?'

'I've been talking to Mandy. We're both been worried about you – that you'd recovered all right – and you have. With her expecting I think she wanted you to meet Josh, then it won't be awkward if we meet up later at family gatherings like her baby's birthday. She wants Josh and the new baby to be friends – and it would be good for Josh.'

Trevor pushed Josh onto the canal path. The smell of the brown brackish water brought back bad memories to Jenny but she pushed them to one side. Besides, the canal with its black and white bridges and lock gates looked so different in the spring sunshine. Josh had never seen ducks before. He sat in his pushchair gurgling delightedly, throwing bread that they snapped up from beneath his feet. Trevor had crouched down beside him and after several attempts he copied his father's quacking noises. This was a side of her children's father Jenny had forgotten through the misery of later years – a father enjoying the company of his child, side by side going 'quack, quack'.

A boat going down through the lock interrupted their fun. Jenny heard again, without regret of her canal journeys, the clink, clink of the ratchets as the paddles were turned on the gates and the water filled the lock, and helped the boaters push the gate open.

Josh was pointing from his chair, 'Chuff, chuff.'

'No Josh. That's not a train. That's a boat. Boats go on water. Like you have in the bath.'

'Chuff, chuff.'

'He learnt that this morning on the way here. We did enjoy the "chuffs chuffs", didn't we Josh?'

'Two words in one day. Well done, Josh.' Jenny

turned to Trevor, 'You didn't come by car?'

'Well, er, no. You see – back in January when it was so cold Josh was quite ill. I had to stay home and look after him. I've had to have so much time off, what with him and Sharon being difficult, they sacked me. It was a firm's car, so that went as well as the job.'

'So at long last you've got rid of that miserable insurance company.'

'Well, yes. I'm living on benefit. It may seem lazy for a man, but it can't be helped.'

This attitude of Trevor's was new to Jenny. Putting another's interests first.

'What are you going to do?'

'Live on benefit until he's older. I'm not happy with child minders or nurseries whilst he's this young, and I'm enjoying it. I know now what I missed with Mandy and Dean. Yes, I'd like to go out with the boys, drink too much beer, then I think of those nights when he was ill, gasping for breath, and I stay in with a couple of cans. Besides, my old mates wouldn't be interested in how I live now.'

Jenny was stunned. The Big Business Trev, if only in his eyes, now apparently happily living on benefit.

'The solicitor, toffee-nosed twit, said you didn't mind for the moment about your half of the house.'

'No I don't. Like you, I want to think about Josh. He didn't ask to be brought into this world and should be considered. If you were kicked out of your home, he would probably end up in care. Nobody wants that.'

Jenny looked down at Josh, big eyed, as though he knew they were talking about him. She bent down beside him, 'Yes, Josh, we are talking about you. Wondering what you would like for tea? What did he have for lunch?'

'Half a cheese roll at Temple Meads Station.'

'Pity you never did home economics at school. Now, Josh, would you like what Dean and Mandy used to have for tea when they were your age?' Josh nodded; perhaps he knew it was a good idea. 'Let's go back to the guesthouse, but wait a minute whilst I talk to the staff.' (That sounds good, she thought.)

Back in the guesthouse kitchen Jenny, trying to look normal, asked Zak how the meal was progressing.

'It's a sausage casserole. Nothing special, and lemon meringue pie.'

'My ex-husband has turned up with his love child. I need to feed them, but I don't want to be in your way.'

'Your what?' exploded Jake from behind the *Bath Chronicle*. He often turned up for an evening meal.

'My ex-husband. As from today. And a rather charming little boy. They're hungry and need feeding.'

'No problem. It's all simmering away,' said Zak.

Jenny fried up bacon and bread. Made marmite sandwiches, found sultanas and grapes.

Trevor and Josh arrived at the kitchen door and Jenny introduced them.

'I need to change his nappy,' announced Trevor and Jenny took him down to her flat. On her return she asked, 'Where did I put all the baby gear?'

'Cupboard, first floor,' said Jake. 'Shall I get the high chair? I remember from the time you had that child who wanted to cross the main road to get to the play park.'

'Don't remind me – that was Charlie.' A few minutes later Jake had set up the high chair in the dining room and Trevor plonked Josh in the seat and food appeared before him as if by magic.

'There's sausage casserole, Trev, if you would like it.'

Josh was happily crunching on bacon and bread.

'No. I'm not hungry. Better be off now. It'll be dark by the time we get back and I don't want Josh getting chilled in the night air.'

'I'll find you a blanket to keep him warm.' Surely there'd be one in the first-floor cupboard.

Fifteen minutes later, a mist now rising over the town and the Abbey tower in the distance, Trevor and Josh took their leave for the station, Josh saying 'Chuff, chuff.'

'Isn't it Josh's first birthday next week. Is he having a party with friends?'

Trevor looked up from the steps. 'He has no friends.' Jenny came down to street level, the cars rushing past.

'Would he,' she paused, 'would you, Josh, like to come for your birthday tea next Thursday? Go on the "Chuff chuff" again?' Josh nodded. 'See you next week.' She smiled at Trevor, 'I mean that. See you next Thursday.'

Once she had got inside, leaning against the front door, she realised she had said this to Trevor for months, outside the youth club, when she was sixteen. 'See you next Thursday.'

Back in the kitchen the brothers looked at her.

'Went OK?'

'Hope so. Difficult situation. I don't know what to think. Perhaps he thought you were my toy boys.' They all laughed. 'Better get on with dinner.'

On Thursday of the following week she made a cake and decorated it with a figure one in Smarties and a single candle. Jenny thought supermarket bought birthday cakes always looked too saccharin and gaudy. This was ordinary home-baked cake. She went to a toyshop and bought some Dinky cars and a road mat as a present. Sausages and cheese were put on sticks, sandwiches and crisps in a bowl. She was surprised that she was enjoying herself and was looking forward to Trevor and Josh's arrival.

As he came in through the front door Josh pointed to the garden and said, 'Quack quack,' so finding some bread they set off up the canal. This time Josh managed to say 'boat' when one chugged past. At Sydney Gardens Josh was released from his buggy and happily trundled around while Trevor and Jenny sat on a park bench watching him.

'How's Sheila these days?' asked Jenny.

'Her operation was successful. She rang up and told me about it in detail. I felt really sick. But she's eating better, so Jane tells me. Now it's her back that's giving trouble.'

'Well, I'm glad the doctors haven't deprived her of her hobby.' Trevor laughed.

Jenny thought back to Sheila's bitter comments at Hestercombe Gardens on waterfalls fragmenting currents, as life's direction can be deflected, and her reply that the currents came together peacefully in the lake. Had her life reached this stage, could there be tranquillity?

Trevor, having no idea of her thoughts, asked her about the guesthouse.

'Do you run it all on your own?'

'Zak does the cooking. He and Jake rescued me on that awful night. Then two students help in the evenings. It's hard work, long hours, but I enjoy meeting so many people.'

'What's the owner like?' So Trev still doesn't know

it's mine, Jenny thought. That's good. I'll keep it that way. 'She's very nice,' Jenny improvised. 'She pays well and keeps out of the way. I seldom see her and can run the guesthouse as I like.'

'Do you get holidays?'

'Yes, I went to Amsterdam in February.' Trevor seemed impressed.

'You've changed. More confident. Not the little mouse you used to be.'

'No. I like to feel I'm in control. I have to be. People don't push me around anymore.'

'Apart from escaped convicts.'

'That's not fair.'

'You need a man to look after you.'

'I wouldn't mind having a man around, but I'll look after myself. It's called self-assertiveness.'

'Being bossy.'

'Yes. Get off that seat and we'll take your son to look at the trains.'

They both laughed at the remark and went up to the railway line that passed through the park in a cutting. As they walked Jenny said, 'You've changed as well. You don't seem so aggressive and bad tempered.'

'That was partly Sharon. Demanding little minx. The office was getting worse. In the old days ...'

'Yes, grandpa. When you were a boy.'

'In the old days, twenty years ago, it was quite laid back – free and easy. When you did something well, like get a new client, it was appreciated. Now it's all targets, this report has to be in yesterday. Training courses, team building – nightmare. Most of the blokes have got high blood pressure and never a word of thanks or more money. Then you see the profits they've made. Looking after Josh is a merciful release. He's been pushed around too much with child minders and I have to be calm otherwise he gets upset.'

'I noticed that last week.'

'It makes me appreciate how you looked after our two. Meals were always there. Clean clothes. And you took them out when you had time, even if it was only a bike ride. I hope I can do the same for Josh.'

Jenny looked into Trevor's clear blue eyes, no longer bloodshot as they had been eighteen months ago, and said, 'Thanks. I did my best, enjoyed it, and they seem to be going in the right direction, which is all we can ask. And we are going to be grandparents.'

But Trevor was more interested in the present and being a father, 'I can hear a train coming, Josh.' Father hunkered down beside his son. 'This looks like an express. A big fast train going to London.' The noise, the rush of air as the train came out of the cutting made Josh's face light up in wonder.

'You'll have to get Kev to lend you his camera. Moments like that should be kept for ever.'

Why was she holding Trev's hand? It seemed so natural.

Then she looked at her watch. 'I have to get back. New guests arriving at five o'clock. When they're settled we can have our birthday tea.'

Jenny showed an American couple, Mr and Mrs Hank Johnson, to their room. On autopilot she told them the fire regulations and where they could find an evening meal while her mind whirled round her own situation. Yes she knew what Trevor wanted, someone to look after himself and Josh. And probably more important for Trevor, a woman to share his bed. Oddly enough the idea didn't repel her, quite the reverse. But could you ever turn back the clock with all the mess in between? Everyone would tell her no, but wasn't it worth a try, for Josh especially? Could Trevor really give him the care he needed, as Josh grew older? It could turn out, with luck, that the fragments of their troubled lives, shattered eighteen months ago, would crystallise into a flawed jewel of love based on experience and understanding.

The tea party was a great success. They sang 'Happy Birthday' to Josh and lit the candle. Having never been to a birthday celebration Josh just stared at the cake in fascination. The Johnsons were just leaving and popped their heads round the door.

'What a happy family occasion! You'll never be one again, young man,' exclaimed Hank. 'Can I have a photo? I'll send you a copy.' With more over-the-top jovial comments the couple left with directions on how to get to the city centre.

Tea over, Jenny suggested, 'Let's go to the play park while it's light and Josh can enjoy the swings.'

'What about your presents?'

'He can open them later.'

With whoops from both Trevor and Josh, as he was pushed on the baby swing, Jenny sat on the bench laughing at them. Trevor placed Josh on a springy caterpillar and sat down by Jenny.

'Nice family occasion, that American said. And it has been. Josh has really enjoyed himself.'

'Trev will you stop trying to turn me on, and keep your hands to yourself. You're supposed to be looking after Josh. He's about to start on the climbing frame and he's not old enough.'

Trevor strapped Josh back in his buggy.

'Give you a final push on the swings.'

'I'm not fourteen anymore.'

'No one's looking and you're very small.'

The sensation took her back to the tingling sparkle of youth and freedom.

As he pushed her Trevor shouted, 'We ought to get going. It'll be dark soon. I don't want Josh getting cold. And he hasn't opened his presents.'

'Better stay the night,' Jenny called back. 'You'll have to get the cot down.'

'I haven't any nappies.'

'Shop down the road.'

Trevor halted the swing. 'You mean this?'

Jenny twisted the swing round to face him. 'Let's give it a try. "Better the devil you know."'

Arm in arm, pushing the buggy, the trio in harmony, however temporarily, walked back to Lansdown View.